I0570707

# THE LAST OF CREED

ALSO BY KELLY SINCLAIR

Accidental Rebels
Lesser Prophets
If the Wind Were a Woman

*Published by Blue Feather Books*

# THE LAST OF CREED

KELLY SINCLAIR

ASEBO MEDIA TEXAS 2011

ISBN: 9780615532462
0615532462
LC Case #: 1-653137411
First Edition

Published by Asebo Media
PMB 111
1610 S. 31st St., Ste. 102
Temple, TX 76504

www.asebomedia.com
email asebomedia@gmail.com

Cover photograph by Lauren Bartlett Cochrane.
Author photograph by Amy Spencer.

*For Bula High School, the final class, and all those who came before.*

# CHAPTER ONE

Dal Creed woke up as the 727 touched down at the Lubbock airport. Pinned between two apologetic Texas Tech football players, he crept with other passengers off the plane. When he stopped in the accordion to shoulder his carry-on bag, he felt a hand on his back.

"Here's your jacket, sir," the flight attendant said. "You left it behind."

She sped away before Dal could ask her a question. What was this space actually called? A passageway, a chute?

The first time Susan flew on a plane was on their honeymoon/cartoonist convention trip eight years ago to New York City. She called the walkway from the gate to the plane an accordian. A phrase existed for this crinkled extrusion—a name he used to know—but one without a trace of his wife. A mystery, then, in no need of being solved.

He found nothing decipherable about Susan lately. He decided that the night before at the Marriott bar, while trying to finish his third Maker's Mark on the rocks. He would never get the hang of drinking to excess.

A genetic bouncer kept him at the level of a pleasant buzz and no further, yet Susan had no inbred limitations. She drank rarely, but when she drank, chaos erupted. Loud talk, manic cheer, breaking glass, club ejections, and harrowing rides home. After the honeymoon debacle, she never again went with him to conventions, or to meetings with his agent in Dallas.

As he strode through the accordion, he pictured her smiling at the gate. The balloon above his head remained empty.

Instead of his wife, he found Levon Porter, tapping his feet impatiently.

"Where's Susan?" Dal asked.

"At home, I guess. Rosanna called and asked me to pick you up. She said it wouldn't be out of my way, since I live here in town. You know how she is. She thinks y'all live in the center of the known universe. I've tried calling both of them but nobody's answering."

Dal made his own effort at calling, with the same result as Levon.

Rosanna Wintersole, a young-acting widow in her early fifties, lived down the road from Dal and Susan. One of his ex-girlfriends used to derive endless amusement from the fact that Dal lived in a community named after his grandfather, saying that she planned to start her own town, "only this time with more people than cows."

In fact, the ratio in Creed was eight to one—eight full-time residents to one cow, which belonged to the Marroquins, a farm family that lived down the caliche road that ran along the southern edge of Dal's property. Mack Wender lived in a trailer at his cotton gin during peak time; however, he was more often found at home with his family in Wolfforth, a nearby town that had become a defacto suburb of Lubbock.

It usually took about twenty-five minutes to get from the airport out to Creed, a spot in the road located in rural Lubbock County.

Levon didn't venture a guess about the holdup with Susan, but then, he and Mack fished Susan out of the Gulf of Mexico a couple of times on their beer-soaked high school senior trip, so he knew what she could accomplish on a dedicated drunk.

"How'd things go in Dallas?"

In addition to the meeting with his agent, Dal attended a comic convention—the organizers called it ComCon DFW—where he autographed the latest collection of Twister Tales daily panels.

"Went okay. We sold some shirts, moved some buttons. Not bad. How did Rosanna sound?"

"Upset, which is weird. Usually, a tornado could rip the roof off, and she'd still be sitting there drinking tea."

Dal tried Susan's number again. No answer.

Rosanna and Susan got along well. They teamed up during canning season, and Susan fed Rosanna's flock of ostriches when needed. In the past few months, Dal and Susan had taken turns using her as a sounding board and a conduit of information. Somehow, Rosanna managed to stay neutral, which was no easy task.

"How's the family?" Dal asked.

"Anita's put out at me right now."

So much for safe questions. Were there any happy couples left in the world.

"Got you in the dog house, huh."

"That'd be a step up from where I'm at. We went to see her sister's family for Juneteenth. That's been two solid months ago and now Shana's telling Anita I made a play for her. And the crazy thing is, I did do what she's claiming, but it wasn't a pass. I was joking around and Shana took it wrong."

"What'd you do?"

"Put a piece of ice down the back of her dress." Levon wore a sheepish expression. "We were alone in the kitchen and I just got in a silly mood and did it. Said something about needing to cool her down. I didn't mean anything by it. Shana's so high on herself. You know how some women can get. Nah, how could you? Susan's never put on airs."

Two-thirds of Creed High School's senior class, Susan and Levon possessed the same restless energy, the same view of basketball as a contact sport, although Susan was a better athlete than Levon and Dal combined. Levon went into sales after graduation and was now regional director for a soft drink company, while Susan moved on to care for her parents until their deaths over a decade ago.

Neither Susan nor Rosanna were answering their phones. Putting his cell away, he saw a helicopter blurring north over the cotton fields and grasslands.

"Did you see that?" Levon asked.

"Just get me home quick."

Best not to overthink the possibilities. Don't think, period.

Levon whipped them off the main highway, another turn off the farm-to-market road, then they drag raced down a strip of erratically maintained blacktop. The land's lack of contour gave them a clear view of the cluster of cars and pickups in his front yard.

At least the house was still standing. Guilt flushed through him in a familiar current. *Nice work, Dal. You're worried more about the house than Susan.* Levon drove his car around the side of the house.

A sheriff's deputy ran toward them while they were walking toward the back door.

"Y'all better move that car, and pronto. We're not through with the investigation yet."

While Levon explained who they were, Dal pushed by the deputy and went inside. Two strangers at his kitchen table were loading plastic bags into metal suitcases.

"What the hell is going on? Where's my wife?"

Expressionless, the taller of the men called out, "Sheriff Verner, Mr. Creed is here."

Wheeling by them, Dal bounced off another stranger in his living room as he called out Susan's name. Any moment she would appear with an explanation. A lie would do.

Rosanna caught up to him in the hallway. A life spent farming gave her long arms a deceptive strength, but she couldn't hold him in place.

"Don't go in there."

How could he not.

He saw the bed first, surprisingly neat. Although Susan helped keep the house tidy enough, she left the bed-making to Dal. Examining the rest of the room, he saw nothing else out of order, except that he couldn't make his eyes focus on what was in front of him.

Sheriff Gene Verner looked as crisp as he did in his campaign commercials.

"You don't have to look, Mr. Creed. Your neighbor already made the identification."

"What happened?"

The throbbing in Dal's head intensified. He cued the attendants to stop rolling their blue-draped cart.

"She got in the middle of a burglary in process—early this morning, looks like—and the perp struck her with a baseball bat. This yours?"

He displayed the Louisville Slugger, resting on a bloodied towel. Dal had used the same bat when he was ten years old to hit home runs toward Lubbock.

Standing by the cart, Dal finally thought to nod his head to Verner's question, then he lifted the cloth.

Shoulder-length black curly hair, matted with dried blood. Reflectively, he traced the high-boned curve of her cheek, cascaded down her strong, elegant nose, and tracked the course of her chin. Her brown eyes half-open and opaque, she bore an expression of faint surprise.

He had seen Susan many times before that spring afternoon in the Wolfforth Thriftway, although idle conversations at Creed school events, then the later funerals and weddings, hardly made for a friendship. Yet, when they tapped eggs for cracks and chatted about the weather, it seemed that the seven-year difference in their ages had faded into insignificance.

Their wedding followed five weeks later. A long acquaintance, a quick coupling, a disastrous honeymoon.

Verner and the attendants waited for him to draw the cloth. There were questions he needed to ask—an outrage needed to be voiced—not this absent-minded stroking of her shoulder, not this crawling into the void.

With no recollection of watching the cart leave, he realized that he was now sitting on the bed.

"I'm sorry for your loss, Mr. Creed. You understand, this is paperwork," the sheriff said. "Dotting the i's, crossing the t's. We know you were in Dallas."

"Do you have some idea of who you might be looking for?"

"No, we're hoping forensics will give us something to go on."

"Was she...?"

"Doesn't look that way, but there's always the possibility. Was she in the habit of leaving the door unlocked? We found no sign of forced entry."

"No, we're good about keeping things locked."

"I expect so, what with all the break-ins out in the county."

"That many?"

Talking consumed all his energy.

"Well, nothing around here 'til now, but it was only a matter of time. Junkies needing that crystal meth—you've seen the stories. Mrs. Wintersole says all she sees missing is the DVD player. If you find anything else gone, make a list. I'll be calling you tomorrow to update you on the investigation. If something breaks, you'll be the first to know."

Verner and his minions gone, Rosanna came in with a mop and bucket and began swabbing the floor in methodical strokes. Sane and deliberate, she described her day.

"We'd planned on going to the mall and eating out. I knew something was wrong when she didn't answer her phone this morning. She didn't come to the door. Then I came in.... I've already called Oralia Wender and the nursing home—did you know Susan'd been planning on changing to full-time?—and the preacher, of course. And everyone else I could think of, so you don't have to worry about calling anyone except your relatives. I didn't see any point in calling you while you were in the air. Nothing you could have done about it from there.

"A TV crew came in a helicopter before you got here, and a man from the paper talked to Levon so you don't have to. From what a deputy told me, the pathologist is awful busy right now, what with the lawsuit and all. In the meantime, I think a memorial service's the right way to go, don't you think?"

He managed a bleak nod.

"The burial's not all that important anyway, though if you want a service when the time comes, I'm sure it can be arranged. It's what you want that's important. I figure Thursday'll give us enough time. Does eleven a.m. sound okay? Good. I'll take care of everything."

The floor wiped clean, she sat beside him and held his hand.

"Levon should be back soon with supper. I know you like chicken, no matter who makes it."

How like Rosanna. She'd cried her tears, shouldered the hurt, and carried on—all in the course of a few hours—while Dal had yet to fully absorb the essential facts.

Susan. Dead.

What was the word he'd been searching for while Verner was talking?

Murder. His wife had just been murdered.

# CHAPTER TWO

*Creed Hill (also known as Mount Rushmore)—Begins about twenty-five yards from Dal's back porch. It rises to a height of over fourteen feet before sloping steadily downward into a grove of fruit and pecan trees. Rose bushes and a quartet of trailing honeysuckle bushes line the cobbled pathway up and down, while on the peak there is a concrete bench facing east. Robert Rushmore Creed Sr. started initial construction during the 1940s in response to a complaint by his West Virginia-born wife, Cora, about the absence of hills. Seeding it in grass, Robert Rushmore Creed Jr. completed the hill in 1960.*

Riotous flowers flooded the altar, threatening to upstage the pastor's eulogy. His epistle included references to Susan's longtime support of Redemption Baptist Church. He failed to mention her recent backsliding, nor the fact that Dal was making a rare visit through its doors.

"I know all of us will miss her work with the children's choir, and she certainly went the extra mile in expanding our clothes closet for the needy here in Wolfforth. She was truly a dedicated Christian. I know her sudden parting came as a shock to us all."

Hearing the weak euphemism for murder, Dal glared at its author. Flustered, the pastor blurted out the rest of the eulogy then the congregation sang "Softly and Tenderly." The service concluded with an invitation to dine in the fellowship hall.

Dal was surprised at the number of mourners, many of them with familiar faces, lining up at the potluck table. Creed having expired as a community, occasions for former residents to gather were few and far between. Pecan pie and condolences. He went through it twice before at that church. The first when Mother died, the last twelve years ago when Junior fell victim to exposure a few yards from his front door during a January blue norther.

On that one, mourners were at a loss for what to say. Locals knew that Junior had a penchant for sleepwalking far afield. A famous cartoonist was expected to have peculiarities—dying strange being one of them.

Dal viewed the move back home as short-term while he wrapped up his father's estate. He was the only heir and sole beneficiary of the will, except for a scholarship fund in Junior's name at Texas Tech.

Junior's first wife had moved back East not long after the nuptials and filed for divorce—on grounds of excessive wind, Junior said on one of the few occasions he mentioned her. A born-in-the-grit Panhandler, Mother taught the third and fourth grade class for a year before accepting Junior's marriage proposal. Their late marriage produced a son who never witnessed Creed in its heyday. Dal suspected that the town had never been a keeper.

He'd seen his father's cartoons all his life, and had already drawn a couple of graphic novel runs for an indie publisher in L.A., so when the comics syndicate asked him to do three months work to finish up, it seemed an easy enough gig.

He could work anywhere, given a decent Internet connection, but he stayed put, and kept at it.

Then came Susan.

"Dal?"

Oralia Wender stood before him plate in hand, a dark-eyed, slender woman looking even smaller in her dejection. Dal searched for something to say appropriate to the occasion.

"Nice dress."

"Susan made—" Oralia fled in the direction of the restroom.

He knew, didn't he, that Susan had sewn that dress for Oralia. He watched the two giggle as Susan took the younger woman's measurements. They were close friends, closer in fact than he and Susan had been for large stretches of their marriage.

Lupe Marroquin, normally taciturn, rose to the occasion.

"The women here sure are good cooks. You know, Elsa brought the pecan pie. The nuts came from your trees. I remember Elsa coming home after cracking with Susan all afternoon. She had blisters on her fingers."

No one had a rejoinder to that.

Coming over from the potluck table, Elsa refilled their tea glasses.

"Someone needs to talk to Mack," she said with a worried expression. "He's sitting in his pickup, throwing out empty beer cans."

Mack Wender and Susan broke up not long after their high school graduation. It didn't surprise Dal that Mack was taking her death hard.

Mack had been named after Colonel Ranald Mackenzie, a famous Indian fighter who rendered the Llano Estacado safe for settlers, railroads, and frozen yogurt bars. Along with his arrowheads, Mack treasured Wild West memorabilia and varied grievances.

When Mack and Dal were around each other, which, thankfully, didn't occur often, he liked to tell stories from his and Susan's high school days. The point of the anecdotes hardly mattered. Dal was supposed to come away instructed on how better Mack knew Susan than her husband.

Mack might have made a more compatible match with Susan, might have fended off the burglar, and might have figured in any number of possible scenarios leaving Susan alive. He lucked out. Dal was the jerk who left Susan alone that night.

He went outside to the parking lot.

Slumped over in his seat, Mack tossed another crumpled Silver Bullet out his pickup window.

"Enjoying the party?" Mack's eyes were bloodshot.

"Not as much as you."

Dal didn't look forward to a confrontation. Then again, he wasn't going out of his way to avoid it.

"Hellfire and damnation, who needs it?" Mack punched out the words out like a TV preacher.

"It wasn't like that at all."

"You'd know all about it, wouldn't you, sitting up there, the Man of the Hour. You don't know a dadgum thing."

It had been a bad idea to come over. Dal turned to leave, which produced another outburst from Mack.

"You had everything, had all your ducks in a row, but you had to snatch her up like you were entitled. You had no business with a woman like her. Hell, you don't know a thing about what matters."

Almost to his car, Dal took Mack's bait. "What, what matters?"

"Respecting the people who came before you, not acting like it don't mean a thing. All your family was that way, fiddling while Paris burned, the whole town falling down around them."

"Rome." Dal slammed his door.

A few minutes later, he was sitting on the hill behind his house. Eastward over the orchard, he saw the Shinnery—a quartet of scrub-clotted mounds—and, over to the northwest, a nubby horizon that at night lit up with the Lubbock skyline.

A three-sixty spin blurred the sea-green cotton fields and blonde grasslands carpeting spaces left by the demise of Creed. It hid the uprooted foundations of houses, churches, a hardware store, a grocery, and other enterprises. A passing stranger wouldn't know that the town boomed and faded for over sixty years along a narrow strip of road. Dal himself would have been hard-pressed to tell where certain houses once stood.

It took no effort at all to see Susan running in her worn gray and gold Creed High School Cavalier sweats down the adjoining dirt road.

She always started from the highway flowing north, her effortless strides taking her by the Marroquin place, where the oldest daughter would sometimes join her. A bobbing form kicking up clouds of dust, she shrank still further until by the time she reached the cemetery, her usual turnaround point, she was but a spot in the distance.

She disappeared.

A slapping sound came from the direction of the school, echoing like wood on brick. Most likely a section of shuttered windows freed by the wind. Susan used to follow a path going from their house to a concrete half-court hidden in a U-shape, formed by the high school Vo-Ag shop, cafeteria, and Home Economics room.

There, she'd play basketball with Oralia, Levon, the Marroquin kids, or Dal. With Oralia or the Marroquins, she took it easy by opting for shooting contests. With the men, there was no mercy shown and none granted.

After Frenship—which was Wolfforth's school district—annexed Creed ISD, an outside wall to the gym was knocked down to create a storage facility for the Culdesac Gin and Tom Wintersole's equipment. It left an ugly gash visible to passing drivers.

When Wintersole, a laconic, weathered man, died a couple of years ago, there was an auction of his farm equipment, save for one small tractor Rosanna used on her lawn. Feeling unaccountably grim, Dal walked over with Susan to the gym to watch. Although they lived next door, neither of them had been inside the building since the school shut down.

The bleachers had been taken up and sold some time back. Buyers and gawkers, leaning on combines, spat tobacco stains onto the badly splintered wooden court.

Faded and peeling from the elements, the Southern Cavalier on the west wall looked much the worse for wear. During the '50s and '60s, Cavalier girls and boys teams won a clutch of state championships, and even toward the end, when the program had trouble fielding the regulation number of starters, Creed teams won more games than they lost.

"We shouldn't have come," Susan said to him as they looked at the bedraggled south goal.

If he were to peer around that last corner leading to the open air court, would Dal see Susan pivoting in the post, launching a fade-away jumper, leaning hard into a lay-up, or slapping the ball out of her opponent's hands?

Susan easily could have earned an athletic scholarship. She never quite explained to Dal why she had turned down all offers. Maybe it had to do with living in the smallest town in the universe—that's what Junior called Creed—and being afraid to fail in the big time. The intimidation factor.

Dal remembered Susan's adoptive father, Floyd Longbrake, as a dour, leathery man who worked long hours on his tractor. He rarely opened his mouth except to complain about cotton prices and the weather. He didn't strike Dal as an inspirational role model.

According to Rosanna, Longbrake attended only one of Susan's games, that being the last Homecoming against Ropesville, during which she scored fifty-two points. Floyd had likely placed all his ambition on his son, who died of appendicitis one week short of his twelfth birthday.

Adopting the infant Susan decades later had been his wife, Dovie's, idea, but the old man, who Susan called Poppa Floyd, did warm up to her toward the end. He'd take her quail hunting up by White River when he was well past eighty and as likely to shoot a Winnebago as a tuft of feathers.

Susan rode a tractor during planting season, moved irrigation pipe, and chopped weeds. She worked alongside her parents and the occasional migrant Poppa Floyd deigned to hire. Dal drafted images of Susan—deeply tanned and not quite adjusted to her height—loping after Poppa Floyd down the turnrows or through the brush, carrying a jug of water or a rifle. Trying to keep up, trying to please.

This Susan he could empathize with, for Junior couldn't abide his son's lack of enthusiasm for becoming a lawyer. To Junior, thin and delicate in appearance with a devout dislike for all things agricultural, the best life for his son was one involving a minimum of sweat.

Dal, who developed along the lines of a cornerback, wanted to plow his Grampa Rush's fields, and later, as a blue-jacketed Future Farmer of America, he raised blue ribbon barrows. After a year at Texas Tech, he transferred to UCLA, where he promptly flunked out, being more interested in bong design than in pre-law.

His friends never met Junior, so naturally they thought his father was the yokel they'd seen in an occasional article or news program. Dal didn't bother explaining that Junior practiced his own form of performance art.

At home, his father stuck out like wingtips in a boot shop. He was a stickler for the proper pronunciation of "theater," subscribed to the New

York Times, and wore a jacket and tie year-round, except for the tire-melting days of August.

While out on the publicity rounds, though, he accepted compliments and brickbats with equal aplomb, a cigar jammed in the corner of his mouth, and a thumb looped in his pants pocket. He topped off the act with a thick twang and a gray Resistol.

Dal as a boy sometimes accompanied his father on those trips. Fancy restaurants, ornate hotel rooms, skyscrapers, and crowded sidewalks—Dal marveled at them all. His father's impersonation of a cartoon bumpkin proved to be the most arresting image. When they returned home to Mother, Junior put away the western hat and donned his usual citified apparel. Dal wasn't fooled. The dry, proper Robert Rushmore Creed Jr. was a fraud, no more believable than the uptown yokel.

Susan had remembered his father as a quiet man except at ballgames, where he stayed true to the Creed fan motto, "We're loud and getting louder."

For graduation, Junior gave her fifty-two silver dollars in honor of the game at New Home. She said Poppa Floyd threatened to use them as a doorstop. Dal, who had been letting the wind rock him slightly back and forth on the bench, stopped cold.

How could he think there were any real similarities between those two elderly men, who lived their entire lives less than two miles apart from one another.

Junior expected great deeds. Poppa Floyd expected nothing.

# CHAPTER THREE

*Culdesac Gin—Built in 1929 by brothers Robert Rushmore and Alva Rudyard Creed, and Tyrone Wender, who were under the mistaken impression that a spur would soon be built to their location from the Wolfforth railroad switch. The Creeds founded Creed community several months earlier, selling lots cut-rate to the first fifty families. Wender picked and dehyphenated the cotton gin's name out of a dictionary. Culdesac's fortunes have shrunk with the town.*

From scraps of paper, the backs of card receipts, grocery bags, and yellow legal pads, Dal collated sight gags for the panel, then hashed out some twenty to thirty roughs. He always kept six weeks ahead of publication.

When he first took over the panel, Dal was concerned about style continuity, so he used three-ply smooth Strathmore paper, Higgins india ink and a Gillot #170 pen—exactly like Junior—and he kept both style and content as much like his father as possible.

Over time, continuity went by the wayside. Dal's tastes ran to less wash, less shadows, less clutter and more puns, more impact panels, where the joke came completely from the sight gag, rather than buried in the tagline or balloon.

For the daily panels, Dal used a Venus drawing pencil. He mailed completed Sunday panels to the syndicate in Chicago where a colorist did her magic. Dailies he scanned and sent via email attachment. He'd tried various software applications but hadn't found one yet that would make him completely abandon paper.

Dal's burst of activity since the funeral had added several more weeks to his lead-time. He had abundant time now to clear his workroom of clutter, mow the lawn, change the oil filter in his car, then sit at his drawing table and stare blankly at the outsized George Herriman Krazy Kat panel spread across the south wall.

In it, Krazy was walking toward the love of his/her life, Ignatz Mouse, with a squiggle of cactus in the distance. A brick hurled by Ignatz remained frozen between the pair.

"Movillis, stipenditz, killotzil," Dal mumbled.

A knock on the front door stirred him to unwilling action. A well-dressed Hispanic man, bearing a briefcase, waited on the porch.

"Mr. Creed? I'm Gabriel Torrez. I'm here about your wife."

Nice suit. Dal, dressed in worn jeans and sporting a week's worth of stubble, poured his guest a glass of iced tea.

"So, any fresh leads so far?" Or leads of any kind.

Torrez appeared uncomfortable. "Look, I'm not with the law. I'm a private investigator."

"If you're here trying to drum up business, forget it. I'm going with the District Attorney."

"This isn't about what happened to your wife. Mrs. Creed hired me some time back to find out about her mother. You know she was adopted."

"She never acted as though she wanted to know anything more than that."

"I guess she changed her mind. She went through her adoptive mother's papers and found out she was born in a private clinic over in Big Spring. I took it from there."

His retainer probably accounted for two large withdrawals from her savings account. That had been a point of interest to a young woman from the District Attorney's office heading the murder investigation. Most of the money came from the sale of the Longbrake farm, and the purpose of the withdrawals mattered little to him, until now.

"Did she owe you more money?"

"Our arrangement was that she'd pay in thirds, the last part when I completed my work, but I've hit a dead end." Torrez flinched at his words' unintended meaning.

"I found an old nurse in Big Spring who told me some things, then the doctor's widow let me look through boxes of his old records. I couldn't find out anything about the mother. I did get the father's name. I've never seen that happen before."

"I appreciate how hard you must've worked, but this doesn't have a thing to do with me. You understand? And I don't believe her father, wherever he is, would want to hear about it. 'Guess what? You have a daughter. And guess what else? She's dead.'"

Torrez seemed unfazed by Dal's rising anger.

"There's a sister. A twin. Maybe she'd like to know."

A twin? Feeling overwhelmed, Dal eased himself into a chair. Torrez pulled papers from his briefcase.

"Here's the birth certificate for your wife. You see how the parents' names are blacked out. Now, look at the twin. Mother's name still blacked out, but this has the father listed. Address and everything. The nurse couldn't tell me much the first go-round, but when she looked at the papers, it jogged her memory some. It helped that they were twins. She told me the father came up and took one of the twins back with him to Lambert. That's over by Houston."

"Were the parents married?"

"No. The father was already married to someone else. The nurse couldn't tell me anything about the mother except that she was from Texas. What a way to narrow it down."

"You said you had the father's address?"

"Yeah, I traced him to his current location. Still the same town. I also dug up the twin's address and phone number. It's right here."

He plopped his folder on the table.

"How much do you want?" Dal asked.

Torrez acted offended.

"Nothing. I identified only one of the birth parents. I thought you'd like to have the report. 'Sides, I kind of feel bad about waiting to tell her. I had all this done, but I needed to get right on another job. Then I saw on the news what happened to your wife."

Dal didn't know what to say. After a spell, Torrez must have figured he wouldn't receive a thank-you, or any response at all, because he gave Dal a decisive nod and headed out the door.

Dal sat on his front porch swing. He started to pull out his Android phone then tucked it back into his pocket. He had no idea who to contact. Susan's adoptive cousins, kindly people who'd been at the memorial service, cried tears at her passing, but Susan hadn't been close to them. They likely didn't know details about the adoption, nor could they offer advice on what to do. Her closest friends were Oralia, who probably didn't need reminding right now of her loss, and Rosanna, who was made of stronger stuff.

Dal rode his bicycle over to the Wintersole place, where he found Rosanna in the ostrich shed, setting out feed in the pens. She owned eight birds separated into four couples, all several months away from breeding maturity, although Rosanna already had the incubator prepared for the eggs.

Making himself useful, Dal took the water detail. He tried not to move too fast since the birds were easily agitated. Preston ducked her head down and tried to snatch Dal's Red Raiders cap, but he had already anticipated the attempted mugging by backing up a few steps.

Rosanna named the birds after Texas governors. Ann and W comprised one odd couple, along with Preston and Sam, Ma and Pa, and Mirabeau and Dolph.

"What do you remember about when the Longbrakes adopted Susan?" Dal followed Rosanna into her sunny, Mediterranean-themed kitchen.

"That's been ages ago. I remember Dovie being so thrilled."

Rosanna grew up helping her parents run a gas station across the highway from his house. Ten years older than him, she'd been his babysitter and then later the object of adolescent admiration when she married Tom Wintersole. Boyishly angular—her short dark hair shot through with gray—Rosanna seemed to be losing a year for every one Dal added.

Pulling bags of black-eyed peas to the table, she continued talking as they popped peas into colanders.

"Dovie couldn't have any more children, so when her boy died, that was it. Then the opportunity came along to adopt Susan."

"Wait a second. How'd the opportunity come about?"

"I don't know. I know that Frannie Lowell was living in Big Spring, and she told Dovie."

"Did Frannie know anything about the mother?" Frannie was an old schoolmate of Rosanna.

"I don't know." Rosanna's pea-popping speed picked up considerably.

"Do you think it's possible she's the mother?" A shot in the dark.

"No. Frannie wasn't inclined that way."

"You mean, she's a lesbian." Dal didn't hide his smile.

"I mean what I mean, Dal. Lesbians have babies, too. Frannie's not the mothering type. Why're you bringing it up now?"

Dal told her about Torrez. Rosanna shook her head.

"Even if all that's true, it's best not to try calling those people. Let sleeping dogs lie."

That night, as a Mad Men download played unnoticed, he read over and over the contents of the folder. Two birth certificates, a record of Torrez's phone calls, current addresses and a note that read "Identical!" How could they tell at that age? Wouldn't it be a matter of opinion, not medical fact, that two tiny, squalling infants were exact duplicates?

What if it were true, that, thirty-three years later, Gina Marilee D'Abruzzo still resembled Susan? The father, Daniel Anthony D'Abruzzo, resided on Eisner Avenue, while the twin was listed as living at the Seabreeze Quarters, both in Lambert.

There was nothing to stop him from calling the twin's phone number listed except common sense.

He regretted pressing the buttons almost instantly, was on the verge of hanging up, when a woman's voice came onto the line.

"Hello?" She repeated the word several times before ending the connection.

Gina D'Abruzzo spoke in a warm, throaty timbre, lacking only a stronger twang to make her a vocal double of Susan. Finally remembering to click off his phone, Dal remote-channeled the show volume up a notch and tried to lose himself in 1960s Manhattan.

Poor bastard, Dal said aloud. He realized at that moment that he had been crying for some time. Crying for Susan, for himself, and for Gina, who probably didn't know Susan ever existed. Was Susan the castoff, the extra daughter neither parent wanted? This D'Abruzzo character might not even care if Dal told him what happened.

That night, Dal dreamed that Susan survived the attack, and he was on his way to Covenant Hospital with Torrez.

"This is great news," he said to Torrez, who was dressed in surgical greens. They kept getting lost on the first floor while trying to find the elevators.

When he woke up, he was standing on the exact spot where Susan had been found, his right knee throbbing from a bump into the bedpost.

## CHAPTER FOUR

*Rudyard's House--The Alva Rudyard Creed house lies directly across the highway from Culdesac Gin. It originally served as the home of the brothers Creed—Rudyard and Rush Senior—and their wives. C.W. Post, creator of Post Cereals, sold a large tract of land, which included the eventual site of Creed, to land speculator J. Butch Tobias in 1904. Decades later, Tobias sold the property to the Creed brothers, cattle investors from Fort Worth. Rudyard's house boasted a spacious veranda, two indoor bathrooms, a music room, four bedrooms, a large kitchen, and cold cellar. Only a battered shell remains.*

Early the next morning, Dal moved some of his things into the guest bedroom, and then drove into Lubbock to see his friend, Raymond Rodriguez. Raymond owned a printing and silkscreen operation downtown on Avenue Q, where Dal used to work when taking a break from his post-college wanderings.

Raymond bore a look of perpetual good humor that went well with his Hemingway beard. Over cups of coffee in his cluttered office, which was plastered wall to wall with prints and posters, Raymond listened to the Torrez story.

"Do you believe him?"

"I think I do, but now what?"

Dal shifted his leg again to relieve the tightness in his knee.

"You got me," Raymond said. "The deal about the father strikes me as really strange. He agrees to take a child, but the mother turns up her nose."

"She might have been underage."

"Maybe so. When're you going down to Lambert?"

"I haven't decided if I should."

"I'd be raring to go." Without looking, Raymond flipped the teabag over his shoulder into the trashcan. "That blows my mind, some gal zipping around who's a proof of Susan. Are you going to talk to the dad first?"

"I don't know what I'm going to do. All I know is that the cops haven't found the son of a bitch that killed Susan. She's lying in some vault, and I don't know when she'll be released for burial. They keep saying there's a backlog—you know that pathologist's in trouble. Ask me if I give a rip what Susan's so-called real father thinks. I've half a mind to send him a copy of the articles that ran, and let Fedex do the honors."

"Be a heck of a way to find out," Raymond murmured.

His voice starting to rasp, Dal flailed on. "Hell of a way. 'Bout as subtle as how I found out. Half the Sheriff's Department in my living room. Her—God—her perfume. I go by her dresser and I can smell it."

He could feel his pulse racing, the muscles in his neck tensing like rows of archers. Even in the nadir of their marriage, he and Susan slept apart only once or twice. In recent weeks, she had begun to relax her defenses, to cede moments of intimacy. They had been on their way back, it seemed.

"Dal?" Raymond looked worried.

"I'm thinking."

About what, he couldn't quite fathom.

Back before he reduced the strip to a panel, Junior never allowed his minor league baseball team, the Windswept Jackalopes, to post a winning season. He told Dal, "It wouldn't be right to spoil such perfection."

When Dal lived in L.A., he attended a charity fundraiser where a magazine writer informed him of the influence Samuel Beckett had on the "classic Twister Tales of the '50s." Dal listened with bemusement while the writer described Junior's creations as absurdist poems of futility.

He told her, "Basically, my father thinks life is dumb. You can call that an absurdist viewpoint if you want to. He doesn't care."

Junior resisted any effort to label his work as art. "Any school kid can do what I'm doing," he'd say dismissively to admirers, though Dal remembered his father reading a book on cartoonists. Dal couldn't get his father to talk about it, even though the chapter that mentioned Twister Tales appeared heavily thumbed.

In the old Twister Tales strip, intellectuals were dolts in black suits, while athletes, even the hapless Jackalopes, were heroes of a sort. In that Twister Tales, Susan would be drawn as Babe Didrikson, who'd set dozens of records in Windswept County for tumbleweed racing and clodhopping.

Though Elmo J. Twister might foolishly endanger her life in publicity stunts, she would avoid serious injury. In the last panel, she'd be depicted waving cheerfully from the back of a produce truck on her way to fame and fortune.

Life is dumb. Boy meets girl, boy marries girl, boy tries to figure out girl for eight years, and then some son of a bitch murders her. Dumb.

"Dal, I've got a book at home about twins."

No surprise. Raymond's ex-partner claimed irreconcilable differences with his personal library as the reason for their split.

"Thanks, but this isn't something I can study my way through."

"You'd be surprised. There was a study done on identical twins who had been raised separately. They found some amazing coincidences, like where twins married women with the same first names, gave their kids the same names, even worked the same kind of jobs.

"Oh, and Delta Avaro wrote a great poem about twins." Her again. "I wish you'd give her a try. You saw her that one time on a talk show and got the wrong impression. She's really a good writer."

"Some other time, Ray."

Dal decided to head back home, where he found Pogo on the front porch.

A German Shepherd with untamable wanderlust, Pogo sometimes dropped by for meals and adulation from Susan. Dal brushed the dog's coat free of dust and stickers and let him in the house. Wagging his tail like a bent windshield wiper, Pogo raced from room to room, looking for Susan.

Disappointed, he reported to Dal in the utility room. He wolfed down leftovers and departed through the flopper.

Flopper. That was Susan's name for a swinging entry cut into the screen door.

Maybe if he went to Lambert, he'd get some things straight in his head. He saw no need to talk to the woman, since the father could clear up the details. Why were the twins raised apart, and why had Susan been exiled to Creed?

It didn't take long to pack. In case Pogo made a return appearance, Dal set out a few foil packages of dog food, then called Elsa Marroquin and asked her to keep an eye on both dog and house.

He kept the speedometer at seventy all the way downstate, following the GPS directions diligently as he drew closer to Lambert. Warehouses, strip malls, and endless car dealerships lined the interstate heading into Houston with no apparent break. Stuck inside a trucker sandwich, he kept missing exits that claimed access to Lambert.

Frustrated, he got off the interstate at the next opportunity. After the usual number of wrong turns and lucky breaks, he came across Lambert, a tropically lush town of some ninety thousand.

At a Stop 'N Go, he bought a map, drew circles around the two D'Abruzzo addresses, then checked his watch. 11:01 p.m. Not a decent hour for dredging up the past with strangers.

At 11:20 p.m., he rolled into the parking lot of Seabreeze Quarters, a trim square of apartments located in a quiet neighborhood not far from I-10. At 11:43 p.m., he extricated himself from his Saturn and walked purposefully into the courtyard area. He stopped to peer at the number on a door. Apartment 109 stood a few feet away. He almost sprinted back to his car.

Early the next morning, after a sleepless night at a Best Western, he parked on a side street next to the Seabreeze and waited. Eventually, Susan came down the walk, slipped into a rose-colored Prius, and drove off.

Freed from his paralysis, Dal pumped the accelerator and barreled around the curve. He caught up to Susan at the intersection, where, two cars ahead, she waited for the light to change. Careful to stay behind a discreet distance, he followed her to a large office building.

He watched as Susan parked near a large sign emblazoned with the TopSound corporate logo. She chatted briefly with a middle-aged black man in a pinstriped suit who'd arrived at the same time, then she walked through the front door with him.

After a moment of dithering, Dal headed to the other circle on his map. Roughly equidistant between the warehouse and Susan's apartment, Eisner Avenue was a small, beige stucco house in a block of small stucco houses, some more rundown than others.

He walked up to the front door, folder in hand, and pressed the buzzer.

A tall, gray-haired man opened the door. Dal pulled an old publicity photograph from the folder and brandished it in his face.

"This is me; this is my wife. I just saw her a while ago. I thought she was gone, I thought she was never coming back, so I want to know what kind of game you have going here, D'Abruzzo."

There was a wheeze in the older man's voice when he responded. "You have the advantage on me, Mister...?"

"Creed, Dal Creed."

"Did you talk to my daughter?"

"I didn't want to scare her off. You have a lot to explain." Dal's body felt like a clenched fist.

D'Abruzzo, looking thin and unwell, unlatched the screen door, took the photograph without comment, then padded into the kitchen. He sat down at the table and breathed into a small bubbling machine while Dal stood awkwardly by the refrigerator.

Small place, he thought. Cozy might be the word to describe it, cramped being another.

"I used to have to go to the hospital all the time to get my treatments. Now, I can do them at home. Technology's something," D'Abruzzo said when he was through.

The man sounded stronger, although breathy. "So, Mr. Creed, you think Gina's your wife."

Faint, feeling quite faint. Sitting down at the table, Dal gaped at the graduation photograph on the wall across from him. It pictured an adolescent Susan—make that, Gina— wearing a black gown with red accents. Susan's portrait back home featured the Cavalier gray and gold.

The name still reverberating through his mind, he replayed the image of Susan's twin walking into the office building. Gina.

She had been wearing black slacks and a soft pink blouse. A shoulder-length hairstyle that looked blow-dried into straight sheets. Urban, slick. Gina.

Susan wore her hair straightened for a while before reverting to her usual natural, untamed curls. He liked the feel of her hair in his hands when they were making love—coils of inky wildness matching their owner. How could he have forgotten she was dead when for days he had thought of nothing else.

His head drooping to the table, he wept.

"When's the last time you ate?" D'Abruzzo asked after a polite interval.

"Yesterday, I think." Hands shaky, but he felt somewhat more composed.

"Marilyn—that's my wife—she left some breakfast. I ain't been real hungry lately."

He scooped some scrambled eggs, bacon, and biscuits off the warmer onto a plate. He added a glass of orange juice at the table.

"I always wondered if Susan'd come looking for me. It never crossed my mind you'd be the one to show."

"You knew she was married?"

"Sure did."

"Who told you?"

"That's not for me to say," D'Abruzzo said easily. "There're other people in this thing."

"Like the mother. Who is she?"

The eggs, peppery and dotted with sliced cherry tomatoes, were delicious.

"I understand how you feel, but the deal was cut a long time ago on how to handle it. I can't go changing the rules now. You want some honey on your biscuits?"

"Maybe a little."

"There you go. Whatever problem you're having with your wife, it'll work out. She shows up, I'll call you. Another thing: Gina don't know nothing about this, so you leave her and Marilyn out of this unless Susan comes 'round."

No wonder he was the picture of relaxation. He had worked out his response years ago on what to say and how to handle it. Dal had come into his home, eaten his food, and now he was about to tell the man that he'd lost a daughter he'd never known.

# CHAPTER FIVE

"I'd tread lightly around Aaron if I were you," Cyril Murray said to Gina D'Abruzzo as they went into the office.

Aaron was Cyril Murray's younger brother, and the head of accounts at TopSound Corporation.

"He got on Garcia's bad side last night. You know he'll want you to go over and make nice to Mister Wholesale."

"Last time that happened, I ended up going out with him."

She wished that Aaron would stop socializing with people he hated. He felt obligated to be on good terms with business contacts—with the entire world, actually—which is why he attended Lambert civic functions, smiled all evening, and popped Nexiums the next day.

"That's going the second mile." Cyril rubbed his mustache delicately. "But if Garcia asks you out again, say no. You've had enough practice turning down suitors. One more shouldn't be much of a stretch."

They went their separate ways—Cyril to a plush suite, Gina to a comfortable office down the hall.

Gina went to work for Cyril right out of high school when his corporation consisted of the Lambert TopSound One-Stop and a handful of outposts statewide, including a struggling strorefront in Houston run by Aaron. Even then, he was better at numbers than customer relations.

Gina had been commuting to the Montrose store with her sister, Linda, who'd drop her off en route to her own job. Gina would then catch a ride back to Lambert with Aaron at day's end.

One afternoon after she had been working there a month, Cyril came by to watch the operation. He arrived in time to watch a customer blister Gina for a minor mistake Aaron made in billing. While Aaron hid behind a CD display, she calmly handled the snafu. The customer ended up apologizing for his tantrum.

After a brief stockroom conference, Cyril emerged smiling and Aaron not at all. He exited via through the back door.

When Cyril told her she'd been promoted to manager, her first reaction wasn't sheer joy.

"I don't have a car. You need someone you can depend on."

Cyril told the other clerk to take over the register, then he drove Gina to a Lambert car dealership where he made a down-payment for her on a used Volkswagen.

Sixteen years later, TopSound's outlets flourished in three states and Gina filled the position of chief buyer, with occasional stints as a fixer at low-performers.

As she emailed an updated order sheet to a vendor, she thought, not for the first time, of how lucky she was to get in on the ground floor of a growing company.

On the other hand, she was never going to climb to the top of the company, not with Cyril's daughter, Charmaine, biding her time two doors down running the company's website and download service. She had recently joined the family business after working with some company in Atlanta. Lately, she and Gina had been desking together—company slang for office lunches. Speaking of...

Charmaine poked her head in the door. "You're still on for the game, aren't you?"

Gina had forgotten about the company picnic tomorrow at the city park. She'd be expected to assume her usual position of first baseman.

"Sure, I guess." There went the shopping expedition with her sister at the Galleria.

"How're we supposed to kick Garcia's crew with a 'sure, I guess'? We're going for two in a row, slugger."

Charmaine flicked a pistachio nut at her as a parting gesture and gave way to Binh Quong, an office assistant. Binh wore incendiary shirts that made her squint when giving orders.

"Gina, are your parents coming this year to the picnic? I have them down on my list."

"Yes, Daddy's been doing better."

"That's good. I wanted to check in case I needed to call in a few more plates to the caterer. Will there be any other guests?" Binh asked with particular alertness.

The Terry question. Even Cyril asked if she'd seen Terry lately. Everyone was acting so civilized, as though she and Terry hadn't engaged in a shouting match a couple of months ago in the parking lot.

"No, no other guests."

The rest of the morning passed quietly. Three calls from outlets about an MP3 player factory recall and order changes, email traffic with vendors, plus she'd updated her daily log of outlet sales. Cyril liked knowing at all times what items were moving and where.

Mom called to remind her, unnecessarily, that it was her turn at lunch with Daddy. Mom's days were tied down managing the West Lambert Stop 'N Go convenience store. She saw to it that her daughters each spent at least one lunch break a week with Daddy.

Linda brought along her twins during the summer, yet even when Terry was still living with her, Gina always came alone. Daddy was no fan of modern romance.

On the way over, she picked up two burger specials from Buck's Drive-In, but Daddy, who usually welcomed his favorite junk food, seemed preoccupied. Not one of his good days, health-wise.

"Babe, we've got a visitor. He's in the john. His wife died recently, so he ain't talking too much."

She wondered why her father was putting so much emphasis on his words.

"He a customer?"

After emphysema forced his retirement from selling cars, Daddy whiled away his hours creating intricate wooden puzzles that, stained and polished, were miniature works of folk art. Word of mouth over time had established a growing clientele.

"Yeah. Tell me, how's work going?"

As she was talking about the picnic, she heard footsteps behind her. Looking up, she saw a sandy-haired man, solidly built, perhaps in his forties. He looked as though he hadn't slept in a week.

"Gina, this is Dal Creed. Dal, this is my daughter, Gina."

When she got up to shake hands with him, she noticed that he was dressed in a rust jacket and beige slacks that might have cost him plenty, but didn't fit in with Lambert's usual late summer swelter. She had a feeling, though, that his shakiness had more to do with grief than humidity.

"I'm pleased to meet you. If you're hungry I can heat something up for you in a jiffy," she said to no effect.

The man sat down, dumbstruck, and still refusing to meet her gaze.

"Dal here draws that cartoon in the paper. You know the one called Twister Tales? We've been reading that for years."

"Sure have. You do good work."

She echoed her father's boosterism. Creed must have come to buy a toy and ended up telling Daddy the story of his life. He looked harmless, and if she continued to make nice, maybe Daddy would have a return customer.

"Baseball. You play baseball," Creed said in stumbling fashion.

"You heard us talking. The only time I play is at the annual picnic. There's this rivalry between the people I work for and the company across the street from us. My boss drafted me due to all the years I spent playing softball in summer league."

"Do you play basketball?" he asked raptly.

"People always think I used to play on account of my height, but no, I don't even do softball anymore. I ride my bicycle when I have time. Who has time these days?"

Why on earth was she rattling on, trying to lift that doleful expression from his face? It must be some kind of misplaced mothering instinct.

Daddy took over the conversation at that point. He did his best to fill in the many gaps until she went back to work.

Daddy might have been trying to set her up with the widower. The man needed time to grieve, for heaven's sake. She thought Daddy had given up on making a virtuous woman of her. He'd actually used that phrase once while talking up an associate minister at their church, and here he was, at it again.

That evening, Carla Johns called while she was chopping up vegetables for stir-fry, and tried to interest her in a blind date.

"You'll like this one, I swear. She's a systems analyst for Dell. Miss Smartypants, but not too arrogant. She moved from Phoenix a few months ago."

Gina and Carla met at a club many years ago when sex split, warped, and reformed many a relationship in their crowd.

Their friendship surviving intact, Gina was maid of honor at Carla's marriage to an associate at a Houston law firm. The answer to Gina's problems, Carla said, was a solid, long-term partnership.

"You've been listening to legal talk for too long," Gina remarked through a mouthful of water chestnuts. She sat the phone down, set it to speaker, and continued working.

"Look, if you don't want a sweetie, I know some men."

"Skip it."

"I don't remember you turning up your nose at Nick."

"Nick the narc. He was okay, and the best part was, he never talked about his work."

Splash peanut oil, soy sauce, chopped onions, and celery in the wok.

"See? There's hope for you yet. Too bad he got back together with that cop."

"No, they belonged together. Matching biceps. I don't consider myself a cold case, merely because I haven't grabbed on to the gusto."

Dump in chopped garlic and more vegetables, then stir.

"I only said that once. Gin, you must have everything I ever said to you filed away in that head of yours."

"That's right, and I also remember you telling me not to rush into anything."

Keep stirring, add sliced asparagus, then cover.

"Like with Terry," Carla said.

"That was a speed bump, not the real thing."

"You acted like it was."

"Okay, I did fool myself for a while. I'm good at that."

"I wish you'd settle down. You'd be so much happier."

"I am happy. Fine, tell me about your hot prospect."

Throw in a bowl's worth of leftover chicken and rice, spiked with Tabasco sauce. Turn off burner.

"Dianne Newberry. She's tall, so you can wear heels for a change. What else. She's a few years older than you—oh, and she's from England, originally. You'll love her accent."

Why not?

"Give me the number."

Write down number, shoot the breeze a while longer, then switch off the phone. Dump food into bowl, whisk wok, and dry. Sit at table, watch Bravo for a few minutes, pick at food.

Clicking off the TV, she punched the phone buttons quickly. A crisp voice answered on the second ring.

"Hello?" British Isles, as advertised.

"Hi, I'm Gina D'Abruzzo. Carla Johns gave me your number. Look, I'm not much on this blind dating thing. I don't do this all the time."

Dianne chuckled. "Neither do I. Where do you live? Maybe we could meet for coffee. I'm not dressed for going out. In point of fact, I was stripping the paint off my kitchen table. That's how exciting my Friday nights have been."

It turned out she owned a townhouse twenty minutes away in Crockettville, a Houston suburb fitting snugly next to the Lambert city limits. Damn, Carla was good.

They felt each other out, over cups of coffee at a brightly lit cafe off Main Street Lambert.

Lithe and smooth, Dianne batted stories back and forth with her about traffic and impressions of the Houston area. The conversation flowed casually into family anecdotes and ended with an exchange of email addresses.

She had peridot eyes and wavy blonde-streaked hair. Attractive, with a warm, loose smile. Gina liked her on the spot.

As they were walking out, a random impulse made Gina invite her to the picnic.

"You don't have to come," she said.

"It sounds like fun."

# CHAPTER SIX

As could have been predicted, Cyril's interest was piqued by Dianne's appearance next in line to Gina at the barbecue.

Following Cyril's beckoning finger, she met him by the tea table.

"Nice-looking young lady." Cyril glanced at Dianne, who was still loading her plate with sausage. "Hungry, too. I didn't think you'd be off the market for long."

Cyril's only real management flaw was his pronounced interest in her social life. Okay, his advice tended to be right on target. Surely most bosses confined their conversations to sales figures and golf games.

Under the shade of an elm tree, Gina, her parents, and Dianne ate at a picnic table and listened to a five-piece band, made up mostly of TopSound warehousemen, play Cyril-sanctioned covers of '80s R&B hits.

Daddy and Dianne hit it off immediately. They talked about carpentry and home repair—dry as dirt to Gina—but they seemed to find new depths to explore in the subject. Mom kept Dianne's glass filled and fetched her a dish of cobbler and ice cream.

Aaron Murray came over while Dianne was scooping up the last of dessert.

He made a pinched try at a company smile.

"Gina, come with me for a minute."

At the outskirts of TopSound's encampment, they peered over to the other side of the park, where Garcia's minions from Gulf Computech were gathered for their own picnic.

"You know we had to reschedule this thing twice? First time, Garcia's ex-wife had an operation, and then he decides he has to go to some wedding."

"His son's."

"All for a stupid game. It'd be a walkover if he didn't keep bringing in ringers."

"I don't know about that. He does have some good players."

"I want you to tell Garcia we'll be ready to go at two, not two-thirty. They should be over their plaque attack by then. And, uh, talk to him, you know."

"Yes, sir."

"Don't call me sir. I hate it when you do that."

It was hard not to be formal with Aaron, who wore an invisible neck brace. With Cyril, the challenge was to not be too informal, especially in the presence of Cyril's fashion-victim second wife.

Off Gina went, across the DMZ, past the baseball diamond, and into enemy territory. She found Ron Garcia talking to several middle-aged women. The awards ceremony apparently had concluded. Glad-handing them efficiently, he turned his attention to Gina.

"Damn, you look good." He took a swallow from his bottle of Budweiser. "If only you were a little shorter, I'd go out with you again."

"Aaron wants the game to start at two p.m."

"You're no fun today. And, don't talk to me about Aaron. I know he sent you."

"What was the fight about?"

"We didn't fight—it was more like a disagreement. You know how the City Council's wasting our tax money on those TV ads. 'Live the Good Life in Lambert.' Jesus, what jerk came up with that? We got too many people coming in as it is, and Aaron's wanting us to advertise even more.

"When I was a kid, there was nothing but trees between here and Houston. I used to go hunting—believe it or not—I used to go hunting out there, and we'd take our dates there to do the horizontal boogie. Did you ever go out there?"

"No."

"I bet you got a lot of offers. Hold on, I'm not through yet."

A clean getaway. Midway, she gave the thumbs-up to Aaron, who started gathering the troops. Mom walked with her over to the car as she retrieved her glove and aluminum bat.

Mom did her best to adopt a casual tone. "Dianne has such a nice speaking voice."

"With that accent, she could read a phone book and make it sound posh."

"Your father likes her."

"I'm glad."

"Who'd you say introduced you to her?"

"Carla."

A worried expression. "Oh, so she's that kind of friend."

"Mom, I like her, she likes me, but who knows what'll happen. I just met her last night."

"Last night."

Mom lapsed into a silence that lasted almost to the baseball diamond. Dianne and Daddy were already in the bleachers.

"Honey, it's just that Linda has her kids. I want you to find someone you can have a family with, someone you can be happy with."

"I'm happy right now."

What would it take to convince people she was doing fine? A wedding, probably.

The lineup hewed to the previous year's players, who were almost all Murray relatives and/or warehouse workers. Gina was the exception to that rule, in more ways than one.

While nepotism might have made warehouse foreman Richard Murray their starting pitcher, he did have a good fastball. He struck out the side, then came TopSound's turn at the bat.

GCC's pitcher was a burly redhead named Booger who had control problems—mostly with his temper, Gina thought. He kept barking at his catcher, but even though he loaded the bases, he managed to produce a double play and a strikeout to end the inning.

GCC mustered two runs in the second inning, one of them a dinger by a jubilant Garcia before Richard regained control of his fastball. Then came Gina's turn at the plate. While she was a solid fast-pitch softball player, she had no illusions about her ability to hit a testosterone bullet. She earned her spot in the lineup strictly because of her glove.

That, and she knew how to draw walks. Booger's boil was so comical she slowed down her jog to a stroll, so by the time she arrived on first, Booger's catcher was on the mound working on calming him down, while player-manager Garcia handled the reaming. Booger sent down two batters, then Richard tied up the game with a cannon shot that bounced off a car in the parking lot.

The rest of the game went in like fashion, punch-counterpunch. She singled, struck out, and walked again, but it was on defense where she earned her keep. She recorded several putouts, including one of Garcia.

Cyril, long retired to the bench, was enjoying a sunflower seed-spitting contest with Aaron.

Down to the ninth and once again, Gina was at the plate, this time with a man on second. Booger zinged two pitches past her for strikes and then wobbled a slider for a ball. After another lecture from Garcia, he scrunched his cap, spat and scowled. Gina resigned herself to a fastball that would send her back to the dugout.

His next pitch slammed into Gina's helmet, which she happened to be wearing at the time. By the time she relocated her feet and remembered how to use them, a fight had broken out.

When order had been restored, she was perched on first base, Booger had been thrown out of the game, and Mom was waiting in front of the TopSound Rappers' dugout.

Garcia had taken over as pitcher. Fumbling with his rosin bag, he failed to notice Richard edging away from third until, warned by his second baseman, his desperation throw bounced in front of the catcher. Richard by a nose. Game over.

If only her left ear would stop ringing. Cyril got to her first, joined by Mom and Aaron.

"I'm fine." She didn't sluff off her escort to the dugout.

"Gin, I want you to go to the hospital," Cyril said as Dianne, Daddy and another man—Dal Creed—crammed into the dugout.

"It's only a bump," she said.

"More like a chicken egg," said Charmaine Murray, who appeared out of nowhere.

"You mean, goose egg," Dianne corrected.

"I don't care what bird laid it, you're going to the hospital," Cyril said. "What's the point of insurance if you don't use it?"

"He's right, dear. I'll go bring the car around," said Mom.

"I'll do it. Give me the key," Dianne insisted. They left, still debating who would drive.

Aaron limped to the rail. "Good game, Gina. Too bad you missed the fight."

When had he been on the field? Oh yeah, while she was crumpled on home plate.

"You're the MVP of the game," said Charmaine.

"Richard's the one who stole home."

Cyril laid an ice bag on her bump. "Whoops, did that hurt? Let's get you up the stairs." He directed Dianne to her other side.

Daddy wheezed, "I'm proud of you, sweets."

"Daddy, you need to go home and use your machine."

"I'll take him," Creed said. He turned to Cyril. "This is very important: don't let them give her Demerol. She's allergic to it."

"Are you her doctor?" Cyril asked.

Daddy managed to say, "do what he says" before running out of breath.

Who was this guy? She'd never taken Demerol in her life. Daddy smiled at her encouragingly as, propelled by Creed, he set off in the opposite direction across the parking lot. Finally, Mom was driving her to the hospital with Dianne's car tailing closely behind. She felt so light-headed. Why not lean back and rest for a moment.

## CHAPTER SEVEN

She'd had a silly fainting spell, hardly lasting a minute, so why bother with the X-ray, the CAT scan, the poking and prodding? Her doctor, Marshall Zhang, fresh from his dance class, had it all in perspective.

"What you need to remember is that when you get beaned, you're supposed to stay down for the count," he said dryly. "People think they're in a video game and jump up as though nothing's happened."

"I'll remember that next time."

"Next time, duck. What you have is a mild concussion, not a fracture. It's okay to put some ice on the knot, but remember it's not a cure-all. Don't leave the ice on too long. Don't drive, don't exercise, don't do the tango. Take it easy. I'll write you a prescription for Vicodin. Okay, the nurse is going to give you a shot and you'll be on your way."

Mom poked her head in the door.

"Come on in, Mrs. D'Abruzzo. Your daughter'll be fine. She'll be good as new in a couple of days."

"The shot—it won't be Demerol, will it?" Gina asked reluctantly.

"No, are you allergic? It's not noted in your records."

"Some man said I was."

"To be on the safe side, I'll add that in," he said and left.

"You gave me such a scare." Mom took over icing the lump.

"Scared myself, too," she admitted. "Dianne's not still here, is she?"

"I told her it was okay to leave. She acted like she needed to be somewhere. Your daddy's on his way here. Sweets, I know you love the game, but you shouldn't play with the men. They're too rough."

"It wasn't my idea to do it. Garcia wanted a token woman and Aaron went along with it. He seems to think I'm a super athlete."

"For softball, yes. I wished you could have pursued tennis. You were so good at that."

"Mom, I only played when I was a freshman. I'm lucky if Linda and I play twice a year."

"I know. If we'd still had the money, we could've bought you membership in that club, and you'd have had more time to practice."

Mom would go to her grave blaming Daddy's bankruptcy for Linda becoming a legal assistant, not a lawyer, and Gina an audio buyer, not a tennis star or captain of industry.

Gina was nine years old when Daddy's financial empire fell into ruins. A constant blur, he hovered at the edge of their family life, trying to balance the spinning plates of his two car dealerships, cleaners, and nightclub until they all came smashing down in a morass of IRS audits and seizures. Afterward, a humble car salesman, he was home in the evening and more attentive as a father. Why be nostalgic for something she could barely remember?

The nurse, followed by Daddy and Creed, arrived with the shot. It brought to a blessed end Mom's reminiscing about their late, lamented split-level house on the "nice side of town."

Daddy continued Mom's theme of giving up the game.

"If they played fair, I wouldn't worry about you being out there, but they're men. They fight dirty."

Whoa with the needle there, lady. "You must not be remembering my league games, Daddy." Ow. "But if Aaron decides to take me off the team, I won't cause a stink. I'd be perfectly happy sitting in the stands with you guys."

"Do you feel okay?" Creed asked in a tentative voice, his eyes still not quite focusing on her.

Attired in pressed jeans, a navy blue tee and a white linen jacket, he looked wilted by the humidity. Gina wondered why he was still hanging around Daddy. Maybe the man needed a sympathetic ear—and couldn't recognize Daddy's ex-car salesman warmth for professional charm and not the real thing.

"It's a bump on the head. It'd take a whole lot more than a baseball to get through this thick skull of mine."

She added a smile when she saw him flinch.

After a certain amount of dickering to decide who would drive where, Mom took Gina back to the apartment, with Creed driving Gina's car behind them. Daddy served as his navigator.

The shot rendered her full of good will, which helped in tactfully easing everyone out the door.

Ten minutes later, Creed rang the buzzer, her car keys in hand.

"I was about to drive off from the park when I realized I still had these," he said with an apologetic expression.

His face looked so woebegone.

"Come on in."

She left the door open as she returned to her nest on the sofa. Don't take too long, she thought. I'm in need of an extremely long bath.

Shifting his weight from foot to foot, he stood clutching a manila envelope.

"Your key chain, it's almost exactly like hers...Texas with a star in the middle." His voice faded to a mumble.

Gina picked her keys up from the floor. "They must make thousands of these each year, maybe more."

He'd gotten too much sun, definitely.

"Do you like tea? I'm thirsty myself, so I know you must be."

Filling the tumblers, she soldiered on.

"I guess you're not used to our weather. Humidity can take the will to breathe out of a person, but at least it wasn't too hot today. Normally, our games don't end in fights. I wouldn't want you to get the wrong impression of us. I guess you being a cartoonist, you've been all over the place, seen everything. Sugar? I don't like it, either. I do like a little lemon juice. You? Great minds think alike."

The last of her baseball adrenaline trickled away as she handed a tumbler over to Creed and sat down. A long bath, a longer nap would be perfect. Let him finish his tea, and then hustle him out the door.

Creed dropped the envelope on the sofa beside her.

"I can't sleep, can't think. I've been racking my brains figuring out what to do. Your father says to take it slow, to wait until the time is right, and he'll tell you."

"Tell me what?" A nutcase, right there in her living room.

"But the right time has long past." He gazed intently at the carpet. "I can't wait on him. It's in my hands. Your voice is...so close to hers. A little more twang and her best friend couldn't hear the difference. The envelope—there're photographs. Take a look."

"Tell me what it is. I don't like surprises."

"If I tell you first, you'll throw me out."

"Then don't tell me. And get out." She tried to steady her voice.

"Sure," he said mildly.

Extricating a notepad from his jacket pocket, he scribbled hurriedly and put the scrap on a side-table as he moved to the door.

He was a bit loony, but harmless. Her initial hunch had been right.

"Look, I'm sorry about your wife, but you know, you've got to move on."

For the first time, he met her gaze squarely. "You're probably right."

Creed safely out the door, she pulled out a stack of photographs from the envelope. The first, a black-haired infant and her—his?—grandmother. On the back read: Susan, 3 mos., Momma. Make that mother, not grandmother.

The second photograph showed Gina when she was three or four years old, splashing in a muddy puddle with a German Shepherd. Except that they never owned a dog, on account of Linda's allergies. Again, "Susan" on the back.

The next photo, the lookalike appeared two or three years older, wearing her Sunday best, standing with Momma in front of a white church.

Her legs wobbly, Gina dug out a photo album from the hall closet and began a side-by-side comparison. She fought an impulse to skip to the end of the stack. The two babies seemed identical, as did the toddlers, the third grade, and sixth grade class pictures. Then came the teenagers.

Tanned and smiling, Susan leaned on a hoe in a field of some unknown crop. An elderly man, on the back listed as Poppa Floyd, was standing in profile pointing at something in the distance.

The next photo, Susan had a basketball in a death grip. She wore a gray and gold jersey.

The next photo, Susan and two boys, all in graduation gowns, were horsing around for the camera.

The next photo, flanked by Momma and Poppa Floyd, Susan was wearing a nurse's uniform and a stern expression.

The next photo, Dal Creed made his first appearance. Wearing a tuxedo, he was being fed cake by a laughing Susan. Her wedding dress was lacy, yet streamlined.

The next three pictures were casual shots. Susan in shorts, astride a bicycle. Susan in close-up, taken by surprise. Susan and Creed, leaning on the hood of a car. A brick house loomed in the background.

Looking up, she saw Creed hovering by the screen door.

"May I come in?"

Hearing no reply, he came in, closing the door behind him.

"I know this must be hard to accept."

"Accept what?" Gina flung the photographs to the floor. "There's a double for everyone. I've always heard that. Your wife and I—we do look a lot alike. It's just a fluke, that's all."

Let it be a side effect from the medication, somebody's idea of a sick joke. Daddy, however, wouldn't have let this man hang around unless—and the Demerol thing. Oh, God.

His voice still steady, Creed said, "This is the hard part, I know. I had trouble believing it. Susan was your twin. You were raised separately."

"Stop."

"Your father brought you back to Lambert—he's your birth father, by the way—and Susan was adopted by an older couple, farmers who lived a couple of miles from our place."

He tapped yet another folder in his hand.

"I saw them, in the pictures," she said haltingly.

"Now, you're probably wondering about the identity of your mother. The answer is: I don't know."

"I know who my mother is. You saw her today."

He sat down on her sofa and said softly, "The birth mother's name is blacked out on the records. The investigator told me your parents weren't married. It was a private adoption, from a clinic in Big Spring. You familiar with where that is? It's up the road from Midland-Odessa. I think the case may be that your father, for whatever reason, agreed to take you, but not Susan. He wouldn't tell me the circumstances, and I felt uncomfortable about approaching Mrs. D'Abruzzo."

"Don't say anything, don't go anywhere near her." Her words and thoughts lurched into a pile-up. "What do—why did you come here, why?"

"You believe me."

"I don't know what I think. Not a flipping clue. Don't you dare talk to Mom."

"She already knows. She has to. You're the only one who's been completely in the dark all this time. My wife, she only knew that she was adopted. She knew nothing more than that."

"That's what this is about? Your wife dies, so you decide to dig up the past? You should have left it alone."

"That's not how it happened. She set the wheels in motion; she paid for the investigation. If she hadn't been murdered, she would've received the report, not me."

"Murdered?"

Gina leaned back on her pillow and tried to concentrate. "Go slow. Who killed her?"

"A burglar. They haven't found him yet. I was in Dallas when it happened." He paused, and then stammered, "It was a blow to the back of the head."

A chill glaciated through her body. "Mr. Creed."

"Dal."

"Mr. Creed, I don't want to hear any more coincidences today. Leave me your address. Maybe—I don't know, maybe I'll call you—just go, please."

She would be calm, no matter what, until he left.

"Sure, and let me give you a copy of the birth records."

A reassuring smile and he was gone. He seemed more at ease than when she'd first met him, but after all, he'd transferred a two-ton weight onto her shoulders. He'd done his duty, if one could call it that.

Gina had a twin, someone who never knew Gina existed, but who set off this chain of events. Susan saw herself everyday in the bathroom mirror, brushed her teeth, and applied her makeup. She mugged for photographs, went to school, fell in love with Dal Creed, and then died at the hands of a criminal.

All that time she wore my face, Gina thought, picking up a photograph. Susan looked happy. If she'd found out in time, would she have left well enough alone? It could have been Susan, instead of Creed, in her living room. If not for a blow to the head.

# CHAPTER EIGHT

Big Spring, Sunday morning. The town rested sleepily in the middle of a wide basin, with contours and trees that made it stand out amidst its arid surroundings. Not much water, however, despite the name.

As he drove, Dal mentally rehearsed his approach to Frannie Lowell. "I know we haven't seen each other in who knows how long, but would you by chance happen to remember giving birth to twins over thirty years ago?"

Maybe this approach: "Did Dovie Longbrake ever mention who was Susan's biological mother?"

An image flashed of Gina falling after the wild pitch, taking him back to the previous day. The shock on her face registered even from his vantage point in the stands. He found himself racing along the fence to the gate. For a long, disorienting moment, he cried out Susan's name until he saw, through the furor, Gina rising slowly to her feet.

He knew the difference in an intellectual sense. Their first meeting at D'Abruzzo's house underscored that fact. Dal was a stranger to Gina—not a lover, not a husband, not an adversary—Dal was a stranger her father had befriended, a man to be dealt with in a polite, but detached, manner.

It occurred to him that he could easily walk away, drive home, and be done with this experiment in masochism.

He couldn't protect her from a wild pitch any more than he could bring Susan back to life. Gina might survive into her eighties, she could die the very next second; either way, did he want to know the outcome at close hand? He couldn't take losing that face again.

"She got her bell rung, but she's up and around." D'Abruzzo stood beside him.

Dal leaned closer. "I want to know why you didn't take Susan, why the girls were split up. Tell me that, and I'll be on my way."

"It's not up to me. I told you that. Look, I'm sorry about your wife."

"And your daughter."

"I knew about her. I knew when she graduated from high school. I knew when she got married."

"But not when she was murdered."

Heavy-lidded and resentful, he stared at Dal.

"No, I didn't. Marilyn keeps up with the news. She would've told me eventually. You want me to shoot my mouth off. You want me to say what a jerk I was. Yeah, it's my mistake, it's my fault what happened, and I have a saint of a wife who forgave me. She took Gina in without skinning my hide in the bargain."

"Didn't people gossip?"

"Some of them wondered. Marilyn made like the baby was hers, that Gina was born premature. Linda was little at the time, so she believed whatever we told her. A few years after that, I lost my shirt. We got dropped by most of our so-called friends. We weren't in their social set anymore. You get the picture. Our real friends don't give a damn how Gina got here. She's our daughter—look at that."

The runner on third slid into home plate. Marilyn D'Abruzzo, a small, gray-haired dynamo, cut through the pack at the gate—Dianne at her heels—and hurried over to Gina, who was being helped off the diamond. D'Abruzzo needed a slower pace.

In the dugout, separated from Gina by a flock of Murrays, Dal studied her face. He searched in vain for an unfamiliar scar, anything alien. As an audio buyer, Gina gave off an edgy, sophisticated aura, but—sweaty and tired—she could have been Susan after a long run.

This isn't working, Dal thought. The longer he stayed around Gina, the more he saw Susan and the less credible her death became.

While driving Gina's Prius back to her apartment, he remarked idly, "Susan would love this kind of car."

"What did she have?" D'Abruzzo asked.

"She drove an old Camaro up until a few months ago, but it kept breaking down so she sold it. She hadn't gotten around to buying a new one."

"'She' this, 'she' that. Where were you in all this?"

"We'd been having problems. I figured when she was ready to unbend a little, she'd let me help. She'd been using our old pickup to get around in."

"You make good money, don't you?"

"I do okay."

"You should have bought her a new car, parked it on the front lawn, and said, 'here it is.' That's what I would've done. There ain't nothing four whitewalls won't smooth over."

"I don't believe a new car would've done the trick, and in case you haven't noticed, it's a little late to be offering fatherly advice."

"Look, Dal, I don't mean nothing. I'm just making conversation."

"Didn't you think it was the least bit strange what happened today?"

"What do you mean?"

"Her getting hit in the head. What else could I be talking about?"

"You're asking the wrong guy. The doc said Gina's gonna be fine."

With a sinking feeling, Dal realized D'Abruzzo did not intend to tell Gina about Susan. He'd put Dal off as long as possible.

"How do you feel about Susan being dead?"

"I feel pretty bad about it. It's a terrible thing when somebody so young dies like that."

Yes, and Martin Luther King Jr. had so much more to offer. How impersonal, how infuriating.

"She was your daughter, flesh of your flesh. I can't get over the way you're acting. It's like I'm telling you about a distant relative—"

"That's what she was." D'Abruzzo looked out the window. "I didn't know her. Never had the chance. I ain't a hypocrite, and I ain't gonna cry like some TV preacher to make you feel better. You want to lay all this on Gina. It's too late for that. Maybe it would've meant something when she was a kid or a teenager. What good it'd do now? I'm sorry your wife is dead, but screwing up Gina's life ain't gonna help."

Back in his car at the park, Dal had almost decided to approach Gina the next day when a glint on the dashboard caught his eye. Her keychain. A jumpy heartbeat later, he was standing in her stylish living room, blabbing like an idiot. Although she put up a good front, the panicked look in her eyes gave her away. She believed him. Rather, she believed the photographs and documents.

After a good night's rest in San Angelo, the best he'd had in weeks, he vegetated during the uneventful drive into Big Spring. The hard part was over. He contacted Susan's twin, something Susan would have done if given the chance. All that remained were a few loose ends.

Frannie Lowell had to be the mother. He remembered her as a vibrant woman with a bubbly sense of humor. She always got Mother to laugh during her infrequent visits to the Creed household. Frannie must have experimented with the other side of the street, then called on Dovie and her old school pal, Rosanna, to come to the rescue. Once Frannie admitted the truth, he could contact Gina and let her decide if she wanted to pursue the matter further.

He found Frannie, trim in a lavender suit, just arrived back home after attending church.

"Dal, it's so good to see you again. I'm sorry I couldn't make it in for the memorial service, but I was down with the flu. I was so shocked to hear the news."

No easy way to broach the subject. "Frannie, I'm here to talk to you about Susan and Gina."

She cocked her head. "Gina?"

"Susan's sister."

Her mouth formed a silent O. "That detective talked to you."

Somebody told Frannie, but who? "And I've talked to Gina. She knows about Susan; she doesn't know about you. There's no need for you to call her immediately. Just take your time, gather your thoughts, and then tell her."

Frannie leaned against the front door.

"You think I'm the mother? Dal, you've gone and opened up a box of troubles. Why?"

"She has a right to know."

"That may be, but is it really your business to stir things up?"

"Who else is going to do it? Don't you want, isn't there some part of you the least bit curious about how she turned out?"

"I'm not her mother," she said firmly.

"Come on, Frannie, I know you. It couldn't have been easy for you to make the decision, but I can understand why you'd do it. You being gay and all, it probably came as a shock being pregnant."

She seemed more amused than angry. "Good try, Dal. But that wouldn't have stopped me from raising a child."

"I just meant, the gossip would've been vicious."

"I'm used to gossip. I take it in stride. Well, if you don't mind casserole, you're welcome to stay for dinner."

Over lemon chess pie, he tried again.

"There's no reason to protect the mother anymore. Does she live here in town? Is she somebody in your crowd? Was she a teenager? I understand why she'd want to keep this secret. I'd respect her privacy, and I'm certain Gina'll do the same."

"How do you know what Gina'll do?"

"I've met with her the last couple of days. She's an executive at a company in Lambert."

"She wants to meet her mother."

"I'm positive."

"She told you that."

"Not in so many words, but it was obvious."

She shook her head.

"Your father was like that. Prided himself on being a good judge of character. He hated admitting when he was wrong. Your mother was a natural-born saint. You want Gina to be thrilled about finding her mother, 'cause that's what you're after. Until she's ready to follow through, there's no point in me helping you one iota."

Deflated, he asked, "How about if I give her your number?"

"Only if she calls you, and only if she asks for it. I won't promise to recite chapter and verse. It all depends on the other person."

"The birth mother has all the rights. You're going to leave Gina hanging."

"Don't take it personally. If it were up to me, I'd tell Gina."

"You would."

"I'm not the Wicked Witch, Dal. To be honest, if it'd been up to me, the girls would have found out when they turned eighteen. That's how it should have been handled."

He exited more or less gracefully. Tooling over the rolling streets of Big Spring, he juggled the facts around in his mind. What was the connection between a Lambert car salesman and a farm couple?

He arrived at the nursing home, home of Lil Sampson, who had worked for the late Dr. Houtchens. Still spry, she was watching a Cowboys game in the recreation room, offering play-by-play for the feeble-sighted.

"What'd you say your name was?"

"Dal, Dal Creed."

"What's that short for, Dallas?"

"No, ma'am. Dalhart."

"That's a shame. I named my cat Dallas. He lived eighteen years. Died the day after Aikman retired. Shoot."

The quarterback had thrown an interception. "There's no such thing as quality anymore. If you pay somebody a million dollars, they don't even have to be worth it, just as long as they look good. That man in the nice suit sure asked a lot of questions."

"Pardon? Oh, you remember Torrez."

Her face crinkled into a thousand tiny folds. "My hip went bad, not my brain. After he left, I recollected more about it. Dr. Houtchens handled many adoptions, but only two sets of twins I recall."

"What can you tell me about the mother?"

He leaned forward eagerly.

"A nervous wreck. Young. She might have been seventeen, if that old."

"Was she single?"

"Said she was, but there was a tan line on her finger where a ring had been. Had a local woman with her—one of those man-haters."

"Frannie Lowell."

"That's not for me to say," she said primly.

"Was the mother from Big Spring?"

"Fort Worth or Arlington. Some place 'round there."

"Did the father come with her?"

"He came after one of the babies had already been given away. He was plenty upset over it."

"The Longbrakes had already taken Susan?"

"I think it was an older woman."

Dovie. Now he was getting somewhere.

"Did the birth mother see the adoptive mother?"

"Dr. Houtchens didn't believe in that. It's real important to keep the birth mother—and the father, in this case—away from the adoptive parents. And he didn't like for them to hold the babies, to get too attached."

"What on earth for?"

"It's for their own good. That way, it doesn't hurt as much."

And that way, the birth mother was less likely to change her mind. Alienate her as much as possible from the experience. What a Neanderthal.

"And he did this with all of them?"

"Why, yes. Hardly anyone ever complained. That's how things were done."

He was starting to feel sympathy for the girl from Fort Worth or Parts Unknown. A new scenario: she was Frannie's friend or lover. Frannie made the arrangements for her with Dr. Houtchens. Frannie was the connection to the Longbrakes.

Somewhere in all this, she or the doctor or someone, sent Susan with Dovie, apparently going against D'Abruzzo's wishes. Who made the decision?

Someone screwed up, he thought. That's why the twins were never told about each other, because the people involved didn't want to explain how it all went wrong.

"That's all I remember. Can I help you on anything else?" Lil kept her eyes on the TV screen.

"I guess not. Thanks for your time."

All he could do now was wait for Gina to call.

## CHAPTER NINE

She spent Sunday barely moving from the sofa, parrying low-content calls from her parents and Carla. Dianne messaged her once.

Did Susan ever come through Lambert and draw stares from people who knew Gina?

An old classmate might have seen Susan and done a double take. At some point, someone from Gina's circle must have seen Susan, or vice-versa.

How strange that their paths never crossed. They lived several hundred miles apart, true, but Gina visited TopSound outlets across the state—somewhere along the way, they could have been in the same town at the same time. No one ever mistook her for Susan, as far as she knew.

Creed was the name of the town and school listed in the copy of Susan's obituary. Dal's family must have founded the town, or were the biggest landowners.

Although Wikipedia had nothing, she googled a Handbook of Texas article about the town. It sounded like a place plagued by bad planning and a poor location. She'd driven through Lubbock a time or two, but couldn't remember much about it, except the flatness of the land and the dryness of the air.

Texas was too big, that's what. If they'd been born in Rhode Island, they'd have met years ago.

Late Sunday afternoon, Carla came by with three-year-old Alice in tow.

"Dianne likes you, but she thinks the people you work for are a bunch of frustrated jocks."

"Some of them are. So, I passed the test."

"I wouldn't call it a test. Alice, don't play with the pictures."

Plying her daughter with a nerf ball, Carla continued. "She wants to go out with you again. She'll probably call as soon as you feel better."

"I feel okay now."

"Hello? Who am I, Cyril the Magnificent? You don't have to be wonderful all the time; I'm not the type to be impressed. Don't forget, I've seen you in the morning before you've combed your hair. Not a pretty sight."

Gathering the photos, Gina handed them to Carla.

"Who's that man with you?" Carla asked, frowning. "I don't remember you having that car."

"It's not mine. Keep looking."

"Wait a minute. When did you get married?"

"You think that's me."

"You're saying it's not?"

Baffled, Carla flipped through the photographs.

Waving one in the air, she pronounced, "That's you. You used to wear your hair that way, and that's your bicycle."

"My bicycle's green, not gray."

"I've known you forever and a day. That's you."

Gina handed her the clipped articles and obituary. "I'm looking remarkably well for a dead person."

Carla stared at the newspaper photo for a long moment.

"'Cartoonist wife found dead. Authorities checking leads.' I don't get this at all. Who is this woman?"

"According to her husband, she was my twin," Gina said.

How unreal that statement felt. Three sprints by Alice around the coffee table, and Carla knew as much as Gina did.

"What'd your dad have to say?" Carla asked.

"I haven't talked to him about it."

"Why the hell not?"

"What if he doesn't want to tell me anything? I don't know what to say at that point. Maybe he had a good reason for what he did. Whatever—Creed couldn't get him to say the woman's name."

"Dang, there's somebody out there who's your real mother."

"I know who my real mother is."

"You know what I mean. I bet Marilyn has the whole story, if you asked her."

"No way," Gina said. "How could I even bring up the subject? This'd destroy her."

"I've seen her at the Stop 'N Go, giving shoplifters the evil eye. She's tougher than you think. Alice, let go of the remote. If you want, I can talk to her."

"Carla—"

"Okay, okay. She likes me about as well as she does the shoplifters. She thinks I turned you. Girl, I wish. Anyhow, you need to get this straightened out. Somebody knows the truth. Now, tell me about this cartoonist. Is he good-looking?"

Leave no stone unturned was Carla's motto.

"He dresses well. He looks okay, I guess. He's real torn up about his wife."

"I imagine. When are you going to see the place?"

"You've got to be kidding. I know next to nothing about the guy."

"Aren't you curious to see where she lived?"

"Kind of. Carla, I've had more things than that on my mind."

"Sure you have, what with you dumping Terry and getting bopped on the head, and then finding out all this stuff. It must have you coming and going."

"What does Terry have to do—that was weeks and weeks ago. I'm not sure I want to know why the other deal happened. Maybe that's ancient history, too."

"Alice, Mommy has a fruit roll for you. Yum. Come on, Gin, haven't you ever imagined having a twin? Everyone does when they're growing up. I had an imaginary brother when I was five or six years old. He used to get me into all kinds of trouble."

Carla's eyes misted over. "Dwayne was so real to me. I could tell you right now what he looked like. Twins. You know what they get away with: trading dates, sitting in for each other on classes, playing jokes on people. And here you had a twin all that time, missing out on the fun."

Gina remembered a pair of fraternal twins in homeroom, and a set of triplets a grade ahead. Although the twins looked more like cousins than brothers, the triplets dressed, talked, and giggled alike well into high school, until one of them—Gina couldn't remember which—became pregnant and dropped out of school.

After that, the remaining pair made no special effort to keep up the doppelganger effect.

When she was a child, Gina wanted a younger brother, but she never imagined having a twin. She never felt incomplete. She never felt a void in her life a twin could have filled.

"Gin, you ought to see that look on your face. If you were Alice, I could give you a hug and a bite to eat, and it'd be all better."

Carla scooted over and embraced her. "If I were you, I'd be bawling, too. Go on, let it all out."

Back under control, Gina thought again of her father.

"That's what I don't get. Why didn't he tell me that she was out there?"

"I don't blame you for feeling pissed off," Carla said helpfully.

"I'm not—fine. Maybe a little. Daddy had to have kept Mom from telling me. I don't want her to think I'm blaming her."

`"That's why you're afraid to go check things out. Marilyn's not going to think you're trying to dump her. Your twin wanted to find you. Would have, too, if not for getting killed. Are you sure this Creed character didn't have anything to do with it?"

"From looking at the newspaper clippings, I don't see how he could have. You didn't see the way he was acting. He's still in shock."

"Not to mention seeing his wife again. Your twin wanted to find you. You owe it to her to at least go see where she lived."

The next morning while she sat in Cyril's office, she tried to get her suddenly developed vacation plans approved without revealing any important details.

Flipping through his desk calendar, he remarked, "Nothing too pressing on the horizon. The convention in Vegas is coming up next month."

"I only need a week. Maybe not that long."

"Certainly, certainly. It wouldn't hurt for you to take a few days off until you get over the beaning."

"I just have a little ringing in my ear, that's all."

Although the bruise on her forehead stretching across her left eye wasn't photogenic, it didn't much bother her except when she showered.

Cyril trotted out his patented 'you don't have to talk about it but I'm here in case' look.

"Don't do that." She couldn't suppress a smile.

"Do what?" Cyril feigned alarm. "Come on, something's worrying you. You didn't even say hello."

"Hello."

"Too late now. Is this about your folks?"

"Sort of." Great. She'd said too much already.

"Your father sick?"

"About the same."

"Come on. You've always been able to talk to me. Shoot, I've told you stuff my wife doesn't know about. What's the big mystery?"

"I wish I knew." A wave of anger crested without warning. "You think everything's running smoothly—optimum levels—then the stupidest thing happens."

"You have cancer." Cyril said, aghast.

"No, no, I'm fine."

A big breath. She recited all the known details, digging out a photograph from her purse for illustration.

His brow furrowed, Cyril said, "All this time there was another one of you running around."

"A twin."

"But straight. Any kids?"

"Not according to the clippings."

'This Creed fellow, did he come on to you?"

"He was upset about her dying. He wanted to see if I looked like her, and to find out more about her family."

"Only your daddy's keeping his mouth shut. Shhh, let me think this through. All right, I've got it worked out. Your whatchacallit—birth mother—she must have been underage or married to someone else."

Cyril the CEO Detective. "Where's the evidence?"

"Why else would he still be protecting her? She must have been sweet sixteen back then. Now she's married, and in no mood for her husband to find out. That's my first scenario. Or, she was already married. Chippied one time too often. You're what, thirty-three now? That gal's sitting pretty. Has grandkids, a nice house, belongs to a country club. Butter wouldn't melt in her mouth. You come out of nowhere, all bets are off."

"You make it sound as though I'm coming at her with a chainsaw."

This reminded her of the old days when he and Aaron would drain pots of coffee plotting ad campaigns.

"That's one way of getting her to talk. You do need to go where that Creed fellow lives. Snoop around. Go through her things if he hasn't already."

"That's where I'm headed."

"Certainly, certainly. You do that, and I'll do a little checking on my own."

"I appreciate your input, but this is my business, not yours."

Cyril pretended not to hear her. "I remember back when your daddy was a high roller. He owned the Fast Action club, out where Houston's taken over. I know a couple of ol' boys he was drinking buddies with back then. A man says a lot when he's juicing."

"I'm not worried about my reputation—it's shot already—but Mom and Linda, that's another thing. If this got out, they'd never live it down."

He seemed disappointed. "Do what you think is best, but you know you can come to me."

Any hopes of quiet on the flight to Lubbock vanished when a chatty woman to her left struck up a conversation with an orthopedic surgeon to her right. Learning more than she cared to about hip replacement surgery, Gina could hear the pair discussing fees as she walked briskly through the corridor. Luggage accounted for, she picked up her rental car and plugged Creed into her GPS coordinates.

As she pulled off the Loop and headed southwest, Lubbock's outskirts looked about the same to her as any other big city, what with the usual warehouses and shiny car dealerships. Maybe about as flat as Houston, but a lot less humidity.

She didn't need to go to all this trouble. What would change if she turned around and caught the next flight home? She'd still be Gina D'Abruzzo, with the same parents and the same history, regardless of how that history began.

Susan's obituary listed her adoptive parents as deceased. No siblings. Even though Susan had to have friends—classmates, co-workers, maybe ex-boyfriends—none were likely to know anything about Susan's birth mother.

Lubbock blended into Wolfforth before she realized it. Where was the turn to Creed? The map didn't match her surroundings. She pulled over at a convenience store and got out to ask directions.

The wind gusted her through the door, making her somewhat breathless as she removed her shades and hailed the clerk. The man's smile veered off his face, leaving a gap-mouthed stare that would have seemed goofy if not for the unmistakable tinge of fear.

"Dear Lord in heaven."

The source of that remark—an elderly, stout woman—leaned on a magazine rack for support.

"Susan, Susan, you're alive."

These people saw her as a walking miracle or a ghost.

"I'm not—"

"Oh, I see the bruises. You poor dear. That must have been so frightening, but you're back on your feet now. How come there wasn't anything in the paper about this? Susan, Susan, wait a minute."

Peeling out of the parking lot, Gina drove over to a nearby grocery store and sat clutching the steering wheel for a few minutes. Twice she stepped out of the door and started to go inside, only to retreat back to the Honda.

As she paced back and forth, a pickup pulled up beside her. An attractive Hispanic woman rolled down her window and gazed at her raptly.

Gina felt thoroughly rattled. "I'm not Susan. I'm not her."

After a bit, the woman spoke up. "I'm going to Creed cemetery right now. We're about to bury her. You here for that?"

"You're kid—didn't they already have a service?"

"The memorial. There's been a big controversy about the pathologist, so the County Attorney brought in someone else to do the autopsy, but he was backlogged, too. You're her twin."

"We never met. I just found out the other day about her."

"Do you know Dal?"

"He's who told me about Susan, but I don't really know him."

Pulling her shades down, the woman said tonelessly, "I can give you a ride over."

They flew down a flat, narrow highway lined by green growing crops and what looked like tall grass. The woman finally spoke as they turned onto an even smaller road that churned billowing clouds of dust as they drove.

"Susan wondered if she had any brothers and sisters. I'm Oralia Wender. Susan and I were best friends. She was a couple of years ahead of me in school. My husband, Mack, and her were in the same class. How come you never showed up before?"

"I didn't know. I promise you, I didn't know. All this came down after she died."

A somewhat disjointed recap later, Oralia seemed satisfied. "If that's how it happened, that's how it happened. What's your name?"

"Gina D'Abruzzo."

"Dia, what?" Gina spelled it out for her. "What kind of name is that?"

"Italian."

"Susan was Italian? She did like lasagna."

The pickup bounced over the ruts leading into a rustic cemetery. They stopped some distance away from the small cluster of mourners.

"I think it'd be best if you tag behind until I tell them you're here."

Standing awkwardly by a headstone, Gina waited for an opportune moment, which came when, as one, the mourners turned and goggled at her. Dal pointed for her to stand by him, which eased the tension a notch. The preacher, a youngish fellow, stammered briefly then the rites were over.

Dal whispered, "If you want, they can open the casket. I looked at her this morning at the funeral home before they brought her over."

The other mourners hung back. She went up to the casket and, fighting off an impulse to flee, waited for the attendant to lift the top section of the lid.

Susan reposed on the satin interior. Someone had picked out a midnight-blue suit with a silver scarf, and matching silver jewelry. Susan's face looked fine. Gina had dug around on the Internet since Dal's visit, but only came across a few images of her sister in all the coverage. She'd found no video of Susan talking, of her doing anything alive.

Gina didn't know how long she'd been staring down into the coffin before Dal tactfully led her aside. The mourners sang a sad, country-sounding hymn Gina might have joined in if she'd known the words.

No wonder people stared, Gina thought. She'd now had a preview of her own funeral.

# CHAPTER TEN

*Creed School--Students met in a one-room wooden building until 1940 when a small brick schoolhouse with an attached gymnasium was constructed. The cafeteria served as the meeting site for family reunions for a while after the school closed, but has been untouched since then.*

"Levon told me they were through with her body last week. Things are still in such a mess over there that So-and-So thought So-and-So had notified Dal, but nobody had."

Oralia drove her through the resolutely flat countryside on a succession of roads that, whether dirt or paved, hardly looked wide enough for one vehicle, much less two-way traffic. It was as if someone took a single Lambert neighborhood and strung it out over a few miles, except they forgot to bring the trees. The sky was a delicate, translucent blue with a bare sprinkle of cirrus the only grace note.

How did Susan fit in, Gina wondered. The nothingness that became something, if you stayed there long enough to fill it—did Susan feel she belonged here?

"Levon thinks somebody may have gotten suspended over it, but it worked out as far as you're concerned. You got to see her," Oralia said.

Yet she'd already seen Susan, Gina thought, when she applied her makeup every morning. What she never witnessed was Susan as a person with her own little quirks and character traits.

"What was Susan like?"

"Laid-back, except when she was playing ball or hanging out at a party. Great with kids. She'd baby-sit our boys when Mack and I'd go out."

"Was Mack there at the cemetery?"

"He doesn't get along well with Dal," Oralia said carefully. "Besides, he's been busy at the gin trying to keep it afloat."

"I guess the farmers are having a hard time."

Gina tried to recall what Willie Nelson had once said on the subject.

"Maybe some of them are. The main problem for Culdesac Gin is we don't have enough farmers. They're taking their cotton to other places. Mack thinks this'll be our last year."

Oralia didn't sound broken up over the prospect.

The pickup pulled into the dirt driveway of a rickety stucco house blemished by golf ball-sized crevices and engulfed by brush.

"I figured you might want to see the old place."

"She grew up here?" It reminded Gina of *The Grapes of Wrath*. "Were they that poor?"

"Uh-huh, but the place didn't look this bad when her folks were still alive. There've been a few hailstorms since then, and somebody's been doing some target practice. The Longbrakes were so old. Susan's really the one who kept it going toward the end."

They approached the house on foot, steering clear of the larger tumbleweeds.

Wrestling open the front door, they ducked under a spider colony and stepped inside. Broken windows allowed enough light to guide them into Susan's room, a claustrophobic cell Gina was only too glad to escape.

Back outside, she asked, "What were her parents like?"

"Old. That's how I remember them. Mr. Longbrake—"

"Poppa Floyd."

"He wasn't what you'd call Mr. Personality. The kids at school, we always invited Susan over to our houses. Nobody wanted to come here."

Not surprising.

"I liked Mrs. Longbrake, though. She was a sweet lady. It's meant to be, your coming today." Oralia switched channels. "You were supposed to come to the funeral. That's why the mistake with the pathologist happened."

"No offense, but there's such a thing as coincidence, and that's what happened today."

"Believe what you want to believe," Oralia said as they climbed back in the pickup. "Whether you know it or not, you were led here."

"By who, Susan's ghost?" Gina said, regretting it instantly.

"As a matter of fact—"

"No, no, let's not get into that. I want to see the places she used to go."

Their next stop was at the school, where they poked their heads in at the gym entrance—as creepy as she'd expected—then they strolled around the back way.

"Did you play basketball?" Gina asked.

"You had to play at Creed. It was up there with the Flag. I was a guard my first year, then Coach switched me to forward. I wish you could have seen her play. She had a hook shot like you wouldn't believe. I mean, it'd go in like clockwork.

"There was one game where she kept throwing it in all night, one after the other. I think it was against Ropesville for Homecoming. That was the last Homecoming, 'cause the school closed down after that year."

Turning a corner, they stood on a cracked concrete half-court that featured a ragged goal. "There were only her and Mack and Levon, by then. Anyhow, after the game—she scored sixty points, at least—she came here and kept shooting. Some of us came over to watch, but I lost count after a while."

"Did she play in college?"

"No, but she did get offers. I remember the scouts that came out to her games."

They turned another corner and headed around to the front.

"Who lives there?" Gina pointed at the brick house nearby.

"Susan did."

She saw Dal coming toward them.

As soon as he was close enough to hear, she tried to take charge.

"Now that I know where you live, let me come back with my car, and we can get better acquainted."

"I can take you," he said.

"Would you? Thanks, Dal," Oralia said. "Gina, you're welcome to come by anytime. Dal can give you the address."

Oralia took off for her car.

"Gina, I want to apologize for coming at you out of the blue. That had to have been a shock. I know I didn't do a good job of preparing you."

Now, she'd returned the favor. Time for a change in subject.

"How long did you and Susan live here?"

"For eight years, together. I grew up in this house."

"Where exactly is Creed? There's hardly anything around here."

Executing a crisp three-sixty spin, Dal said, "Tah-dah. This is it. You see the gin down there?" He pointed southward. "From there to here is Creed proper."

He then directed her attention to a house some distance north up the highway. "That's the Wintersole place. Rosanna still lives there. You could call it the suburbs. By the way, Rosanna and Susan were good friends, if you want to get with her sometime. I'm sure she has all kinds of anecdotes."

"Would she know anything about the adoption?"

"Probably, but she's like the rest of them. It's like pulling hen's teeth."

He started back to the house. "Let me make you a glass of tea."

If Susan had a hand in decorating, she chose a modern, minimalist style. The sectionals and Monroe chairs came in bisque, and the throws were in terracotta. There was a plush wool ivory rug—major money, major upkeep---while the curtains had a parquet-style motif in ivory and terracotta.

"You look surprised."

"I guess I was expecting something more—I don't know—more rural."

He led her into the kitchen, chuckling. "We do have indoor plumbing—and Susan liked ordering things online."

"I don't mean to sound condescending."

After the tour, they sat on a bench atop a grassy knoll behind the house. Dal seemed oblivious to the blasts of wind rattling through the honeysuckle bushes. The air felt a touch cooler than she'd expected for mid-September. Her glass of iced tea wasn't helping matters.

"Where did the burglar find her?"

"In our bedroom, by the closet. The pathologist said that it happened so quickly he didn't think she felt any pain."

They always said that. Better to think that she died quickly instead of lying there helpless for hours.

"What was she like? If it's too hard to talk about, I understand."

Despite having buried his wife less than two hours ago, he appeared more at peace than he had in Lambert.

"Beautiful, but she didn't believe it when I'd say so. She was down-to-earth. Practical."

"Give me a for instance."

"For instance, she did all the bargaining when we shopped for big-ticket items. The salespeople talked to me at first but she'd be the one doing the figuring. She knew the value of a dollar."

Not quite the intimate details she was hoping for.

"What was she like around people?"

"It depended on the circumstance. I'm invited to charity functions in Lubbock now and then, on account of what I do. We'd get dressed up and schmooze with the local gentry. Most of the time, she seemed to enjoy herself. She could have made more of a splash if she'd wanted to, but that wasn't her style."

"Well, given where she grew up, she probably didn't feel too comfortable around those people." He looked surprised. "Oralia showed me the Longbrake farm. It never occurred to you she might feel insecure?"

"I knew," he said unconvincingly. "What you don't realize is that she was very observant; she noticed things. The first time we went to a function, she read the society pages for several days beforehand, went through a bunch of fashion magazines, then bought the proper outfit. I can tell you this: she came off as having more class than some people I've met. She was sophisticated about people, if maybe not an intellectual."

Susan's background was clearly a touchy subject.

"What did Susan think of her adoptive parents?"

"She loved her mother. When we started going out, she'd recently buried Dovie, so she was still getting over that. Susan said she knew early on that she was adopted, since Poppa Floyd used to bring it up whenever she was being mischievous."

"Did she get along with Poppa Floyd?"

"If he said jump, she'd ask how high, if that's what you mean by getting along. If you mean a genuine father-daughter relationship, no. Gina, I don't think they told her anything about the birth mother, or your father, for that matter. Except once. Dovie told her that the birth mother was a good Christian girl. Susan said she couldn't have been too good a Christian, but Dovie said that bad things happen even to the best of people."

"And?"

"And that's all. You were hoping for more."

"I wonder why Dovie put it that way. 'Bad things.'"

"I'm sure she didn't mean that you and Susan were bad, just the situation."

If that's how Susan was raised to think about being adopted, no wonder it took so long for her to hire an investigator. Which brought up another point.

"I want to talk to the investigator. I may hire him, if he's any good."

"I don't think you'll have to. You see, on the way back from visiting you, I went by Big Spring to talk to someone who, to be truthful, I thought she'd be your mother. Now I'm not so sure."

He told her about Frannie Lowell, the nurse, and Dr. Houtchens.

"Frannie didn't want me to give you her number unless you wanted it," he said as they descended the hill.

"You bet I want it. You don't think she's the one?"

"I don't think so."

"Why?"

"Frannie's not the kind of woman who'd hold back on the truth simply to protect herself. There's someone else."

"The girl from Fort Worth."

"According to the nurse."

Standing in the kitchen, she pressed the numbers Dal gave her. A woman picked up on the second ring.

"Hello?"

"Frannie Lowell?"

"Yes," the woman said with a note of hesitance.

"This is Gina D'Abruzzo."

Frannie said calmly, "I know what you're going to ask, and the answer is no. I'm not your mother."

Without knowing precisely why, Gina believed her.

"Then tell me who is. Please."

An extended pause. "This is what I'll do. I'll get in touch with her and see what she says. Where are you now?"

"At Dal Creed's house, but I've booked a room at the Hotel Estacado."

"Oh." Another pause. "Are you going to be there a few days?"

"I can hang around, at least through the end of the week."

"Then what I'll do is contact her, and get back to you as quickly as I can."

After she got off the phone, Dal invited her out to dinner. After she deposited her rental car at the hotel, she rode with him to a small Middle Eastern restaurant that served excellent baba ganoush and garlic chicken, followed by a choice of baklava. Not quite what she expected from Lubbock, but Dal was unwilling to leave it at that as he talked at length about some local winery that had won gold medals, artists that he knew in town, and West Texas musicians who were stretching the experimental envelope.

"Listen, I appreciate the trouble you're going to, but I've never thought of Lubbock as a cultural backwater."

Or thought of Lubbock, period. "Maybe it's a step or two behind, but that's okay."

***

Gina D'Abruzzo neatly bisected her wedge of baklava and ate both halves before taking her first sip of Turkish coffee. Susan always did that, even though the coffee was supposed to accompany the act of eating. A minor, yet unsuspected similarity.

He must have been twenty-one or twenty-two, home from college—no, he'd already dropped out by then—out on the hill talking with Mother, when a gangly youngster came from behind the school steering a rickety, too-small bicycle down the turnrow behind the Creed orchard.

"That's Susan Longbrake. You remember her," Mother said, waving to the girl, who waved back before vanishing behind the trees. "I remember that being Mitchell's bicycle."

"He must have put a lot of miles on it."

"Now she does. She rides up here a lot, always playing basketball."

Dal recalled a curly-headed girl down in the lower grades who towered over her classmates.

"Still growing, I see."

Mother tsked. "That bicycle is too old and too small for her to have to ride on, especially when it's that far to her house."

"Floyd's not a windshield farmer."

"He has enough money to go hunting after quail. He ought to set enough aside to see after that girl better. Ten dollars a month and soon enough she'd have a bicycle, but no, men like Floyd don't ever think that way. If it's not a shotgun or a tractor, it doesn't exist. That tears it. I'm going to talk to Rosanna about getting her a bicycle for Christmas."

"Y'all doing charity work together?"

"Oh, we've been helping Dovie on buying Susan pretties now and then."

"Dal?" Gina stared at him.

"I'm thinking," he said with a grimace. "I didn't mean to drift away on you like that."

"I don't mind. About the investigation. Who's handling it?"

He told her of the turf battle between the Sheriff Department and the District Attorney's office over who should handle the lion's share of the case, the particulars of which Dal heard from his source in the D.A.'s office.

Thus far, the only clues were a couple of fingerprints and Caucasian hair fibers not belonging to either Susan or Dal. No viable suspects yet among the handful of junkie burglars questioned.

"At least, you know I'm not in the running."

"I never thought you had anything to do with it. From the photos, it looked to me like the two of you made an ideal couple."

"Susan and I, we had our problems."

"Nobody's perfect."

Enough with the platitudes. She had to hear the truth.

"We didn't always get along, and in the last year or two, relations had become difficult. I didn't move out. I mean, neither of us were the type to throw dishes at one other."

"But you weren't getting along," Gina said with an impersonal manner.

"I honestly think we were making progress."

Why did he feel compelled to explain?

"When I left for Dallas, she...kissed me. Nothing earthshaking, but I took it as a positive sign."

"What was the problem? Sorry, that's really none of my business."

"I pulled you into this, so it's only fair you hear it all. The thing is, I want you to know that I was mostly responsible for the situation, because I didn't handle it well. I probably made it worse. You see, Susan had a problem."

"She drank."

How did she know?

"Not that often," he said.

"But when she did, it would get out of hand. She didn't want to admit it. I was that way. A few years ago, I quit. Haven't had a drink since then."

"Then it must have been hereditary. She couldn't help it."

The similarities were beginning to overwhelm him again.

"No, Dal. She had the need for it like me, but what I've learned over the years is to take responsibility for my actions, and that's why I quit drinking. Susan never made it to that point," she said evenly. "Do they know if she had been drinking before it happened?"

"Yes, she had. Over the legal limit."

"Maybe if she'd been sober, she wouldn't have let that man in, or left the door unlocked."

"That's a hell of a thing to say." Dal felt his face flush. "It's not her fault this happened to her. A lot of times she drank to get back at me. I wasn't as supportive as I should have been. If it's anyone's fault, it's mine, for not being there, for not putting in a security system. I thought we were so far into the country, no one would bother us.

"I was living in a dream, that's what, a perfect little dream. No one's entitled to that. People must have thought: he has a beautiful wife, good money, a place in the country. Man's got it all. But I didn't, and Susan knew it, and she's the one who ended up paying for my pigheadedness."

***

Gina apologized, but the damage had been done. Polite and to the point, he dropped her off at the hotel, promising to call her the next day. Maybe he would. Why didn't she keep her mouth shut?

Gathering her notes, she drew up a list of people to contact, starting with Susan's co-workers at Tumbleweed Senior Center. She needed to call ahead first, to prevent multiple shocks of recognition. Some old man might stroke out seeing Susan back among the living.

What was she thinking? Anywhere she went in Lubbock, someone might think he or she was hallucinating. Talk about a face that could launch a thousand accidents.

Nothing she'd heard thus far about her sister came as a surprise. Her sister. How strange that phrase sounded.

At that moment, her sister, Linda, was probably trolling for male prospects at a Democratic party social. Linda, who once punched a neighborhood bully for tripping her kid sister. Heaven knows how she'd take the news that they had different birth mothers.

The biology of it wouldn't change her feelings toward Gina, but the politics of it—whose ox was gored, why the birth mother was holding out, whatever possessed Daddy to become involved with the woman—that would drive her until she nailed down every last detail of the triangle. Linda could probably wrap up this little mystery in a couple of hours, but her scorched earth philosophy would split the family into warring factions.

Gina preferred the slower, more polite approach. If that didn't work, then call in Big Sister.

## CHAPTER ELEVEN

*Louie's--Vandalized pumps, a square of cracked concrete and a burnt-out husk south of the Rudyard Creed place are all that's left of Louie's, a filling station/store owned by the late Louie Shines. Louie's was a community institution, where farmers drank coffee in the morning, farmwives bought a gallon of milk, and Mrs. Shines ran a small post office in the back. The Shineses raised three daughters: Dinah, Rosanna, and Carlina. Dinah's closing of the station and the post office's dissolution marked the official end of the community.*

Dressed in denim cutoffs and a gold tee, Susan had him down 20-10. She amassed her lead on silky jumpers and hook shots, never entering the paint where Dal's hack fouling gave him the advantage.

"Go ahead and shoot, let's get this over with," he said, trying to catch his breath.

Glancing over his shoulder, he saw the sun scoot behind the school, leaving a trail of magenta streamers. Susan laughed. He turned and saw her arch a twenty-footer from beyond the top of the key that careened off the backboard.

He tracked down the ball and bounced it over to her.

"It's your turn now," she said. "I'm through."

"No, you're not. Give me one more shot," he said.

Her smile vanished. "I told you, I'm through. Go play with Gina. You can beat her."

And with no further prompting, Gina stood beside him, wearing her TopSound Rappers jersey. At the same time, Susan began racing around the corner, away from their house.

He started after her, but then a door appeared out of thin air in front of him.

When he woke up, he was rattling the back door knob loud enough to rouse Pogo outside, who set off to barking.

Another walkabout.

***

The director, a block of ice in a plaid dress, welcomed Gina with understandable suspicion.

The older woman questioned her at length about the sequence of events that led Susan's previously invisible twin sister to visit Tumbleweed Senior Center. After extracting a promise to not visit with patients, the director sent Gina to the staff room and said she'd send in one of Gina's coworkers.

After a few minutes, an attractive brunette nurse came into the door and frankly stared before making a recovery.

"For once, Edna was right. You're a dead ringer. Where on earth have you been keeping yourself?"

Her accent sounded European.

"Downstate—" Gina began.

"Where are my manners? I'm Helene Pielowicz. Susan and I were friends. We'd go to the clubs, or to a dinner and a show. She was great fun. I can see why I'm not supposed to let you near the patients, but let's see if we can get to someplace more comfortable."

Helene led them to chairs in the lobby, where they sat in chairs next to a picture window. The place smelled of bleach and old-lady perfume, but there were cheerful prints on the wall, and the walls had been painted recently.

A fuzzy-haired woman wandered over from a nearby room and complained to "Susan" about the dirty sheets on her bed. Not convinced by Helene's explanation, the woman went away muttering to herself.

"I wanted Susan to become an RN," Helene said. "If she'd put in a few more months she'd have earned her license."

"Why didn't she?"

"For a time, I thought the problem was at home, but Susan swore that Dal was not opposed." She fell silent for a long moment. "I think I'm adjusted, then it hits me all over again. I miss her. She had so much more to give, if she'd had the time."

"What about her and Dal? They seem to have had problems."

"Sometimes they didn't get along very well."

"Because of the alcohol."

"She tried not to drink. That was only part of the problem. I think she and her husband were two very different people, who hit it off in bed, and thought that was enough to start a marriage on. Sometimes that's enough, but not for Susan."

"She wanted more."

"She wanted to, I don't want to make her sound like a tourist, but she wanted to see the world, to go places she hadn't been before. Not our Dal. He wouldn't take her anywhere."

"What do you think of him?"

"Concerned about appearances. Too much so."

"In what way?"

"He was afraid she'd get tipsy in public, ruin his image. I think that's why—never mind."

"No, tell me. Tell me everything."

"I don't want you to think badly of her, or think that all she ever did was drink and fool around."

Whoah.

"Fool around? She had a lover?"

"He came by sometimes when she was working nights. They'd go talk by the back door. She didn't like for him to come over, but the man was quite persistent."

"What did he look like?"

"A little taller than her. Always dressed in boots and jeans. Handsome. Brown hair, mustache, soulful eyes. Also married."

"How long had they been seeing each other?"

"Two or three years, I think, but she'd known him a long time. They'd gone to school together."

"What was his name?"

"Mack or Jack, something like that."

Mack Wender. Oralia's husband, and Susan's classmate. For someone who wanted to see the world, Susan didn't stray far from home.

"The name is familiar?"

"Afraid so."

Through the remainder of the visit, Helene shifted the focus to Susan's work performance and popularity with the other nurses, little of which stuck with Gina. A few more layers have been stripped away today, she thought.

Underneath the church-going Florence Nightingale was a complicated woman who carried on an affair with her best friend's husband. What other revelations lay ahead?

***

Almost exactly a tenth of a mile from his porch to the Wintersole mailbox. Dal used to run several round trips religiously each morning until he stepped in a prairie dog hole by the side of the road that broke his ankle. Thereafter, he stuck to walking and a more careful judging of the terrain. It took more time but involved less wear and tear on his anatomy.

Seeing Gina's car approaching, he waited at the Wintersole mailbox. A stiff western wind rustled the tall Conservation Reserve Program grass flanking both sides of the highway.

She drove up beside him and rolled down a window.

"Out for a stroll, I see."

"Rosanna invited me to lunch."

Glancing at her watch, she frowned. "Lost track of time. I was going to visit with her, but I can come back later."

Rosanna came out on the porch and waved.

"Too late. Why don't you join us? She'd take it as an insult if you didn't stay."

Over Mexican quiche and salad, Dal listened to Rosanna describe Susan as considerate, thoughtful, and devoid of imperfections. That was gilding the lily much too much, but he held his tongue.

After lunch, Rosanna dragged out old photo albums and Creed school annuals. Taking that as a cue, he volunteered to check on the ostriches, who were taking turns dancing with a curious grace down their runways.

***

Rosanna wore khaki slacks and a maroon blouse, a casual look at odds with her demeanor. She acted ill at ease throughout the meal and only began to relax during the photo talk. Pausing over a shot of Rosanna and Tom with a church youth group that included Susan, Mack, and Oralia, she recalled in glowing detail Susan's instant mastery of roller-skating.

"It was something to see. Not ten minutes after she laced on those skates, she was doing spins and going twice as fast as anyone else. She had so much natural ability, she could have starred in any sport."

"This is fascinating stuff, I really mean that, but what can you tell me about my birth mother?"

Rosanna popped up from the table and began loading the dishwasher.

"It's too soon."

"Does she still live in Fort Worth?"

"No more questions on that, please," Rosanna said, her back to Gina.

Slinging her purse over her shoulder, Gina muttered, "So helpful," then left out the kitchen door.

****

Dal caught up to her at the car. "I'm going to go through Susan's things this afternoon if you'd like to come by." Her clenched jaw spoke volumes. "Then again, tomorrow would be fine."

"Let's do it now," she said with a staccato delivery. "I want to wrap things up."

"You're not planning on going back to Lambert already, are you? Frannie said later this week—"

"Do you really think it's going to happen?"

He scrambled into the car before she whipped her car out of the Wintersole driveway. She ranted about a conspiracy of silence by people who would never reveal the truth, developing that riff as she drove over to his place. So much for being unflappable. He couldn't help but smile.

"You think it's funny?"

"You're finally acting human."

"What, was I a reptile before?"

"Never mind."

Home again.

"Okay, I don't loosen up with people until I've known them a while. It's nothing personal. I was raised that way. When I was a kid, we moved from neighborhood to neighborhood until my parents' finances settled down. I always had to deal with new kids. They can be real judgmental," she said, slowly returning to earth.

Susan also used to save up her anger and blow it all at once. It probably wouldn't do to mention the similarity to Gina.

The night before, he'd gone through all the closets in the house, looking for material traces of Susan, reducing the memorabilia to a couple of boxes on the living room coffee-table. He'd take her clothes—most of it bagged and boxed by the back door—over to the church tomorrow, where it would eventually end up on the backs of the destitute. Susan would have liked that.

He'd keep the photographs, some other odds and ends, but why not give the Marroquin kids her bicycle, since he already had an operational Schwinn.

Gina inspected Susan's trophies and medals. "Most Valuable Player, All-District, All-Regional, All-State. She must have been something to see. I didn't win them, so it wouldn't be right to claim them for my own."

He couldn't throw them out. A box in storage, then.

"What about this?" She tried to twirl an autographed basketball.

"It's the game ball from their bi-district game against—I don't recall the other team."

"Was Oralia's maiden name Iglesias?" He nodded. "Then I'll drop it by her house. She'd probably like to have it."

Going through the photographs briskly, Gina picked about a dozen, plus Susan's senior year annual, then stopped at a sweetheart pose of Susan and Mack. Dal told her about the two going steady in high school, and offered the photo to her.

"Did they get along after the two of you got married?"

"I think so. It helped that she and Oralia were such good friends, otherwise there might have been problems."

"Problems?"

"Well, you know how wives can get about former girlfriends. They got along fine. You might also want to talk to Levon Porter. He and Susan were friends their entire lives. They played basketball a lot, either here or at his house in Lubbock. His wife has a radar gun when it comes to women. If she thought Susan was safe company, that should tell you something."

It was too much to expect Gina to be visibly torn up about Susan's death, but still he wished she'd quit acting as though all that mattered was learning about Susan's social life and their birth mother. If the situation had been reversed, Susan would have been more sensitive to the husband's feelings.

An image came abruptly to mind of the last time he and Susan made love, incoherent and mindless, several nights before she died.

Was murdered. He had to keep adding that phrase. Looking at the vibrant woman before him, he wondered if he'd be able to tell the difference between the two in bed. Dal warned himself: don't play that game. Don't speculate.

# CHAPTER TWELVE

Gina had hoped to talk with Oralia for a while, since Mack was nowhere evident, but Oralia kept chitchat to a minimum.

Tomahawks displayed above the Wender living room sofa, arrowheads and Elmer Kelton novels on the bookshelves, framed western scenes on several walls, Navajo rugs—this was not a house grasping for a theme.

Oralia checked the clock. "Not to run you off, but I need to round up the boys from the neighbors. We're going out tonight."

There went her chance to check out Mack.

That evening, Gina ate at the Texas Bon Temps Cafe with Helene Pielowicz, who recommended the Cajun-spiced tamales and jalapeno gumbo. No one she'd met thus far in Lubbock wanted her near a steak, she thought as she polished off a green chili breadstick.

"Did Susan ever talk about Mack?"

"Not really. I asked her once why she kept seeing him. She said Mack understood her better than anyone else."

"Why wouldn't he? They grew up together in Creed. What I can't figure out is why they didn't get married when they had the chance."

"She didn't love him," Helene said firmly. "She told me that. Mack seemed happy with it. I think you call it a draw."

Gina wondered why Susan didn't cut one of the men loose, then chastised herself for falling prey to the 'could have' syndrome. The situation with Mack worked for Susan, and who knows, maybe being an LVN was the height of her ability.

"What are you thinking?" Helene inquired.

"The people I've met, they expected so much of Susan. They all sound so disappointed."

"Not me. I wanted her to be an R.N., but I'm not disappointed about it. If anyone should feel cheated, it should be you. We got to know her;

you never had the chance."

***

The peach and cherry trees had long been picked over, but there were plenty of pecans left for Raymond Rodriguez to collect. Dal had told the Marroquins to harvest what they wanted, but to freeze a few bags for him to pick up later.

That had always been the routine, for the Marroquins to do the work and get the greater share of the harvest. When Susan came, she worked alongside Elsa in shelling, freezing, canning, and drying everything in sight. Since the utility room shelves and the deep freezer were still laden with past harvests, he planned to let the Marroquins keep as much as they wanted, for now and probably for the future.

Raymond scooped pecans off the ground with his net, all the while quizzing Dal about Gina.

Satisfied finally, Raymond said, "She's not going back home, not yet. She may be pissed at the good ol' gal network, but they're going to come through for her. Otherwise, they would have stonewalled her completely. Wish I could be there for the fireworks."

"I wish I could sit the whole thing out. You didn't see Gina blow her top all of a sudden. Susan was that way."

"What do you mean?"

"It's a simple comparison."

"I know you, Dalhart. That was a big part of you going down to Lambert. You wanted to see Susan again."

"If you'd been in my shoes, you'd have jumped in your van the minute you heard the news."

Raymond pointed his net at Dal.

"When my dad died, I would've gone to Timbuktu to meet his twin, but I wouldn't have confused the two like you did."

"I know the difference, Ray. I know Susan's gone. God, I know it. You weren't there when Gina lost her temper. Susan would save three months of mad and dump it all at once. She'd be fine after that. Gina did the same thing, exactly. Call it a coincidence, I don't care, but I know what I saw."

Over bowls of frito pie, Raymond returned to his theme. "Here's the problem: you think you're Mr. Altruism, that what you're doing is completely normal."

"Isn't it?"

"Any man would want to see his dead wife's twin sister. You get it now. Saying it aloud is weird enough. You're in new territory, Dal. That woman is a total stranger. She may share a few traits with Susan, including the incidental fact that she looks like her, but I promise you, Gina's an iceberg: ninety percent is completely unknown. When the birth mother shows up, anything might happen."

Heartburn already, and he was still on his first bowl.

"After the mother comes, it's all cut and dried. We already know D'Abruzzo's the father. One plus one equals two."

"You think Gina and the mystery woman are going to fall into each other's arms like all is forgiven. You don't know, Dal. You don't know. Anything can happen, from bouquets to bullets. If I was Gina, I'd be mad as hell."

"Over being adopted?"

"Over the twins being raised apart. Susan was treated like a spare tire in the deal. If you ask me, the birth mother has a lot of explaining to do."

"I think it's entirely possible that she was bullied into doing what the other parties wanted."

"Other parties?"

"The doctor and D'Abruzzo. I'm not going to condemn the lady before I hear her side of the story. Besides, D'Abruzzo had all the time in the world to let Gina in on the secret."

"You think he should have broken his word and destroyed two—no, three—families, like that's how it should have gone down."

Dal's phone rang, thankfully cutting off Raymond's sermon. It was Frannie, who said that she and the mother would be arriving separately in the morning. Gina would meet with Frannie at Dal's house, after which the birth mother's debut. It would be up to Dal to notify Gina.

Off the phone, Dal studied the bottom of his bowl. A queasiness overtook him. This is what you wanted, he thought. *You can't back out of it now.*

## CHAPTER THIRTEEN

Helene Pielowicz wanted them to visit a nightclub, but Gina declined, reckoning that a bar full of drinkers made a poor audience for the second coming of Susan. On her way into the hotel, Dal called with the news. Frannie came through, after all. She clicked off, relieved, and stepped into the hotel lobby.

"Oralia was right," a shaky baritone voice sounded to her left.

She saw Mack Wender, mustached and older than the sweetheart photograph, but with the same cerulean eyes.

Gina took his hand and shook it forthrightly. "I'm glad to meet you, Mack."

"How do you know who I am?"

Wandering in an unsteady line over to a chair, he plopped down and stared at her, amazed. She explained about seeing his face in a photograph.

"I could hardly believe it when the preacher told me you'd been at the graveside service," Mack said. "I called home and Oralia told me you'd been by. I didn't figure Dal'd tell me a damn thing, so I had to call half the hotels in Lubbock trying to track you down. I've been sitting in this lobby over an hour waiting on you to show up."

He must have dropped by a bar on the way. He seemed more startled than drunk.

"Did someone punch you in the eye?"

"I was tagged by a wild pitch. I imagine the bruise'll be gone altogether in a couple of days. Why don't we go up to my room and talk? It'd be a little more private."

He looked abashed. "I don't know. It wouldn't look good for you."

"Nothing's wrong with conversation, since that's all we're after," she said, in case he had a contrary opinion.

She'd had better conversations, as it turned out. Mack tried to parry her efforts to connect him and Susan as more than old classmates. She finally went with the direct approach.

"A friend of hers from work told me you and Susan were lovers."

Mack pushed back his chair. "That's a damned lie. I'd never do that to Oralia. You better not go flapping your lip to her."

Bingo.

"I'm not judging you, Mack, and I'm certainly not running to Oralia with this little news flash."

Oralia hustled Gina out the door and failed to tell Mack that Susan had a twin sister—she had to know about the affair.

"Then what do you want?" he asked, suddenly in tears.

Taken aback, she said, "Nothing. I don't want anything from you."

Pulling out a handkerchief, he blew his nose and tried to pull himself together as she apologized for her attitude.

After a bit, seeming more composed, Mack remarked, "Susan liked that color, too."

She was wearing a purple blouse.

"I don't really have a favorite color in clothes. I know I don't look good in yellow."

"You know, Susan hated bright yellow," Mack said a trifle too brightly. "Our school colors were gray and gold. True gold she didn't mind but when I bought her a yellow shirt on our senior trip, she wouldn't wear it. Said it made her look like she had hepatitis. I thought everything looked good on her."

His mood turned pensive. "We were close. We kind of got into the habit of being together. We never could break ourselves of that."

"Like I said, I'm in no position to judge. I'm just curious why the two of you—"

"Never got married," he finished. "My father didn't like the fact that Susan was adopted. He was worried about her bloodlines. I decided to wait until I finished at Tech, then he couldn't tell me what to do. Susan must've thought I was putting her off for good. She returned the engagement ring a few weeks after I started at Tech. We'd fought a few times before that, but when she gave me the ring back, I knew it was a done deal. Past a certain point, you could never get her to change her mind."

"The fights, were they over her drinking?"

"Drinking was the thing to do back in high school. We'd pool our money and get someone's older brother to buy a couple of kegs. Then we'd go over to the pit."

"The pit?"

"The caliche pit, about a mile down that dirt road by the gin. We'd be out there under the stars, drinking and telling jokes, having a good time."

He assayed the beginnings of a smile.

A charmer. No wonder Susan allowed the affair to continue. Gina thought it best to send his smile and mustache back to Oralia. Before he left, they exchanged insincere promises about calling each other sometime.

She never knew what to do when people cried. The only time Daddy ever shed tears was the day he came home after being at an AA meeting. Gina was eleven years old at the time. Seeing her father unhinged scared her. Gathering the family around, he apologized for being such a rotten father. Gina couldn't understand why he acted so upset, though in retrospect the reasons were clear.

Not the Lambert Car King anymore, he was Dynamo Danny, a used car salesman working on commission and barely making payments on his debt to the IRS. What's worse, his wife made more money than him working as a cashier.

She couldn't recall any incidents where Daddy's drinking got out of hand, but it must have been worrying him that he might end up like his father, who died young from cirrhosis of the liver. Whatever prompted the outpouring, the tears never happened again. Why was she thinking about that?

The cover story she left on their answering machine was that she had gone on a TopSound business trip, yet what was the point of the lie. Daddy had to know that Dal talked to her about Susan. Ditto for Mom.

There are no secrets anymore, she thought, except the only one that matters. After calling Dal to confirm the time and place, she made one more call.

She interrupted Mom's hello to say, "It's me. Can I talk to Daddy?"

"Gin, how's the trip going?" She sounded worried.

"Fine. I really need to talk to Daddy."

A moment later, he came on the phone.

"How ya doin'?"

"I'm okay—no, that's not true. Let me start over." She fought to keep her voice from trembling. "I'm going to see her tomorrow. Frannie Lowell is bringing her down to Creed. I want to know who she is—something about her—so I'll be prepared."

"Sweets, I can't tell you nothing."

"Bullshit." She immediately recanted. "Oh God, Daddy, I'm so sorry. I didn't mean to yell at you. All you have to do is tell me her name, tell me something. I don't want to walk in there cold."

"She may not show herself. She may back out of the deal. Until she comes through, I can't tell you a thing. I'm sorry, but that's the way it's gotta be."

She knew better than to push him but she did anyway.

"Did you know her well?"

"No."

"What about Susan? Did you ever see her?"

A long pause.

"Once, when she was six years old. Frannie Lowell took me by the schoolyard and I got to watch her play. She was a cute little girl. Real lively."

His voice trailed off, then she heard the receiver click. Why did she bother calling? Should have known Daddy wouldn't say anything revealing.

It had been a strange, unsettling day, followed by a night spent repeatedly brushing aside images of Susan in her coffin, Dal tenderly handling photographs, Mack bursting into tears, and Helene laughing about some anecdote involving her sister.

My sister, she thought. What would Susan have thought of Gina D'Abruzzo? Big city, alien customs. Bisexual. Unacceptable. Perhaps they would have worked it out, would have discovered a common ground. She finally drifted off to sleep around four in the morning, waking up an hour later.

Conceding defeat, she took a shower. Then came a room service omelet, a stint before the mirror applying makeup, and watching the news on MSNBC.

Life was getting complicated in the Middle East, the commentator said. It wasn't getting any simpler on the Texas Panhandle.

# CHAPTER FOURTEEN

*The Senior/Junior Place—Robert Rushmore Creed Senior built the original Creed homestead. When it burned down in the late '40s, he constructed a brick house in the same location, where he and Cora lived until their deaths in the 1950s. Junior added a sheltered front porch and swing that gave the house some character. Dal demolished the old wooden garage and put in a brick two-car attachment. Susan oversaw the extensive remodeling.*

"That's Frannie," Dal said as the red sedan pulled into his driveway.

"What if she's pulling a fast one?"

Gina drew closer to the door.

"Oh, she wouldn't come if she didn't have a mother up her sleeve."

"No, I meant what if she's really the one."

"Take a look," Dal offered, stepping aside. "What do you think?"

Crisp and cheery, Frannie took one step onto the porch and looked up at Gina. Her red hair blazed in the sun.

"Why, Gina, you're just the prettiest thing."

She came through the door, her smile unchanged by Gina's lack of response.

Glancing over at Dal, Gina shook her head. Allowing Frannie to hug her, Gina felt airy, almost weightless. It was an effort simply to mumble an inanity about being glad to meet her.

"Why don't we get comfortable, and I'll tell you about your mother."

"Birth mother," Gina interjected quietly as they eased down into the sofa.

She couldn't trust her reactions—whether to smile or to act sober, to play it open or poker-faced. The mystery guest had yet to arrive and she was already on shaky ground.

"That's important to you. Birth mother. Then that's what I'll say.

Your birth mother was only seventeen when she met your father. She hadn't been married but a couple of months when she and her husband went to Fort Worth for a convention."

"So she didn't come from Fort Worth."

"That's right. They decided to visit Dallas after the convention was over, to see the sights and eat out, but they had car trouble and had to stay over a couple of days. While they were at a motel, they met your father, who helped them find a mechanic and drove them around. He was in town to help a relative."

"That would be my aunt. She lived in Dallas back then."

"Your birth mother can tell you more on how they met. When she turned up pregnant, she came to me. I helped her get in touch with Dr. Houtchens. She stayed with me till y'all were born. I don't know everything, but I'm darn sure of this: her husband couldn't father a child and for a time he was willing to go along with the story, but then he changed his mind. That's when your birth mother moved in with me. It was still early enough in the pregnancy that she wasn't showing much, and then y'all were born a little premature. After that, her husband took her back."

"Without us."

"That was the arrangement. Think about it. Two babies, born out of wedlock. Money was tight back then. She didn't have any options."

Not necessarily. "What about my father? He took me."

Her voice caught in her throat and went no further.

"Gina, he was married, too."

"I'm not talking about the woman. I'm talking about Susan."

"The birth mother needs to be the one to tell you about that."

"Then bring her on." Gina felt back on top of her emotions.

"Dal, would you call Rosanna and relay the message?" Frannie asked.

Dal leaped to the phone and made the call. He went over and stood at the front door, his foot tapping nervously. Moments later, Gina heard a car crunching over the gravel in the driveway.

Turning back from the door, an agitated Dal had to visibly restrain himself from saying anything. Frannie asked him to show her his workroom, then led him by the hand down the hall.

Rosanna walked in the door.

"Hello, Gina. You're looking very pretty today."

Gina waited for another woman to walk in.

Rosanna closed the door behind her.

"You were the first one born, by ten minutes," she said, trying to smile.

Looking at her closely for the first time, Gina saw a tall, green-eyed woman whose short dark hair was spiked with gray. Her birth mother.

"Whatever you want to know, I'll tell you."

Too much complication, Gina thought, trying to frame a question.

"I don't get it. You lived right down the road from Susan. You didn't tell her. Why?"

"Because I'm a coward." Rosanna's eyes fixated on the wall behind Gina. "I didn't want to risk losing her friendship. She was very dear to me. Telling her the truth might have made me feel better, but what would it have done to her?"

A reasonable explanation. To hell with that.

"You lived for decades in the same place with Susan yet you couldn't be bothered to tell her the truth. You can call it being a coward, but it sounds crazy to me. Absolutely insane. You could have said something, if not while the Longbrakes were alive, then after they were dead. You had plenty of time to make it right with Susan. You blew it."

"You're right," Rosanna said with a leaden, uninflected voice.

"And another thing: why did you split us up? If you couldn't take Susan, why didn't you let Daddy know? He would have taken her in a flash. Then she'd have been with her real family."

"There are things you don't know about what happened," Rosanna said haltingly. "Things you should ask your father about. I made mistakes—a ton of them—but the mistakes weren't all on my side."

"Oh, so my father's to blame for getting you pregnant."

What a miserable excuse. Gina rose to leave.

"I'm talking about afterward. If only he was here to explain it to you."

Furious, Gina wheeled around.

"You've had long enough. Don't be trying to drag my father through the mud, just because one night you wanted to cheat on your husband. I don't know why I wanted to meet you. I'm glad Susan never found out. I wish I hadn't."

***

The voices rose sharply, then a door slammed. Dal followed Frannie back into the living room where they found Rosanna standing shell-shocked.

Over glasses of tea, they clumped together at the kitchen table and waited for Rosanna to speak. In the meantime, Dal and Frannie meandered through the usual topics of weather, politics, football, and crop prospects. At length, Rosanna's shoulders relaxed and her eyes began to focus.

"That's why I didn't tell Susan. That...anger, I didn't want to see it. I didn't want to face it."

Frannie refilled Rosanna's glass. "At least you got it over with."

"It's over with, that's for sure. She won't return."

"Ah, once she gets over her mad, she'll be back," Dal said. "Give her time."

Hollow-eyed, Rosanna stared into the middle distance.

"I can wait till hell freezes over. She won't forgive me, and I have no right to ask."

At the hotel, he found Gina in no mood to talk, jamming clothes and photographs pell-mell into her suitcase.

"When does your plane leave?"

"The next flight's in two hours."

"You have plenty of time to drive to the airport."

She zipped the suitcase with added emphasis.

"I don't want to be here in case she decides to follow me."

"She won't do that. She thinks you're never coming back."

Gina emitted a sharp, toxic laugh. "Got that right."

"Five minutes. Give me five minutes."

"How thrilled you must be, to finally meet your mother-in-law."

"I know you're angry. You have every right to be," he said.

Raymond was right about the iceberg. Dal felt like the captain of the Titanic.

"So now you know, we both know. What happens next?" he asked.

Gina flew out the door with Dal tacking behind her. It was pointless to continue, but he did anyway.

"Susan told me Rosanna was like a second mother to her. You don't know Rosanna, but Susan did. I know they loved each other. I don't understand it either, why Rosanna didn't get around to telling Susan. Maybe she thought that since they were already close, the truth was irrelevant."

He hewed to that line of reasoning, until her car spun out of the parking lot. A perfunctory hug, no attempt at a smile, and she was gone—returning to God knows what kind of situation with her father.

Dal didn't have to follow up on the private eye's investigation. Dal was under no dictate from on high to tell Gina a solitary word about Susan. Rosanna would have been at peace with her memories of Susan.

Now Rosanna was traumatized, Gina was repelled, and the worst part for him was that, instead of providing a picture-perfect closure, he'd only further tangled the threads. He still hadn't discovered exactly why the twins were raised apart.

To judge from the expression on her face, it'd be a while before Rosanna could open up on the subject, if she ever did.

Why did he still want to know?

Because of the split, Susan came into his life, allowing him to fall hopelessly in love with her, for better and sometimes for worse.

How could he quarrel with a long-ago decision made by one or more parties, except for the fact that because of the split, Susan was in his house the night she was murdered.

## CHAPTER FIFTEEN

After hearing of Gina's adventures up north, Carla spent most of the drive to Gina's apartment trying to talk her friend into confronting the elder D'Abruzzo.

As Carla saw it, Daddy had been a ladies man in his money days, so he probably sweet-talked Rosanna into going to bed with him.

"My father doesn't treat women that way."

"You don't know how he was back then. He might have been a Casanova. People change, Gina."

"Not that much. Not my father. I can't talk to him about personal stuff, anyway. We don't do that.

"Do what—talk?" Carla shook her head. "I forgot. Y'all don't act like normal people. Don't get me wrong. I'd like for my family to keep their mouths shut, now and then."

Mom delivered unwitting proof of Carla's claim in the message on Gina's answering machine when she got home. Mom issued a Sunday dinner invitation to Gina and "your new friend, Dianne, if she wants to come."

While doing her laundry, she pored over photographs of Susan, trying to match them with the life Susan's friends and relatives described.

In one photograph, Rosanna and Susan were standing on the Wintersoles' back porch. Susan had her arm around the older woman's shoulders. Could it be that Susan suspected the truth?

One moment Susan didn't want to know the story behind her adoption, and the next she did. She took what passed for an inheritance—money from the sale of the Longbrake land—then sank it into the investigation.

What would Susan have done if she'd found out? Confronted Rosanna, or kept it to herself? Where did Rosanna get off talking so mysteriously about the separation, trying to blame Daddy? Although, come to think of it, Rosanna didn't trash Daddy as much as she could have.

It took Gina much too long to drift off to sleep. In desperation, she dug out a sleeping pill Terry had left in the bathroom cabinet.

Feeling dopey the next morning, she sat in Cyril's office and tried to talk about sales trends. All he had on his mind was the Fast Action club.

"I talked to a man who worked as the bouncer there until it closed. He remembers a lot of things about your father."

"I asked you not to get involved."

"Certainly, certainly, but you did tell me the story, and you know that I'm going to help you wherever I can."

If she didn't want him involved, she shouldn't have told him.

"Did you meet the lady?" Cyril asked.

"Yes."

"Is she tall like you?"

"Kinda. Maybe five-eight."

"I knew that woman would have some height."

"I don't look like her. What did the bouncer tell you?"

"There's a man, name of Rubio Corrales. He managed the club back then. Your father might have gotten into trouble with a couple of women, but you'll need to talk to Rubio to get the details."

Rubio had visited Daddy a few times over the years.

"Corrales lives in Galveston." She knew that already. "I've got all the information here if you want to pursue it."

"I figured you'd be down on the beach interrogating him."

Cyril pretended to be hurt. "What do you think this is, *Cotton Comes to Harlem*? I'm no detective. Why don't you take the day and go see him? You still have plenty of vacation time, and Binh's doing fine holding down your desk."

"Thanks, but I'd rather do that over the weekend. I need to get some work in."

"The offer still stands."

***

"Thanks for calling us." Anita Porter scooped pecans from the ground with efficient strokes. "The kids even asked when they'd get to come out, but picking pecans, that's the last thing on their mind."

Down the road, the younger Porters were competing with the Marroquin crew in throwing rocks at a broken sandfighter.

"Funny how little things remind you of someone. Like Levon asking when I was going to make pralines again. Susan and I liked trading off, you know. My pralines for her pecan crunch. Lord, she was a good cook."

"Yes, she was."

"The kids loved her so much. Now Levon tells me she has a twin sister."

"They were raised apart."

"Levon hoped to meet her before she left town. Maybe someday."

Levon, who was over at the outdoor court, poked his head around the corner and yelled for Dal to come over.

He'd found the source of the flapping sound, a section of wood paneling that had come loose on a window. Levon unwrapped cord from a nail underneath and pulled the paneling up. Dal saw a dusty mattress with bedding, sitting in the shadowy middle of what used to be the Home Economics classroom.

"He must have been a migrant worker," Levon said. "Stayed here until something scared him off or he ran out of money. There can't be too much work around here nowadays. He'd be better off up north, down south—anywhere but Creed."

He tied the paneling down securely. "If it gets loose again, you might want to borrow my drill and make a new hole for the nail. I know it must have been real irritating, especially hearing it at night."

Dal nodded, thinking that he'd filed the sound under natural occurrences. Had he noticed anything lately? Around the kitchen table, he swapped stories with Levon and Anita, along with Elsa Marroquin, as they played Skip-Bo. Levon started telling an anecdote about Susan, then dropped it for one that included Dal.

Their friend, Levon's classmate, and an occasional babysitter, Susan was the glue between the Porters and Dal. What was he now but a reminder of the missing link? Before Dal could produce a headache as a means of letting them off the hook, Levon proposed a game of one-on-one.

With Anita, Elsa, and the kids watching, Levon won a 21-15 affair that had its share of elbows, but nothing like a typical battle with Susan. On the way to their car, Levon extracted a promise from Dal to continue the weekly court date, claiming to need the exercise.

That night Dal dreamed of a lustrous full moon under which he and Susan made love on the hill. Flanking honeysuckle bushes provided camouflage. Their fragrant scent hung in the warm summer air. He felt her long legs wrapped around him, her hands clutching his back. Deep inside her, he felt an ache settle in his spine as he tried to peak.

"Relax," she said. "You're doing fine."

Resting his head between her breasts, he listened to her breathing, the rate increasing as her rocking intensified. He could have stayed in that position forever, locked into the warmth a moment away from onrush.

Pogo was barking. He awoke in darkness, chilled by the mid-October air, standing naked on the back porch with Pogo pressed against his knee.

***

"Saturday night's alright for fighting."

Dianne sang tunelessly along with the car radio as she and Gina sat at a traffic light, Houston's finest hookers lined up on the nearby street corner.

"Make that Friday night. Look at those pros, all of them hot to trot."

They were inside the loop on Westheimer, a block away from Freddie's.

"I don't know about you, but I'm hoping a certain someone isn't there," Dianne said.

"Lupe. There's someone I'd rather not see myself."

"Terry."

The light turned green. Instead of moving forward, Dianne hung a right and asked for alternative destinations. They settled on the June Bug, a blues bar on White Oak they'd both been to before. Roomy, not a tasteful fern in sight, and loud, funky music.

She could have danced all night if Dianne hadn't ripped a seam in her jeans rubbing against an exposed nail on the wall. Back at Dianne's place, they took turns sewing up the tear until Dianne pronounced it healed. The needle and thread put away, Dianne initiated a kiss that went on for a while but failed to shoot off rockets. Taking it no further, they sat on the sofa and talked nonstop.

An only child, Dianne came to the States at the age of twenty with the intention of earning a degree in philosophy at Columbia University—a career change, an ex-partner, and a cross-country move landed her in Phoenix.

Another failed relationship sent her to Houston. "I don't want you to think that I move every time a relationship doesn't move out. The job at Datapac—that was a great opportunity. I had to take it."

"If I moved every time I split up with someone, I'd have to buy stock in U-Haul," Gina said. Her admitting to being a failure in romance—probably not a smart move.

"People at work say next year I'll run the department once Junie moves into management. What about you?"

"I don't know. I haven't talked to Junie yet."

It was Dianne's turn to laugh. "No, really."

"I'm not going to move much higher up the ladder, I know that. It's a family business and unless I marry in, I'm going to stay chief audio buyer until everyone in the Southwest loses their hearing."

"Work getting you down? You seem rather subdued," Dianne said.

"It's not the job, it's me."

"The sister thing, huh," she said sympathetically. "Oops."

"Oops is right. I bet Carla told you every last detail." She slipped out of Dianne's arms. "That's why you asked me out."

"Give me some credit, why don't you? I wanted to see you again, if only to watch you catch a baseball with your ear. Not everybody can do that. Now you're smiling."

"Clever disguise."

"It's a good one. Tell me: what was your sister like, what'd she look like?"

Strange question. "Like me, of course."

"Carla said you saw her at the funeral. You mean, you couldn't tell any difference?"

"Her hair was curly. Natural, the way mine was a few years ago."

"That's the only way you could tell?"

"Could we talk about something else?"

"Alright, then," Dianne said, clearly puzzled. "Did I understand you right the other day? You said you never attended college."

"That's right."

"No offense, but you sound better educated than that."

Gina could take offense, and call Dianne a cultural elitist. Why bother when she thinks she's giving out a compliment.

"I guess you can blame that on Cyril. A few months after I started working for him, he came into the store, and he got to talking about some book he'd finished reading. Naturally, he had the book right there with him. He left it on the counter and said he needed someone to argue with about it. Took me a month but I finished it."

"What book was it?"

"The Godfather. I realize now he'd had the copy a long time. He thought it'd be a good one to start me on. All those Italian names. After that, he'd bring a book by, I'd read it, we'd talk about it, then he'd start me on another. He's into the Civil War so I've marched through Georgia any number of times. I eventually took off on my own tangents, but we still trade books."

"Were your parents not into reading?"

Unaccountably, she thought of Rosanna.

"No. When we were kids, we'd all run around in the park, or play board games. Daddy liked driving us around on Sundays to look at cars."

"What has your father said about your twin?"

Straight from the ozone. She'd bet the rent that Carla asked Dianne to rag her about Creed.

"Nothing. We haven't talked about any of that."

"Sooner or later—"

"No, Dianne, I don't have to do anything I don't want to. Not sooner, not later. There's not one good reason to bother Daddy with it."

Talking about her father while she was nose to nose with Dianne gave her the yips. Gina shut her up with a kiss.

# CHAPTER SIXTEEN

Laying out his favorite Esterbrook penstaff and a fresh stack of Bristol paper, Dal sat on his stool and thumbed through ideas for op-ed panels. After a few minutes of negative brainstorming, he set them aside.

As he doodled on the borders of his scratch pad, Dal realized that he couldn't care less about current events. He'd never been a news junkie. Why not drop the op-eds, he thought, and then said as much in the subsequent phone call to his agent.

"Next thing you're going to tell me is that you want to drop the whole thing."

Dal realized that he was tired, so damn tired of doing the same thing day after day, year after year. Past the novelty stage early in their marriage, Susan didn't pay much attention to his work, other than to make approving comments when a fan letter or a check came in. She absorbed his attitude that life with a cartoonist was no different than life with an accountant, except that the hours were better.

He should have thought of this years ago, roused himself from the muck, but he'd been too satisfied, or too obtuse, to notice the problem.

Susan had been on the verge of forgiving him. All the signs were there—the looks, the moments of intimacy. He hadn't understood the truth of the matter. She was about to give up again, to accept his blank slate of a life. He failed Susan, not the other way around.

Dal quit on the spot, but it took longer than that to convince his agent.

"I've backlogged enough dailies to take up two months, and by this time next week I guarantee you I'll have the last contracted month. I have four Sundays in the can, so I'm needing ten panels to finish up. About the ad accounts: there's a company downstate I'd like you to send a prospectus."

"What's the company?" His agent's voice sounded heavy and resigned.

"TopSound, located in Lambert. I don't know their corporate address offhand."

"I can look that up. Dal, I hope you're not making the biggest mistake of your life."

# CHAPTER SEVENTEEN

It could be worse, Gina told herself. If she'd invited Dianne along to eat with the folks, her guest would have aimed some serious eyebrow action in their direction, thereby further confusing Linda.

Linda settled a dispute between her twins about a broken bicycle seat, and tried again to make headway on her spaghetti carbonara.

With a note of exasperation, Linda said, "For God's sake, somebody say something. I want to know why you're all acting so screwy. I've had more fun at precinct meetings, and believe me, that's saying something."

"Nothing's wrong, dear."

Nice try, Mom.

"Tell me another one, about the Easter Bunny this time."

Flashing non-verbal cues to Daddy, Gina kept waiting for him to make the first move. He sat there placidly soaking up sauce with a hunk of bread, immune to subliminal suggestion.

"Linda," Gina said. What next.

Linda pushed her bangs out of her eyes. "Yes? Gina, it's your turn to talk."

Mom volunteered to take the girls out for ice cream—a suggestion they pounced on eagerly—and off they went, abuzz with talk of sprinkle toppings.

This isn't working out right, Gina thought. She wanted to ease into the subject slowly, first with Daddy, then with Mom. Linda would come last.

"What's the matter, Gin? You look tired," Linda said as they cleared the table.

Impassive to a fault, Daddy fiddled with his breathing machine, never once looking up that she could tell.

"That trip I took to Lubbock the other day wasn't for business."

There, she got the first words out.

"I went to see some people, one in particular. I can't do this."

She dropped the tableware in the sink and headed to the living room.

"Gina, wait a second. Hold up."

Linda clutched her by the elbow and turned her gently around. Linda looked up at her, her face worried.

"Is this about Terry?"

"Not in a million years. Daddy," she called out, a hard knot twisting in her stomach. "Daddy, don't make me be the one to tell her. Say something."

Linda's eyes were tinged with apprehension. "You went to see the twin."

"You knew?"

Anger pulsing her into action, Gina grabbed her purse and hurtled out the door. Linda, her touch light on Gina's back, stopped her on the front porch.

"I wanted to tell you."

"Why didn't you?"

One more person who knew the truth, one more person who'd let her down.

"Mom begged me not to," Linda's voice shook with emotion. "I had a sick headache one day back in high school. When I got home, the folks were arguing. Mom was home from work. They didn't hear me come in. I thought it was weird that they were fighting, when they hadn't done it in years. I remember Mom saying she didn't want 'that woman' anywhere near you again. You know me. I barged right in and made them tell me what was going on."

"That woman?" Rosanna tried to see her. "Why didn't you tell me?"

"I thought you might run away and never come back. Sounds silly, I guess. You were about twelve then, and a little on the wild side."

At the time, Gina and her pals were throwing rocks at streetlights and switching their neighbor's mailboxes. "Wild side" was an understatement.

"Then, as you grew older, I knew if I told you the truth, I'd also have to explain why I didn't tell you sooner. I kept putting it off. I told myself it didn't matter anymore. Look at me: I'm still afraid you're going to leave. I love you, Gin. I know that's no excuse."

Linda, the fiery floor general, the strong-willed sibling. When her husband went on a sales trip and never came back, Linda didn't waste any time mourning. Her sister obtained a divorce, moved into a cheap apartment, and dove back into the dating scene without skipping a beat. Her sister, who at that moment looked terrified.

"Linda, I'm not mad at you. I'm a little confused, that's all. Why would I leave my family? Jeez, don't start crying on me."

While Linda collected herself, they sat arm-in-arm on the front porch steps, and watched a pair of inline skaters race down the block. It was a lush Lambert day, not as humid as usual, although in Creed, Dal would probably mistake it for rain.

"What's she like?" Linda asked tentatively.

"The birth mother? I didn't talk to her long enough to find out."

"I meant our sister."

From the moment Dal told her the news, it had been Gina's twin—Gina's problem—and the less the others knew, the better. I was wrong to keep Linda out of this, Gina thought, selfish, and ignorant not to think Susan was her sister, too.

"I tried to ask Mom once or twice if she knew anything about her, but I didn't get anywhere," Linda said, her face expectant.

"I don't know how to tell you, but she's…"

Linda divined it instantly.

"Oh God, no, I'm so sorry. I'm so sorry." She erupted into tears.

It finally felt real to her, Susan's life and death, as Gina held Linda and released her own emotions. If they'd both been raised by Mom and Daddy, or if they'd both been adopted, that Gina would have accepted. The separation made no sense to her.

How painful that must have been for Rosanna, Gina realized with a start, and how confusing for Susan, if she'd found out. Had Rosanna been there one afternoon in the D'Abruzzo's neighborhood, watching Gina at play? Daddy would know, she thought, but he's not going to say anything without a major fight. Not yet.

Full of questions about Susan, Linda got most of them answered, except for the last one about how Gina and Dal got along. Gina's non-committal answer didn't suffice.

"Did you tell him you're bisexual?"

"Why would I risk tangling up the wires if he turned out to be a bigot? And no, he didn't come on to me. The man just lost his wife."

"Oh yeah." Linda pondered that point. "You have so much in common with him."

Susan had been a straight, churchgoing country wife, as well as a hardcore jock with a secret lover. Gina had very little in common with Dal—or with Susan, other than a shared taste for alcohol.

She had a feeling Linda planned to roast the folks. Gina knew better than to try and talk her out of it. No matter how shut out Gina had been all these years, she knew her parents had her best interest at heart.

On the phone that night, however, Carla pursued a different line of reasoning. The folks selfishly kept the birth mother away. They were jealous. No one needed protecting anymore. Gina shouldn't keep making allowances for them.

"You should be suspicious, very suspicious of anything they tell you." Carla concluded her opening argument.

"They haven't told me anything yet," Gina said dispiritedly. "You're trying to work up some grand mystery, when there's probably not much to it."

"Maybe. On the other hand, your parents haven't lifted a finger or said one word to help you through this."

"I don't blame them. This must be so embarrassing to them."

Carla blew up. "I don't believe what I'm hearing. Is that what you think you are? An embarrassment?"

"I didn't mean it that way."

"Yes, you did. You've been acting totally unlike yourself. The Gina I know wouldn't be afraid to ask the right questions, to blow through the roadblocks. When Terry messed with your head, you didn't let it drag on. You cut the strings. You verbally kicked her butt all the way down Westheimer."

Not the Terry angle again.

"They owe you an explanation," Carla said. "They owe you that much. I know you're scared. I would be too, but this isn't going to fade away."

***

A restless Wednesday.

He had locked the back door—even put a chair in front of it—but he still awoke to find himself, wandering through the back yard around three in the morning, with a basketball in his hands. Clothed in pajama bottoms this time. Why a basketball? Although he liked the game, it was more Susan's area of expertise. Sleeping in the guest bedroom made no difference.

A psychologist would have a field day with this, he thought.

He decided to give up on sleep and athletics. Time to turn out another Sunday panel. His eyes cast once again to the corner of the drawing board, where long ago he'd pinned a sketch of Susan wearing a quizzical expression. He'd drawn the portrait on their first date when he said she didn't have to get undressed to serve as a model, but he wouldn't object if she did.

She didn't.

On impulse, he searched through drawers in his desk until he found an old sketch of Susan sitting in the bathtub. Asked for a sexy look, she obliged, though not before splashing him with soapy water.

One showstopper Rockette leg stretched along the rim, she waited patiently for him to finish, then remarked, "That better not end up in some porno magazine."

"If it does, I'll buy you a copy."

"Only if Johnny Depp's the centerfold."

Along about noon, he microwaved a chimichanga, popped open a beer, and checked his e-mail. Hello. A message from Gina.

> I'm sure you didn't expect to hear from me again. I want to apologize for my behavior toward you and Mrs. Wintersole. My usual manners went by the wayside. There's no excuse, except that I felt under pressure, which was not your fault. I should have been more understanding of your situation. Again, please accept my apology. Please Mrs. Wintersole know that I'm sorry for my behavior.

As Raymond had predicted, she appeared to be coming around. She mentioned Rosanna twice, two times more than he'd expected.

## CHAPTER EIGHTEEN

Tracing the words with her fingers, Rosanna pored over the e-mail copy as Dal, perched on the edge of the sofa, waited for a reaction. She appeared rapt in thought.

"I've arranged a plane ticket for her, Rosanna. I know she'll be back."

She set aside her reading glasses and shook her head.

"Don't be so sure. All this tells me is that she doesn't completely hate me. You don't apologize to people you despise."

"I thought you'd be happy to see this," he said, disappointed.

Her face brightened for a moment. "I want a miracle to happen: for her to accept me and not reject her father at the same time."

Reject her father? "You know something about Danny. Tell me."

She regarded him thoughtfully.

"I'm a stranger to her. How can I expect her to believe what I say, to understand the reasons for what happened."

"All I want to know is why, why were they separated?"

"That involves Danny."

"Rosanna, listen to me. It all started with the split, a chain of events, one after the other. It sent Susan here. It put her in our house the night she was murdered. If she'd been sent to Lambert, she'd still be alive today."

"You don't know." She stared out the bay window. "You don't know how her life would've turned out. I know the two of you were having a rough time, but please, please don't dwell on all the things that went wrong. I wasted most of my life doing that. Weren't we blessed to have Susan in our lives? We should try somehow to have that joy, that absolute joy she had for living."

Back home, he sorted through scraps of paper searching for gags. He settled on five contenders that would complete the last batch of dailies.

The day before, he finished the Sunday boards. No more Elmo. Dal stretched in his chair as he tried to work the kinks out of his back.

His agent said that a press release had been faxed yesterday announcing Elmo's demise. Any journalists who called would probably connect his wife's murder to the death of Twister Tales. Let them. The first casualty had been his marriage, and he'd been too stupid to realize that until time ran out.

***

Sunday on Galveston Island. On the phone, Rubio Corrales suggested he meet with Gina at a murky bar on the Silver Strand. White-haired and barrel-chested, he looked unchanged from the last time she'd seen him, which had been around two years ago during Daddy's spell with pneumonia.

After a brisk hug, they ordered drinks—a coke for Gina—then played verbal hide and seek for a few minutes. The conversation touched on tourists and oleanders until he stopped ignoring Gina's obsession with the Fast Track club.

Rubio looked at her with a rueful expression.

"There were two girlies I know of. One, a local. She shut her yap after we gave her some money. The other one—ever since you called me, I've been thinking about those days. Going down memory lane, guess you call it. Danny, he was a go-getter back then. Big guy. Not too hard on the eyes. Your mom and him weren't getting along back then. I don't think I should—hell, I told you I'd talk to you. He worked during the day on all those schemes he had going, then at night he'd be working the club, sugarlipping contacts left and right."

Rubio, pick up some speed.

"Yeah, he stepped out with the girlies. Hold on, Stretch, I'm getting somewhere with this. I remember a kid coming by the club one night. She hung around for hours 'til Danny showed up. He'd been partying with some high rollers. Next thing I knew, they were off in the storage room."

"What did she look like?"

Sweat was rolling off of her like it was August in Hermann Park. Maybe he wouldn't notice.

"Brunette. Pretty. Nice legs. Call me a dog but I have an eye for the girlies. Don't ask me her name. Never knew it in the first place. Danny came out and told me to go get her five hundred bucks out of the safe. I go in thinking she's a bimbo out for a free ride, then I get a good look at the kid, sitting there under the lamp. Thinking to myself, 'man oh man, why is Danny messing with jailbait?' She was starting to show. The real thing. Just sitting there."

He slowly shook his head. "After I gave her the money, she still looked so blue I took her to my place and fed her supper. My wife didn't like me letting the kid spend the night on the couch, but I didn't think it'd be right to dump a pregnant girl at the bus stop. Lot of hoodlums hung around there at night."

He scooted his chair closer and took Gina's hand.

"I know she rode back home on the bus. She weren't no whore. I'd lay odds it was her first time in a juke joint. Not a whore, Gina. She was only a kid in trouble."

"Did Daddy say anything?"

"Nothing, Stretch. He never said a word."

Driving back into Houston, she turned onto Westheimer and stayed there until she entered the Montrose district. She parked in front of a tattoo parlor as a light rain began to fall, and she watched women go into the Best Bar. That was an old hangout for her and Carla. Back then, Bee Bees welcomed all sexual persuasions, even collegiate boy-girl couples out for over-priced margaritas and cheap thrills.

Way too many thrills for Gina, who drank herself into a coma on a regular basis until she got tired of finding out second-hand that she'd had a great time. The steamy nights she couldn't remember, the hot dates that blew up in her face—how did she avoid pregnancy, DWIs, and the mystery corpse spotlight on Channel 11? How did she manage to avoid her parents' mistakes, and how did she get so lucky.

Daddy gave Rosanna money, and agreed to take at least one of the twins, or did he. Perhaps Rosanna, wanting to punish Daddy, rejected his offer to take the twins. Maybe the money was for an abortion or to pay her off, and then he had a change of heart when someone told him about the twins.

Daddy and Rosanna knew the truth, yet neither was talking. Gina knew one thing: she didn't like any of the scenarios.

When Gina was nineteen, she had a six-week relationship with a cokehead county paper-shuffler on the fast track to marriage. He thought a ring on her finger would settle her down, and straighten her out. He brought out her worst tendencies of self-destructive behavior and me-tooism. You like Chinese food, staying out all night, and drinking gallons of tequila? Count me in.

When he brandished the ring again during a four a.m. margarita 'n coke binge, Gina had enough presence of mind to say no, after which he cracked her Joan Jett CD and screamed that she was nothing but a closet dyke who liked ripping off normal men. Two minutes of his eye-popping hysterics left him crumpled beside the car, and her nursing a throbbing left foot.

The next day she slunk into TopSound, having missed two days of work. A glowering Cyril, who declined to fire her, greeted her at the door. Over the next few months, however, he regularly lent her books that, when boiled down, all preached backbone and self-reliance.

The ex-boyfriend moved back home to Michigan shortly after that. He hated Bee Bees and considered Carla to be his rival. He made no secret of his desire to father a child, but she managed not to get pregnant, a piece of luck made possible by his frequent equipment failures. So much for cocaine being an aphrodisiac.

After the break-up, Mom and Daddy celebrated with apple pie and vanilla ice cream. A perfect time for Daddy to take her aside and reveal the truth about Rosanna in order to impress upon his youngest child the dangers of unwanted pregnancy and loose men, a perfect time, except would she have listened through the Jack Daniels brain wax.

Later, she began a now full decade of sobriety, drinking vats of coffee during the bad spells and devouring lethal amounts of Hershey's bars at work. She amused Cyril no end with her newfound devotion to chocolate and sales targets. All that time, Daddy kept his mouth shut. What made her think he'd talk now?

No more Rubios. The only people she needed to talk to were Daddy and Rosanna, Daddy most of all. A drink or two at Bee Bees and she'd have the guts to confront her father, to scream her anger until she broke him down completely. A tall glass of bourbon on the rocks, only it wouldn't be only a drink or two, and she'd end up in bed with a friendly stranger, no closer to the truth.

A trio of young lesbians roistered into Bee Bees, their laughter echoing down the block. Barflies in training. Go home, Gina, go home.

# CHAPTER NINETEEN

Charmaine Murray had an enormous desk, even bigger than Cyril's, Gina thought as she laid waste to a thick ham on rye with spicy mustard. She politely batted aside Charmaine's inquiries about the "hot blonde you took to the picnic."

"That queen bitch stepmother of mine was up in arms over that. It's none of her business who you're with, or what you do with them."

Charmaine reached across the desk for more pepper to sprinkle on her salad.

In Charmaine's brief time at TopSound she had proved herself to be a true daughter of Cyril, what with her weakness for practical jokes, and pizzas with strange toppings. Charmaine had quizzical eyes, a solid, curvy frame, and a warm smile. It was nice having another woman to hang with at work.

"That's right. She's no fan of gay people, and she definitely holds it against me," Gina said.

"Who says?"

"Your father."

"He said that 'cause he didn't want to hurt your feelings. She thinks you lack the proper background. Apparently, your blue collar needs a lighter shade." Charmaine said the last part with the proper haughtiness.

Charmaine continued to dish enough dirt to leave Gina feeling a touch peevish for the remainder of her workday. Peevish, and undecided about the contents of Dal's recent email. Not only had he paid for a round-trip ticket to Lubbock, he'd also sprung for a hotel room "if she needed it."

But, did she want to go up there again, knowing her birth mother lived right down the road from Dal. Could Rosanna be persuaded to tell the truth?

I owe it to Susan, Gina thought. It didn't make sense, to feel an obligation to a stranger, yet that's precisely how she felt. The only question being when to go.

Her mother called later in the evening while Gina was watching Rachel Maddow talk to a sharp-eyed man about politics. Mom inquired about Gina's health, her job, Dianne's health, and other surface topics.

Gina felt so tired of the run-around, of the lies said and the lies her parents didn't even have to use because she hadn't challenged them. Time to cut through.

"How come you never told me about Susan?"

A sharp intake of breath. "It was a terrible situation for your father. The one thing that woman did right was giving you to us."

"But not Susan."

"Honey, the moment your father found out, he drove up to Big Spring. Susan had already been taken somewhere. That woman was so hardheaded on telling us about the adoptive parents. Took years, as I recall. Thank God, you were still there."

The cracks in Mom's voice showed the strain.

"You had a headful of curly black hair, red-faced, and yelling. So tiny. I fell in love with you the moment Danny brought you through our front door. He was sick that this had happened. He wanted to make things right somehow. He did his best, honey."

With an increasing sense of detachment, Gina listened as Mom called Rosanna a hick tramp who forced herself on Daddy, then tried to break up his happy home.

Hmm. The ceiling in the corner showed signs of peeling, possibly indicating a slow leak in the roof. That meant a call tomorrow morning to the complex manager.

"...I don't care what stories she told you, they're all lies."

"I talked to Rubio. Daddy got in trouble with women at least twice. Not only that, when Rosanna came down here and told him she was pregnant, he gave her five hundred bucks."

"That's not true. Rubio doesn't know what he's talking about. They're all in it together, trying to tear Danny down, trying to drive you away. That woman. That woman wasn't there when you had the measles, or when they called me down to the station after you and your friends got in trouble for throwing those water balloons at the patrol car. I was there; I picked you up. I wiped your nose, not her."

"Mom—"

"She can't go claiming to be someone she's not."

Though round-faced—almost cherubic—Mom could manage, when angry, a stony glare worthy of a football coach.

"She hasn't said hardly anything, certainly nothing against, or even about Daddy. I want to find out what really happened. I want to hear both sides of the story."

"You know his breathing gets out of kilter when people upset him. Don't hit him with this. You're not gonna go off half-cocked and make him sick."

According to the doctors, Daddy's health would continue its slow, steady decline unless a bout of pneumonia sped up the clock. Mom's version had Daddy rushing to his grave if Gina uttered one word about the past.

"Gin, I know this is a terrible shock for you, finding out you had a twin. It was a shock for your father when that woman's friend called after she'd given birth. I wish we could have found the baby soon enough, but they wouldn't tell us anything. We did our best."

While lying in bed that night, Gina kept realigning the facts as she knew them, searching for scenarios that absolved both Daddy and Rosanna of guilt. None of them worked.

If Daddy gave Rosanna money, then why did he act so shocked to hear about the births? Unless it was nothing but an act for Mom, unless the money had been intended to pay for an abortion.

If Rosanna carried the pregnancy to term against Daddy's wishes and never wanted him to know, then why did she allow him to take Gina, yet refused to talk about Susan? Unless Daddy lied to Mom about the real sequence of events, unless he grabbed Gina over Rosanna's objections, unless she allowed Frannie to contract the D'Abruzzos, and never seriously considered giving Gina to anyone else.

Unless, unless, unless.

Rubio described Rosanna as a simple girl in trouble, Daddy as a carouser—descriptions that at times could have served for Gina in her wayward years.

What was stopping her from talking to Daddy? Sheer terror, that's all.

# CHAPTER TWENTY

> Twister Tales has been called 'a slice of rural Americana,' 'a peculiarly comfortable marriage between Salvador Dali and Ma Kettle' and, in its later years, 'a beloved reminder of comics' Golden Age.' My father viewed his work as merely a fantastical portrait of Creed, which was a dying rural town named for and co-founded by his father. A proto-Sontagian, Junior Creed resisted any interpretation of his work by critics, or even by his non-intellectual farming neighbors.

"Proto-Sontagian"? That would go over well with the editor charged with updating and editing the late Padgett L. Shearer's book on cartoonists. She had called earlier to suggest Dal pen a few words about his father. She had been solicitous of Dal's feelings regarding the death of his wife and the impending demise of Elmo.

A few weeks ago, he could have produced five pages of analysis seasoned with half-baked semiotics, never mind details of family and town history, or the emotional knots in Junior his son failed to unravel. Now, the dry stuff felt utterly trivial to him.

> A taciturn man with a taste for Stan Kenton, my father didn't know any cartoonists when he began his life's work. He grew up in a Texas village that had been hit hard by the Great Depression.

Not entirely true.

> When my grandfather and two others founded Creed, they had every expectation that tracks would be laid from the railroad spur in nearby Wolfforth. An agriculture-centered community lacking access to a railroad may as well pack up and leave. This is what eventually happened. There were other factors, however, in the town's decline. While the Dust Bowl didn't hit Lubbock County as badly as much of the Panhandle further north, it did leave its mark, as did economic disruptions caused by the Depression. Then the tornado hit in the 1950s, causing more Creedonians to move away.

The tornado. Oh yes. Tell them something they might want to hear.

> A destructive natural phenomenon for the farmers, the tornado led to the creation of a cultural icon, as

Icon? Tell the damn story.

> Junior dealt with the tornado's aftermath by spoofing it with sketches depicting cows flying in the air and farmers doing back flips. It must have been his way of conquering the enemy. Elmo showed up in the early drawings as a shorter version of his father, developing the familiar potbelly and twirling mustache years later when Junior, always a reluctant farmer, retreated into what he called his "doodlings."

Junior began the first of many all-night sessions as he struggled to find the angle that would make fans out of the syndicate bosses in Chicago.

Junior didn't break the nightly pattern, even decades later.

Dal felt a familiar tightening of his throat and a twinge in his stomach, twin hallmarks dating from Dal's childhood, when Junior would summon Dal to the workroom, supposedly to keep him company while he was working.

Instead, Junior prodded Dal into criticizing the work in progress, forcing his son to the brink of tears and beyond. Dal never could figure out the reason for the interrogations: boredom, frustration, or malice? A need for company, perhaps, which sometimes came over Dal during extended sessions. The need made him seek out Susan or Raymond for a coke and chat.

Susan. Every memory somehow tracked toward her. Not right now.

Rush Senior, who had watched the population dwindle despite his loans to residents, decided that since he had started the town, he could end it. He called in all the notes, which forced over twenty families into moving on short notice. After their departure, he sold the houses to a company in Lubbock. After that, the deluge.

Mother said his blood had turned to vinegar, his heart to caliche. Great-Uncle Rudyard's response was to specify that his house never be torn down, which accounted for the wreckage across the road from the gin.

Why Rudyard and the Wenders refused to intervene, and why Rush Senior continued to sell vacant houses for lumber or relocation, were two more mysteries never to be solved.

Dal only knew that he started first grade with seven other Creedonians and graduated high school with five. Susan ended with two. Ended with a small article in yesterday's paper headlined "Murder of Cartoonist's Wife Still Unsolved." The District Attorney's office denied that the case had been backburnered, but did admit that they had run out of leads.

What else could they say, Dal thought as he switched off his computer. What else could the paper run on its website? That murderers too often go uncaptured, that the current innocent face would be replaced in due course by another victim, that the sheer volume of media tragedy had created a public attention span of one degree above absolute zero.

He couldn't remember the name of the baby who fell down the well all those years ago or the celebrity who survived a back alley stabbing last week. Why should anyone else remember a damn thing about the cartoonist's wife.

A flick of the eyes over to his Scrooge McDuck clock. Three a.m. No more delaying tactics. Positioning a fresh sheet, he drew what had come to him while sealing trays of work.

The final panel: Elmo, one hand on his hat, and the other clutched around the tail of an ascending tornado.

The tag read, "All that hot air I produced finally caught up with me. I'm off to a far, far better place—dagnabbit!"

To sleep, only to awake in transit, walking down the path leading from the house to the basketball court. He jogged back inside with Pogo on his heels, then made a pot of coffee. He dismissed scheduling a visit to his doctor. Dal had already made the diagnosis: like father, like son.

Recommendations would likely entail reducing stress, drinking less caffeine, and installing double-bolted locks—none of which prevented Junior from dying when Dal, on a skiing vacation with Raymond in Ruidoso, New Mexico, left his father unattended.

"I wouldn't hang around if I were you," Dal said aloud to Pogo, who was investigating a monster dust bunny behind the distilled water dispenser.

"The minute I'm out of town, you're a goner."

# CHAPTER TWENTY-ONE

"You understand, don't you, Mr. Creed, that TopSound conceptualizes all of its own advertising. An agency here in Houston takes it from there. Quite frankly, I don't see a niche for you here, although the price you're quoting does have its appeal."

Charmaine Murray waited for a response as she tapped her pen against a coffee mug that read "Are you a friend of Dorothy, or someone with a ruby shoe fetish?"

Whatever that meant. She was a curvy woman with mischievous eyes and carved cheekbones.

"Ms. Murray—"

"I did like the humor in your specs. The little girl dragging her father through our store. I am curious about one thing, however."

She leaned forward in her chair.

"Why you went to this much trouble in order to see Gina. TopSound is not in the habit of laying land mines at our front door."

Still not smiling, but a definite twinkle in her eyes. Or a glint.

"I'm not doing Twister Tales anymore."

"Is that right? I kind of liked the geezer. However, I can see why you'd want to leave cartoons for the far more creative field of advertising."

With a face like that, she could be holding a royal flush and who'd know.

Prepared to blab on if necessary, Dal instead watched as Ms. Murray summoned Gina via her phone intercom.

"Look, if you don't want me here, I can leave."

"Sh-h-h," she said amicably.

A moment later, Gina came through the door and executed a perfect double-take.

"Surprise. Your brother-in-law has offered his services. I'm afraid we can't use him right now, but first of the year I'd like for him to work with us on a campaign."

"Dal, I wasn't expecting you. That is, I'm glad to see you." She seemed rattled yet pleasant.

"I hope you don't mind me trying to drum up some business here. Figured since I was coming down anyway...Look, I can get back on the plane. No hard feelings."

"No, stay."

"I hope you haven't made dinner plans. Things were so hectic up there, we never really got acquainted. There's so much more I want to tell you about Susan."

"I want to hear it." She grimaced. "I have a date tonight. Wait, do you mind if—Charmaine, would you?"

"A foursome? Why, yes, Ms. D'Abruzzo, I'd love to go out tonight."

Charmaine flashed a warm, toothy smile. It wouldn't hurt to have two more conversational partners in case he faltered.

"I went ahead and made reservations at Lodgett's. I'm sure they won't mind if I make it a party of four," he explained.

"Lodgett's?"

Charmaine and Gina spoke simultaneously, with Charmaine carrying the ball after that. "Don't you know how much it costs?"

"It's my treat."

"Dal—"

"Gina, I want to make up for dumping the news on you in the first place."

Not much of a fight was put up after that, not even at the restaurant door by Gina's date, a stylish, somewhat chilly woman Dal remembered from the ballgame.

Mark up one big difference between the sisters. Gina appeared to be gay—or perhaps bisexual—and, to judge by Ms. Newberry, attracted to sophisticated types. Even if one adjusted for gender, Susan would never have gone out with that kind of person. Dal himself wouldn't have passed muster with Susan, if not for her having seen him so many times dressed like a farm hand.

While waiting on his sea urchin ceviche appetizer, Dal remarked, "I understand they have good food here."

"That's like saying Paris has a couple of nice cafes."

A smile formed on Charmaine's lips. He had a feeling she would make short work of him in a verbal dispute, not that one appeared imminent. Gina acted only slightly more relaxed than she had been at the office.

Here, on neutral ground, they felt one another out in polite conversation orchestrated, more often than not, by Charmaine. No mention of Susan. Or Rosanna. Or her father. Midway through their entrees, Charmaine politely excused herself and carted Gina off to the restroom.

Dianne dabbed her forkful of venison in a tangerine gastrique. "I don't know why Gina's so moody tonight. Perhaps something at work's bothering her."

"I keep dropping in on her. That's the problem. I guess I'm afraid she'll back away if I give her the chance—and then I'd never get to know her."

"Why is that so important to you?"

He thought about it for a moment.

"I wasn't much of a husband to Susan. That is, I thought I'd done reasonably well until after she died. Recently, I figured out the obvious fact that I'd been a total screw-up as far as my wife was concerned. Then the adoption thing came up. For whatever reason, she wanted to find Gina."

"You found her. Why continue?" Dianne asked with a cool expression.

"Who's the most important person in your life?"

"My father."

"What if someday you were to lose him?"

"I wouldn't try to create a relationship with his twin brother overnight. I don't know if I'd traipse off to see him after the first time. Imagine seeing his face again like that," Dianne said with a slight shudder.

"Gina missed out on knowing her sister. I want her to know Susan the only way she can now, which is through me."

"Look, I'm getting to know Gina myself. I'm no expert on the lady. All I know is what I would feel: confused, curious, and bloody scared. I don't know if you've thought this thing through."

"Not as much as I should have, probably. As far as I'm concerned, it's Gina's call. The moment she wants me to leave, I'm out of here."

***

"What's the problem? He seems like a nice guy. You're over there acting like Homeland Security's on its way."

Charmaine checked her hair in the restroom mirror.

"I think I saw a Cezanne on the wall. This is going to cost him an arm and a leg."

Dal had ordered a bottle of Chardonnay with dinner. The wine was on the verge of sprouting wings and attacking her if the others didn't hurry up and finish it.

"He's not buying the painting, just the meal. Besides, it's a print. Gina, you've been in fancy restaurants, so I know the décor's not giving you fits, it's Dal. If it's that hard on you, tell him to go back home."

Why couldn't she? What did it matter that she had a sister who lived and died with Gina's face? It could have been Gina's life, spent across from a cotton field with a semi-famous cartoonist, spent caring for elderly people and the children of friends. Picking pecans, and shooting baskets. Messing around on her husband.

Another life, not hers. Maybe Dal needed to see the difference.

"Have you ever been to Freddie's?"

"I've heard about it," Charmaine said. "I don't know if Mister Normality can handle it."

"That's the idea. I want to find out more about Susan, but that's going to be hard if Dal keeps thinking I'm a knockoff of his wife."

"Who says he does?"

"I get the feeling he needs to see me as more of an individual."

"What if your ex is there?"

"Then the night is totally screwed."

An hour later, they were sitting around a corner table in Freddie's, taking in the scenery. Studying Dal intently, she saw him react when two men glided by on the dance floor, react, then relax without a second glance.

Freddie's boasted a sound system less deafening than usual, a bartender renowned for being a dead ringer for Humphrey Bogart, black walls, and a neon pink ceiling and floor.

Dal cocked an eyebrow at her. "I don't have a problem with you being gay or whatever."

"We can leave if you like."

"I'm happy. I've finally found a bartender who knows how to mix a proper Bloody Mary. Wasn't he in *Key Largo*?"

"No, but you ought to see him play both Bogie and Bacall in the whistle scene."

The night's conversation had revealed new, reassuringly normal layers to the man, but she hadn't expected a country boy to be so nonchalant about being in a gay bar.

"You've been in one of these before."

"Three or thirty times. Some of my best friends are straight."

Dal didn't bother with further details. Whatever else one might say about the man, he didn't waste air on scoring brownie points. She liked that.

"Do your parents know?" he asked.

"They know I date both men and women. Mom thinks that all I need is the right man, while Daddy thinks…"

What does he think? "He's friendly to whoever I bring over. Do you want to dance?"

That was a time-honored method of shutting down a line of questioning. Surprisingly agile, Dal kept up with the deejay's mood swings from dance pop to a grinding neo-soul ballad.

The song seemed to be taking forever, but then suddenly it couldn't last long enough. They slid closer together, heedless of Dianne and Charmaine, who had decamped to the pool table. Before she was ready for it, before she'd even conceived of it, they were breathing too close, sweating too much even for Houston, acting as though they knew what they were doing.

***

How they arrived at that point, he had no idea, but there she was in his arms, offering no resistance, perfectly at ease as they danced. How natural it felt to pull her closer, to bury his face in her hair. He stopped cold.

A stranger.

Susan, the thought began in his mind, then vanished. He pulled away from Gina and walked over to the pool table where Charmaine stood crowing over her victory.

"Rack 'em up, Dianne, rack 'em up, and go again."

This is Gina's world, Deal repeated to himself. Her world, not Susan's. Take the tour then get off.

"What's up with you, Dal, leaving a lady on the dance floor like that?" Charmaine cuffed him playfully. "That's a dangerous thing to do around here. Next thing you know, she's off choosing place settings with the waitress. Dal, Dal?"

Gina, who didn't act offended by his quitting mid-dance, maintained a light mood all the way to her apartment. She kept cracking jokes with Dianne and Charmaine. They made a deliberate effort to include Dal in the fun.

Gina saw him out to his rental Volvo. "I had a lovely time. I appreciate you coming down. I mean that."

"Sure. Come up and see me sometime."

He tried not to flinch when she hugged him.

Not until the next morning, safely aboard a flight home, did it occur to him that he never bothered to ask if she discovered anything new about why the twins were separated.

Hadn't that been a major reason why he made the visit, yet it never crossed his mind while he was with Gina.

## CHAPTER TWENTY-TWO

Dianne left shortly after Dal, acting all the way to the car as though something about the evening hadn't set well with her. It left Gina at a loss for words, and Charmaine in no apparent hurry to leave.

They were cozy together on the sofa with tortilla chips, salsa, and Cokes, watching an old Barbara Stanwyck movie.

Charmaine asked bluntly, "What's going on? It's obvious Dianne doesn't do it for you."

"I like her okay."

But she doesn't fire you up."

"No, I guess not," she said with a tone of regret.

"Then you and Dal have a traffic accident on the dance floor. Major collision. Instead of following up, the two of you play diplomats the rest of the night. Boring as shit."

"I don't know what happened. I don't think I'm attracted to him, yet when we were dancing, something happened."

So confusing, how a relative stranger could do that to her, and a grieving widower at that.

"Curiosity, that's what it is," Charmaine opined. "You put yourself in your sister's shoes for a moment, and Dal went for it. No harm done. Dal had a good time. He probably hadn't been out since before your sister died."

She reached over to turn the endtable lamp down a notch. "I think the evening's turning out fine."

***

"You did what?" Raymond Rodriguez said incredulously.

They were out for a Sunday stroll through Raymond's West Lubbock neighborhood. Dal avoided a waist-high wobbly pass from the two preteen boys next door. They retrieved their soccer ball with apologies.

"I almost kissed her," Dal confessed. "Hormonally stupid, wouldn't you say?"

"No, I wouldn't say that. Tell me this: who did you think you were with when you were dancing with her?"

"Gina," Dal said with absolute assurance. "But I thought of Susan at first."

"That's only natural."

"This isn't a natural situation."

"True enough." They veered around a tricycle on the sidewalk. "What you've said about her tells me you know you're not dealing with a clone of your wife. This gal is smart, sophisticated, and well-read."

"Susan was smart."

"In her own way. And it sounds to me like Gina opened up after she came out as a lesbian."

"Bisexual—and why haven't you asked me if we went to bed together?"

"It's way too soon for you, and she's really most sincerely gay. She'll kiss you, but she won't do anything more."

"I made a fool of myself, trespassing on her turf. She seemed to enjoy my company. Am I being crazy here, Ray? Am I?"

"No," he said with a sober expression. "There must be a reason for you and Gina being in this situation. God must have a plan, even if we don't always—"

Dal cut his friend off with an expletive and trudged on in silence. He left minutes later having said little more. Raymond tended to turn religious on him.

Although that kind of spiritual reflex might work fine in theory, it didn't hold up to real life. Or death.

Susan did more for other people in one week—out of goodness, out of natural generosity—than Dal did in a year, yet guess who got snuffed out.

God has a plan, Dal mused. A great, beauteous strategy for how Dal and Gina would meet. Such a wonderful plan that God had to kill Susan in order to carry it out.

Back at work, he doodled unproductively as he weighed and discarded successive long-form ideas. What about the Joe Pericles concept, where a modern-day dentist becomes a missionary for the Greek Gods in order to bring in new believers?

Another break. In the freezer, he found a Tupperware container of peach ice cream that Susan had made. He settled in with a bowl as MSNBC blatted the day's highlights.

Trouble in the Middle East, a huge explosion in South Africa, a racist attack in Boston, and a cute baby contest in Salt Lake City. Nothing new.

Licking his spoon, he remembered dancing with Gina in a subtle havoc that now evoked no twinges of guilt, only a blankness.

The Bogart bartender slipped in without warning, clutching a cigarette as he held forth for a table full of adoring upwardly mobiles. Why not?

Back at the drawing table, Dal roughed a full pager of the faux-Bogart tough-guying some blonde minx as Gina—definitely Gina—glared from her seat at the bar. He drew her in a leather jacket and miniskirt, with major attitude.

What do I have here, he thought. A crime epic, or a gay club comedy, or both? And what role did Gina play—a love interest, a spy, or an enemy?

Susan didn't have a complicated bone in her body. She hated you or loved you, stayed sober or got roaring drunk, played merciless basketball or cuddled the children she babysat. Gina debuted as a subtle corporate type with a short fuse, only to display an unexpected warmth and humor at the bar.

Best to draw her as a mystery woman.

***

"Millie Becker's alligator sent over a discovery and I told him, 'discover this, you prick.' Gina, Gina, pay attention."

Linda snapped her fingers. They were drinking cappuccinos in Linda's kitchen while the twins played Nintendo in the living room.

"I'm sorry."

"You'll never grow up to be a legal assistant. Okay, tell me more about our brother-in-law. I wish you'd brought him by."

"He only stayed one night."

"With you?" Linda asked eagerly.

"Good Lord, no." Gina decided not to mention that she and Charmaine had slept together. It was a nice, if unplanned capper to the night, but she hadn't quite worked out how she felt about it yet.

Gina regrouped. "Dal and I did...uh...sort of connect before he left. We went with Dianne and Charmaine Murray to a club. He was cool about it. We almost kissed. I guess it's because we were dancing."

Betty Boop-eyed, Linda digested the news.

"Did he get all hyper again talking about Susan?"

"No. We started to once or twice, but it felt weird. Does that make sense?" Gina clawed her napkin.

"A guy's dancing with the spitting image of his dead wife—I give him credit for not running screaming from the place. I don't know. He probably needed to get out of the house and kick up his heels. Tell me, honestly, what do you think of him?"

"A little too well-mannered for my taste, but not a snob. He makes little jokes about himself. Doesn't go on and on about his work. It's like he feels it's his duty to put people at ease. Noblesse oblige."

"Whuzzat?"

"Probably didn't say it right. He doesn't rub your nose in his money."

The napkin was quickly turning into confetti.

"Fine, that's all great. Do you like him?"

"I think so."

Sensing a theme beginning to develop, Gina added, "Don't jump to conclusions. He's a nice guy. He's told me so much about Susan. There's a lot I'd like for him to tell me."

What would Susan think about that almost-kiss. What would Susan think of her? Not much, probably.

Hello, Earth to Gina."

Abstracted, Gina said, "I need to be careful."

"About what?"

"Dal. That whole situation. I need to be careful."

# CHAPTER TWENTY-THREE

"I came by to drop something off for Oralia. I know you're always busy drawing your little pictures." Mack didn't wait for an invitation to come in the door.

"I'm not busy at the moment."

Peering out at the sky, Dal saw black clouds clotted in the southwest. Tornadoes didn't usually visit in the fall, but anything could happen with Texas weather. An offer of tea meeting with a frown, coffee with a shrug, Dal gave up on citing fruit juices when Mack raided the fridge for two bottles of Young's Oatmeal Stout.

Mack chugged down the better part of a bottle, then fished a thin gold bracelet out of his shirt pocket. He explained that Oralia had found it under a cushion in their den. A probable casualty of Susan's roughhousing with their boys.

Dal searched his mental Rolodex for a fresh topic with Mack, one that didn't involve Western history or sports. Ah, cotton.

Mack's face shuttered at the mention of his gin.

"I might as well quit. One of my farmers called this week and said he'd decided to take his harvest over to Ropes. A business decision. Hell, he made his mind up months ago. The little coward didn't have the nerve to tell me. That's three in the last week alone. They should have told me back in the summer, then I wouldn't have tried to hold on through one more season. All they care about is going to the gin in Ropes or New Home, and shooting the bull with their buddies. Daddy said 'an honest man's word is as good as gold.' Not these assholes."

Mack dove into another beer. "Can't say that I blame them. When your grandfather made all those people move, this place went to hell. Grampa said he begged him to give the folks more time to pay, but Old Man Creed wouldn't do it. He sat on your uncle's veranda and watched those pickups roll by. Your family killed this town."

An old subject given a stale rehashing.

"My grandfather had help, Mack. A tornado, drought, the Depression, never getting the railroad spur—about the only thing that didn't happen here was an earthquake. My grandfather just gave it the send-off. I'm sorry you have to consider closing the gin, but I can't carry the load for you. Keep the gin open, shut it down, do what you're going to do. Leave me out of it."

Beer number two drained, Mack pondered his class ring. Tears rimmed his eyes.

"We ought to get along better than we do. I can't seem to shut up. Look, Oralia wants me to pass along an invitation to supper. The boys miss you. You doing anything Thursday night 'long about six-thirty?"

Dal accepted the invitation. He felt like blaming his moment of weakness on Mack's please-don't-kick-me Dalmatian eyes.

Shortly after Mack left, Dal received a call from Rosanna, who needed help corralling Ma and Pa, her oldest pair of ostriches.

The sky a discordant mix of gray and indigo, he found a duster-clad Rosanna pacing by the shed. She had two nylon ropes coiled in her hands. He could see Ma and Pa loitering on the nearby grassland, their giant black and white plumes standing out against an expanse of gold.

"I fixed the fence. A lot of good that does after the fact. I figure if you come at them from the left and I come from the right, we'll shoo them toward the pen. Keep your rope handy, though."

Following her plan of attack, they eased closer to the escapees, who appeared indifferent until a rattle of thunder kicked them into high gear. Ma being the closest, he tried to lasso her but failed miserably, even as Rosanna had Pa well in hand. Ma faded into the distance.

Dal stroked Pa's wings, clicking his tongue and singing the Dixie Chicks' greatest hits, while Rosanna led them both back to the shed. The fine mist skipped hurriedly into a downpour. Back inside the pen, Pa dashed for the protection of the shed.

"Whaddya know, he's not as dumb as I thought."

"He's hungry, Dal. Rain doesn't bother them. If you need to go on, I can take it from here."

A wave of thunder drowned out his response.

"You'll make a hand out of me yet."

He made a futile attempt to wipe the rain from his eyes.

Twenty minutes later, they were within roping distance of an agitated Ma. Punting the muddy grass around her, she was in no mood to be trifled with.

"Let's give her time to get used to us," Rosanna hollered.

"Okay," he yelled back, and then mumbled, "I'll pull up a chair. We'll get acquainted."

Once Ma seemed to have lost her interest in plowing, Dal looped the rope over her neck as Rosanna approached from the side. Ma didn't take it well. She knocked Rosanna to the ground and sprinted a few feet before she shuddered to a stop.

Unrattled, Rosanna ordered from her mud bath, "Loosen the rope, Dal, before she chokes to death."

"I'd hate to see that," Dal muttered.

This time, Ma let him touch her.

"Now you want me around. Isn't that like a woman."

The rope loosened, Ma remained tractable during the trek penward. Rosanna took over the singing while Dal contented himself with stroking Ma's feathers and wishing for an umbrella, an ostrich-feather umbrella.

Rosanna spritzed them both down with a hose before they went inside. He ducked into the pantry and changed into an old bathrobe of Tom's while Rosanna put his clothes on to wash.

Rosanna microwaved bowls of homemade stew and cornbread. As she worked, she made rude comments about the knobbiness of Dal's knees. She looked somehow stylish in a faded blue nightshirt. It had been months since he'd heard her laugh like that, he thought, then told her as much.

Drizzling her bowl with tabasco sauce, Rosanna took her time responding.

"Between you and Susan having problems, then...all the other stuff, it's been pretty rough around here, but I'm doing better."

"That's my fault. I never treated Susan—"

"Stop that. Stop that now," she said sharply. "The fault went both ways. Y'all were wrong for each other from the start."

"I loved her."

Her face softened. "I know you did. And she loved you. You should have lived with each other for a while. I know that's not the proper way of doing it, but a few weeks in each other's hair would have done the trick. You'd have known that, intellectually speaking, Susan wasn't in your league and never would be."

"She wasn't stupid."

Rosanna flashed a Mona Lisa smile, reminding him of the twins. The cheekbones, the area around the eyes, the curve of her face.

"I remember...I remember taking picture books by their house when she was a toddler. The next time in church, Dovie brought them back to me. Floyd didn't approve of them. He called them charity. He took the money for clothes, but he turned down things like books and toys, so he could prove he was the man of the house. You need to give a child dreams beyond this world at a time when it truly matters."

She shook her head. "I was such a fool, thinking I could make a difference with presents. That is, when I could slip them by Floyd. They were her parents. They could do what they wanted. Tom and I, and your mother, fought Floyd to a standstill to give her a bicycle. I couldn't expect to do much more than that."

"What did Tom think of Susan?"

"You saw him around her, Dal. He was crazy about her. Good heavens, he gave her away at your wedding."

"Then why was he against bringing the twins home?"

A straight answer, Rosanna. Don't drag in D'Abruzzo as an excuse.

"He wasn't against it. I wrecked the deal. Let me talk a while. You might remember hearing that Tom couldn't father children, on account of his hunting accident back in high school."

Tom's brother peppered him with birdshot, which led to an infection. Tom always said he fired blanks.

"He got angry at first when he heard the news. Spent the night in the barn, then the next morning he said, Rosie, let's name him after my brother Bob if it's a boy.'"

"Frannie said Tom kicked you out."

"Frannie thinks I've been lying to protect Tom all these years. Frannie's wrong. What happened was, I was barely seventeen when I got married. I'd graduated from high school a year early, and was taking some courses over at Tech. They all told me at the wedding that Tom'd be a good provider. Even though I didn't feel any sparks, I thought that might come in time. And it did. Just not soon enough. I rode down on that Greyhound bus, chasing after a man who said he loved me. Afterward, when I knew better, the only thing I could think to do was to go stay with Frannie."

"Wait a minute." Dal wrapped the robe tighter around him. "What happened down there?"

"You'll tell Gina, and don't try to convince me otherwise. Anyway, what counts is what happened afterward. Tom sent me a letter while I was staying with Frannie. He said that he still loved me, no matter what, and I could come home any time. I didn't feel it'd be right to come back big as a cow. His family, they'd all be gossiping, trying to figure out who was the natural father. I finally learned something about not being selfish, and I learned it from Tom's example. That's the kind of man Tom

Wintersole was, and that's the man I fell in love with."

She rose to check on the laundry. Later, dressed and waiting for the rain to dial down to a sprinkle, Dal told her about the evening with Gina.

"It's too soon—"

"I know that. I don't know what happened." He felt utterly miserable.

"She's a beautiful, intelligent woman. Your body reacted before your mind did. I wouldn't worry about it if I were you. You know, I thought my whole world ended when Tom died, but then a new world opened up. I took those classes over at Tech, bought the ostriches, and re-did my kitchen. I made new friends. My life's not the same anymore. It's not better than it was with Tom, but it's different. Not a day goes by that I don't think of him, not a day. I think about him and Susan being together now and that makes me happy. There'll come a time when you'll think of Susan and smile. I'm praying for that day, as I've always prayed for Gina to be happy.

"We all have our lessons to learn. The hardest lesson I ever had to learn was in how to accept Tom's forgiveness. I remember reading and rereading Tom's letter, hoping against hope, then about a week after the twins were born, I was alone at Frannie's house. Tom came up the walk, carrying a dozen yellow roses in his hand. I knew. I knew everything was going to be alright."

## CHAPTER TWENTY-FOUR

Friday morning, in Cyril's office. He meticulously cleaned his nails until Gina was ready to scream, then he sailed, unperturbed, into a summing up of Gina's career with TopSound.

It sounded so much like a power resume—the hands-on triumphs at various outlets, the astute purchasing decisions, the people networking—that Gina knew she was about to be fired. Cyril then took an inexplicable turn into the dynamics of managing a family business.

Something about Charmaine being the future of the company, although, at age twenty-five, she still needed polishing. Even so, the company needed fresh blood in a top management position.

"That's why I can't make the obvious promotion. Charm's not ready."

"A promotion?" She felt quite dim.

"It's too soon to make her executive vice-president, so there you have it."

Have what?

"Aaron and I feel that the best solution is to call you our senior marketing director. Same office, new title, but more pay. What do you think?"

"Why?"

A miscued question, but all she could think to say.

"You got plugged in the head by Garcia's cracker, that's why. It made Aaron and me think about the responsibilities we've given you over the years—how it all added up—and how hard it would be to replace you. This way, we keep you in the company for life."

She thought she was already a lifer.

"What would I be doing?"

"Monitoring trends. Trouble-shooting. What you do now, but more of it. Also, you'll be working with Aaron on developing new locations.

There'll be a lot more travel, but that's the trade-off you make moving up the ladder."

Finally, she'd regained her footing. This wasn't about promotions at all. Cyril must have found out somehow about her fling with Charmaine. Gina had done better than Charmaine at keeping the flirtations to a minimum, but there had been that kiss in the snack bar, and the knowing smiles back and forth.

"Cyril," she said quietly. "The deal with your daughter. I'll do better at keeping things professional. It won't happen again."

A small, almost delicate smile crossed his face. "Certainly, certainly. You're not ready to settle down. How do you feel? Ready to move up?"

Feeling shell-shocked, she replied in the positive. She returned to her desk, after handshakes and congratulations from Aaron, who poofed in from his adjoining office.

That was an odd statement from Cyril. "Not ready to settle down." As if he was trying to protect Charmaine from getting dumped, and not simply putting his daughter's lover out on the road.

Then again, everyone in the office knew about the blowup in the parking lot with Terry, so why wouldn't Cyril want to protect his daughter from public humiliation. Gina wasn't the most stable person around when it came to relationships, and maybe the mixed signals she'd been sending Charmaine weren't helping. She thought of the hurt look a few minutes ago on Charmaine's face when Gina brushed by her at the water cooler with a breezy hello.

What happened now? A raise and promotion, yet she couldn't shake the notion that she had been weighed and found lacking, in some vital area. Character, probably. If that were the case, then why didn't Cyril fire her instead of bringing her, for all intents and purposes, into the power circle?

She was being tested to see if she belonged in their family.

"Gina?" Binh stood in the doorway. "Your brother-in-law called to confirm on your flight tonight. It's a good thing you had the time written on your calendar. Oh, and your father called. He didn't leave a message."

She hadn't decided whether she should go, but Binh made up her mind. No message from Daddy. What else was new?

***

"More meat loaf?" Oralia stood ready to dollop at Dal's request.

"Sure, why not," he said, although he felt close to stuffed already on fried squash, home-made tortillas, and salad.

Thus far, Mack had been on his best behavior. He kept tabs on the table manners of Colt, a six-year-old sports announcer in the making, and

Austin, a slight, bookish seven year-old more interested in Dal's line of work.

When Dal's chance mention of Susan slammed the conversation shut, he tried to rebound with the boys by discussing their video game scores.

Again and again, Dal was reminded of the fact that he wasn't the only person affected by her death. Susan had been around Levon's kids and the younger Wenders their entire lives, serving as babysitter, coach, and confidante. Overnight, she disappeared.

A murderer walking the streets left a gaping hole in these people's lives, all for a DVD player. Susan was nothing but a victim to such a man.

"Dal." Oralia, thankfully, broke his train of thought. "You said you'd seen Susan's sister recently."

Colt piped up. "Does she play basketball?"

"She's more into softball. She's planning on coming back up here."

"This weekend?" Mack asked.

"Maybe."

"Mama says she looks like Susan," Austin said, wide-eyed. "Does she talk like her, too?"

Oralia explained the difference to him, although the boy still didn't seem to grasp the concept.

After supper, with the boys outside and Oralia busy in the kitchen, Mack told Dal he had to give his two last gin hands their notice. He thought they might be able to hire on at another operation.

"I've got a buyer lined up already for some of the equipment. Another man's coming over next week to look at the rest of it. I can probably sell off the building for wood and scrap metal but who knows? Some of it may be there until Armageddon, or until I find a buyer for the land, whichever comes first. You know, my boys think I'm joking when I tell them about Creed. They don't believe that there used to be an honest-to-God town. They think I'm pulling their leg. Daddy's telling stories again."

## CHAPTER TWENTY-FIVE

Odd how at times she didn't remind him of Susan anymore. Dal had invited Gina to eat at the County Line restaurant, known for its steaks and barbecue. Gina complained about missing out on local favorites during her first visit.

Rosanna came in while they were being seated. Through the round of greetings, Dal studied his dinner companions, yet detected no surface tension.

He knew women had the ability to conduct merciless warfare without so much as a change in pitch—much less topic—yet there they were, mother and daughter, yet not mother and daughter, ordering rib plates as if they were on a family outing.

They talked about Gina's promotion and flight turbulence with a loose, chatty tone he envied. Toward the end of the meal, Rosanna offered to put Gina up for the night. She accepted with the proviso that she come over after a talk with him.

Afterward, the two of them alone, Gina leaned back in her chair. "I'm glad that's over with."

"What do you mean?"

"The preliminaries. Having to engage in all this lovely repartee, when all I want is the truth. She seems like a nice enough person. I can see why she and Susan were such good friends."

"Is that all that matters to you, finding out why the twins were raised apart?"

"I already know the scenario on that. I talked to a man who used to work for Daddy, and Mom told me a little bit. Looks to me like Rosanna did it to spite my father. She knew he was coming to Big Spring, so she sent Susan off with the Longbrakes to break up the pair. That's how she got her revenge."

"Your mother—Marilyn—isn't a neutral party."

"Neither are you. I'm not saying Daddy is completely innocent in all this."

Her face clouded. "I think he gave her money for an abortion."

"Are you sure?"

"No. Are you sure Rosanna did everything right on her end?"

Conceding her point, he switched topics as they left the restaurant. He mentioned that Levon Porter and his family were looking forward to a visit from her. Tomorrow for lunch, if possible.

"And now, I'd like to show you some of the sights in Creed."

***

"What's this place?"

Gina saw nothing but a crumbling concrete slab under the light of the full moon. They were a few car lengths down from the entrance to Dal's driveway.

"Your grandfather's store. His name was Louie Shines. He had a little country store with a gas pump in front."

On impulse, she clambered through the brush surrounding the slab, stopping in the middle.

Dal followed her route. "There's nothing to see, even if it were high noon," he said.

"I know that. What did it look like?"

"Rosanna probably has a picture. It was a clapboard building with a tin roof. He had an electric heater in a corner where old folks would sit and gossip during the winter. I remember when I was a kid Louie had these jars of stick candy lined up by the cash register. All different flavors. The post office was in back until they moved the boxes to a trailer, then the post office closed, too. He died not long after that."

Striding away from the slab, Gina came to a halt in the middle of the road. She saw nothing, not a car, not anything in either direction.

The light from Dal's house, the moon, and a zillion stars allowed her to see his expression. Pensive, yet more relaxed than she'd ever seen him.

"I could stand right here all night and never see a soul. No wonder you got burglarized."

"And that's why people live in the city. Nothing ever happens there."

He sounded more amused than upset.

The wind was beginning to pick up.

"I don't see anything, Dal. I don't see a town. I don't see my grandfather—I wish I could see Susan. Don't get me wrong. I appreciate your stories."

Dal sat on the hood of his car. "To me, she's everywhere. The farmer that owns this land puts in a patch of black-eyed peas every season, so Susan'd come over and gather a basket to put up. Or, she'd go riding her bicycle down this road. She'd take a walk in the evening, sometimes with me, sometimes with Rosanna. I can understand why this place means nothing to you, but to Susan, it was home."

She took a few tentative steps closer. "How much alike are we? Now that you've had time to compare."

"You lose your temper the same way, have certain little habits in common. Otherwise, you're completely different."

"But right now, could you tell us apart? Sorry. I don't know why I said that."

"When I first saw you, I thought you were Susan. It seemed like her coming back to life made more sense than the hell I'd been going through. I'm glad I found you, but you've been put through a lot because of it."

"I may have lost a few illusions about my family, but nothing like what you've lost."

He started to speak then stopped, unable to go on. She murmured a few words intended to soothe, then he turned into her arms and held her tightly for a long moment.

She couldn't be sure that what she heard was his sobs, or the roaring of the wind.

## CHAPTER TWENTY-SIX

A trio of coltish girls, a Susan Sarandon look-alike, and a tall, dark-haired man stood in front of a tiny A-frame house. There was a cluster of tumbleweeds caught in a barbed-wire fence next to them.

"At first, we lived out in the country, but then we moved into that house behind the store," Rosanna explained.

What did she define as living in the country, Gina wondered.

Two of the girls, now teens goofing for the camera, posed on the hood of a Ford Fairlane. In the background, a brown field stretched into infinity.

"That's my sister, Carlina, on the left and me on the right. Tom loved that car."

"When was this taken?"

"Right after we got married."

"And you were seventeen at the time."

Must be the makeup they wore back then. She looked older.

"Just turned. Carlina and Dinah were nineteen."

Twins on both sides. That didn't happen too often.

The Sarandon look-alike, now graying and stooped, sat primly on a sofa, her twin middle-aged daughters flanking her.

"Your grandmother's name was Rachel Golozy—"

"What?"

Rosanna spelled the last name. "Mama's parents were from Hungary, but she was born and raised in Caldwell, Kansas."

"She was beautiful," Gina said sincerely. "What was she like?"

"Artistic. Stubborn. My grandfather was a dentist. They came down to see us once when I was a little girl. He had a thick accent and bushy eyebrows. I don't think he liked anything about us—not Daddy, or the store, or us girls."

"Why?"

"I have no idea."

Hearing Rosanna use the word "Daddy" sent a peculiar sensation through Gina.

"How did your parents meet?"

"Daddy worked as a salesman with his father through Texas and Oklahoma, and for a while in Kansas. Daddy and Mama met, got married almost on the spot, and he took her on the road with her. They were going through Lubbock when they heard that the store here was for sale dirt-cheap."

"Maybe not the best decision."

"When I was a little girl, there were still a few families, a few houses up and down this highway."

"Why did you split us up?"

Rosanna recovered quickly. "Your father's not here to speak for himself."

"Lay it out for me. I can take it," Gina said quietly.

Sober and reflective, Rosanna stroked a photograph of her father.

"It was raining when our car broke down in Dallas. Right down the street from a motel. I thought we were in luck when a man pulled up behind us, jumped out of his Cadillac, and went to work helping Tom under the hood. It was your father.

"It turned out the car needed a new part, so, after he helped take our luggage over to the motel, he went with Tom to a parts store. It was already closed. Danny called the owner at home and got the part that was needed, but after all that, he didn't have the right tool to install it. We had to wait until the next day to get the car fixed. Danny took us to eat at a fancy restaurant, then out to a nightclub. Tom and Danny were both several years older than me, but they were so different from each other. Tom had never been to a club before, and neither had I."

"What'd you think of him?"

"Danny? Handsome, and so full of energy. He talked as though he came from back East, which made me think he was sophisticated. He bought us steaks and Bananas Foster at the restaurant. I was so impressed by the flames. At the club, he knew exactly what to order and how to act."

"I don't remember my father being that pushy."

"People change. I know Tom and I did some things out of the ordinary that night. We got drunk, for one thing. You know us Baptist drinkers. It doesn't take much to get us plastered," Rosanna said ruefully.

"Danny took us back to the motel. After Tom passed out, Danny and

I got to talking. I told him I hadn't really seen much of Dallas 'cause it'd been raining during the day. He drove me in his Cadillac up and down the avenues. I thought I was riding in the lap of luxury. Then he took us to a hotel where he was staying."

"That's why you went to bed with him, 'cause he had a sweet ride?" Gina couldn't hide her disbelief.

Rosana shook her head. "He was so magnetic, like a movie star. I was young. I was stupid. A few weeks after Tom and I went home, that's when I knew I'd gotten pregnant.

"I covered at the store during Daddy's lunch breaks. One day, I called your father at his car dealership. I didn't tell him then that I was pregnant. Danny said on the phone he wanted to see me again. He didn't wear a wedding ring, so I had no idea he was married. I called him a few more times from the store, trying to build up my nerve to tell him. I started wearing a jacket all the time, and going to bed before Tom—pretended I had a problem with eating too much—but I was running out of excuses. Twins, you see. One day your—I'm sorry, Susan's mother—Dovie came in to the store when I was on the phone. She swore she wouldn't tell a soul. I called Dovie one morning while Tom was out on the tractor, and she drove me to the bus station in Lubbock."

Flushed, Rosanna paused to catch her breath. "When I got to Lambert, a young man at the dealership gave me directions to the club."

"Did my father give you money to get rid of us?"

"He did give me several hundred dollars. He said that it was my problem, and that I should take care of it quickly."

"Quickly."

"'Don't waste any time,' he said. I don't know what hurt me more, him saying he didn't love me, or watching him pull that gold money clip out of his pocket like I was some floozy he needed to pay off."

The heat was stifling. Gina stepped out onto the back porch, desperate for a breeze. Above her head, a cluster of bugs sizzled around the blue-lit zapper, each casualty sending out sparks into the darkness. Susan had been on this porch many times, told Rosanna her troubles, and laughed over stories. They watched exquisite sunsets sink into this level, unfathomable horizon.

Rosanna came in and sat on the swing. "It's warm for October, though nothing like Lambert, I'm sure."

"You split us up to get back at Daddy."

"Frannie wanted to help me raise the baby. She didn't make much money back then, but I felt that if I took in sewing, babysat for women in the neighborhood, I'd help pay the bills. Then I found out I was carrying twins. That changed everything. There was no way we could afford both. Frannie called Dovie, and she agreed to take one of the babies for a few months, just until we could get better situated."

"A temporary arrangement."

"When I went into labor, all our plans flew out the window. Frannie knew he'd given me money, but I didn't tell her what for. She called his home number, thinking she could get more money out of him to help on our expenses."

"But Mom answered. Daddy would have taken both of us, right?"

Rosanna tapped the armrest nervously. "I thought maybe I could get both of you back, eventually."

"But you didn't. I want to understand you, but you're not making any sense."

"I signed papers that took away my rights," Rosanna said in a rush.

"Tell the truth, why don't you," Gina said. "You knew exactly what you were signing. You didn't want Daddy to know where Susan was at, 'cause you were afraid you'd never get to see her at all if he took her. You let the Longbrakes keep Susan, which saved your reputation and your marriage at the same time. You got rid of us, and you kept your meal ticket. You took the easiest route possible."

Blinking steadily through the fusillade, Rosanna emerged from her trance.

"Easy? I talked Tom out of giving Floyd Longbrake money to get Susan back. It would have destroyed Dovie to lose another child, and yes, it would've hurt my marriage, though not in the way you think. Getting drunk wasn't like Tom. It upset him so much that he prayed and prayed over it. He thought taking in Susan would be a way of paying for both our sins. I knew it'd always be in his mind, how she came into our lives. I wanted Susan to have a chance. And yes, I chose to keep Danny away from her. You keep asking why I split the two of you up, but you haven't asked why I let Danny take you. I didn't have to. Frannie was willing to help me."

Gina slowly sank into a chair. "Tell me."

"Frannie had gone home for the evening." Rosanna swayed back and forth in the swing, her eyes cast toward the ceiling. "Danny came in the room. Before he said anything, he started crying. Sat on the corner of my bed, and cried. The first words out of his mouth were an apology. He asked about Susan. I told him she was with a good family, and that was all he needed to know. He offered to take you. I told him to get out, but he wouldn't stop talking. He said his wife had given her blessing for him to come up to Big Spring, and that she longed for a baby—he didn't tell me your older sister. He had a silver tongue that night."

Her rocking slowed. "Two single women making dirt wages—how could we afford to raise children on our own? I know now we could have done it, but I didn't know that then."

Rosanna met her gaze without wavering. "Dr. Houtchens came in, some papers were signed, and that was it. Franny bought a yellow baby blanket a few days before I delivered. That's what I wrapped around you. I didn't see you again for six years."

Neither spoke for a while.

Feeling a shade less than comatose, Gina asked, "What had you been planning to name us?"

"I was going to name you Rachel Louise, after my parents. Susan was Susan from the start."

A different name, a different identity. What if she'd grown up with Susan? At the least, her sister could have escaped being murdered. With a start, Gina figured out one reason Dal had tracked her down.

"Poor Dal," she said aloud, and then explained. "If things had been done differently, Susan could still be alive, somewhere."

Rosanna sighed. "I wish Susan hadn't been at home that night, but only God knows how any other road would have ended."

No more questions tonight, Gina thought. Time to go to bed, and hope that the house was burglar proof.

## CHAPTER TWENTY-SEVEN

"She's in the shower," Rosanna said. "She should be ready in a few minutes. Would you like some coffee?"

"No, thanks. I had two cups with breakfast. That's enough to keep me buzzing." Dal sat in the easy chair. "How'd it go last night?"

"Better than I expected. We went for a long walk this morning. I don't believe she got much sleep."

"How about you?"

"I woke up once and went to check on her. She was reading a scrapbook I'd kept about my family, and things that happened in Creed. She's so much like Susan. Very direct, without being mean-spirited, and you should have seen her with Pogo."

"He's over here now?"

"Pogo goes where he wants to, except when I take him to the vet. He fell on her like it was old times again. She romped with him up and down the road."

"He thinks Susan's back."

"Dogs know when someone's loving on them. That's all they care about."

A subdued Gina came into the living room. Bidding Rosanna goodbye, she seemed less cordial than the night before. On the way into Lubbock, she recounted her conversation with Rosanna.

"It's hard for me to picture Rosanna staying with Frannie," Gina said. "Living with a lesbian—everybody thinking she's one, too. She got scared."

Dal snorted. "You're big on that. Courage, doing the right thing. You have a loving family, a boss who doesn't care about your private life—you practically live in Houston. You don't have to worry about losing anything because of your social habits."

"Social habits? That's a strange way of describing it."

"You can have children with or without a partner, and as long as you pay your bills, who'd say a word against you? Try doing that back then, especially around here. You're straight, but living with a lesbian, and pregnant, but no husband. You're broke, and you're convinced you're going to hell for what you've done. You do what you think is best, what everyone around you says is the right thing. It tears you up inside so badly, you invent a story to explain why you'd give away your babies, and what happens? Your grown-up daughter comes along to poke holes in your story. So what if Rosanna is fudging a few details? What does it matter?"

Silenced, Gina studied the landscape until they arrived at the Porters' house.

Garth Porter came out of the garage and called excitedly, "Robbi, Robbi, come quick. They're here."

Anita stood at the front door, her face a mask as Robbi emerged with a basketball in hand.

"Wow," Robbi said with a gasp.

Her ball bounced down the steps and rolled to a stop in front of Gina.

Garth said exuberantly, "Dad said you'd look like Auntie Susan, but Robbi didn't believe it. I won the bet."

Chiding her son for his manners, Anita introduced herself, adding, "Levon is out back, checking the meat on the grill. This is Robbi."

"Hi," Gina said.

The girl still looked stunned.

"She's my ten year-old. And this—"

"I'm Garth. I turned twelve in July. How come Auntie Susan never brought you over?"

"Hush up now," Anita cautioned.

"No, it's okay," Gina said as Anita steered them inside. "We didn't know each other."

"Oh, wow," Robbi uttered. "The Prince and the Pauper. I saw that on Disney. Which one are you?"

"Do you want to play ball later?" Garth asked.

"Sorry, but Susan was the basketball star, not me."

The boy's mood abruptly deflated.

Out in back, Levon Porter, small and trim, busied himself at the barbecue grill. Turning toward his visitors, he smiled at Dal, then he stared for a long moment at Gina.

Casting his eyes downward, Levon said to the ground, "Pleased to meet you."

"I'm sorry, Gina. We thought we were ready, but I guess we thought wrong," Anita said.

"Levon, Dal tells me that you and Susan were best friends."

"Uh-huh," he mumbled.

Still unable to look at her, he said somewhat louder, "Back in school, I'd help her with math and English, and she'd help me with my shot. We were best friends from day one, and the kids, the kids were crazy about her. I'm sorry if I seem a little rattled. Oralia saw you at the burial. She told me you were a twin, but."

Dal waited for the end of Levon's sentence, but none was forthcoming.

"I knew you weren't Auntie Susan," Garth claimed. "She didn't dress like you."

Gina was wearing skinny white jeans, high-heeled sandals, and a sleeveless black top with random silver threads woven into it. Dal knew little about fashion, but she looked sleek, expensive, and profoundly uncomfortable.

Lunch, with its distractions, came to the rescue. Robbi finally decided to smile by the time dishes of banana-pecan ice cream arrived. Levon never did loosen up, despite Dal and Anita's efforts.

This is how I acted around her at first, Dal realized. How unnerving it must be for the both of them. As soon as Gina pronounced herself full, Garth and Robbi drafted her for duty on the court, which was a tidy square occupying a corner of the Porter's backyard.

Watching Gina miss most of her baskets, Levon observed, "She has no arch in her shot, and she barely leaves the ground. Susan would have demolished her. Even you could take her."

"Thanks, Coach. She's better with a bat and glove."

"You saw her play?"

"Saw her take a fast ball right above the ear."

Levon let out a sympathetic whistle. "I would've gone nuts if I'd been you. What's she like?"

"Hard to know until she decides you're okay."

"Like Susan."

"Susan wasn't standoffish," Dal said with a note of irritation.

"With you, maybe, but I knew her from first grade on. We'd be on school trips or playing road games, and she wouldn't say a peep to strangers unless Mack and I laid the groundwork. I'm not saying this girl is anything like Susan, except, you know, their having the same fingerprints and all. You ready to play?"

He took no pity, whipping Dal soundly even though Garth twice tried to distract his father by hooting in his father's face as he was attempting a lay-up.

***

"You have a great family," Gina said to Levon, who was intent on teaching her the importance of follow-through.

The others were on the porch. Garth and Robbi were battling over who would show Dal how to play the latest handheld computer game.

"Thanks. You need to keep your body under control. Make it all one move. That's better. Okay, one more time, and this time bend your knees a little."

"Let's take a breather, shall we? I was wondering about something, if you don't mind answering. How well do you know Mack?"

"Not as well as I knew Susan," Levon said evasively.

"I haven't said anything to Dal, and I won't, but I don't understand certain aspects of Susan's relationship with Mack. Why didn't they get married?"

His back turned to the porch, Levon scrutinized his shoelaces.

"She didn't talk about it much. She never said a word to Anita, as far as I know. Susan liked Mack, but he loved her. Always did. Mack's father threatened to cut him off if he married her, so Mack booked. By the time he came around again, Susan had dug in. Susan never ever changed her mind once she was set."

"How come you never dated her? You had so much in common."

He chuckled. "That sort of thing wasn't done in Creed. Now, there was this one time a while after she broke up with Mack. She was wanting to shoot some baskets, so we went over to the court. One thing led to another. Right in the middle, we both started laughing. I thought I'd bust a gut."

"What was so funny?"

"Look at us. You're a good three inches taller than me. There we were, scraping our knees on the court when I said something about how I wished I'd brought a stepladder, and we both lost it. We didn't try that again. She was too good a friend to me, and anyhow, I met Anita not long after that."

While Dal and Gina were in the midst of saying goodbyes, Garth—up to that point a blithe spirit—burst into tears after giving her a hug. Mortified, he ran back into the house with Anita following close behind.

"Sorry about that," Levon said. "He was real sweet on Susan. We should be a little more together next time."

Gina didn't think another visit was likely. She reminded them of their loss every time they looked at her face. No sense in adding to their pain.

"Dal," she said once they were back on the road. "After the Wenders tomorrow, that's it. Call it a lack of courage, but I can't handle seeing any more of her friends."

And neither can they, she added silently.

## CHAPTER TWENTY-EIGHT

The Wender boys acted spooked. Austin wouldn't talk at all, and Colt hid behind Oralia's skirt.

Gina whispered to Dal as they walked across the Wenders' front yard, "The only thing left for me to do is tell them Santa Claus is a fake. They'll be completely traumatized."

"I told them you were coming for lunch." Oralia nudged Colt out of his hiding place. "I told them about Susan having a twin. I thought they were old enough."

"Still, it's hard for little ones to understand."

Reacting to her voice, Colt said timidly, "Aunt Susan?"

Kneeling on the grass, she said gently, "No, I'm Gina. If I could be Susan for a day so you could see her again, I would."

"But I'm seeing you now," Austin blurted out. "I know who you are."

"Austin, she's telling the truth," Oralia said to no avail.

Time for a demonstration. Before a captive audience, Gina launched a few jump shots at their basketball goal. She gave it her best slipshod effort. One went in by accident.

She made a believer out of Colt. "You're no good."

"Didn't Aunt Susan show you how to play?" Austin asked.

"We were raised apart from each other. I never knew her."

Austin seemed convinced. "You would have liked her, and you could have worn each other's clothes."

As the boys, young and not-so-young, shot baskets, Gina sat in the kitchen while Oralia finished prepping enchiladas for the oven.

Oralia revealed that Rosanna had told her the other day that she was the twin's mother, but after the shock wore off, Oralia could see the resemblance, though mainly in the way Rosanna and the twins acted.

"And that has to be something inherited, 'cause you've hardly been around her."

When the hoopsters came back in, Mack beckoned to Gina, saying he had something to show her.

In his den, Mack drew out a tray from a glass case.

"What do you see?" he asked.

A sharp black rock with ridges. "An arrowhead?"

"Close. It's an archaic spear point dating back 4,000 years, according to the steward for the county archaeological society. Susan found it at the Shinnery mounds two years ago and gave it to me. She found a lot of points and cherts for me. Could spot them from twenty yards away."

He turned his limpid eyes on her.

"Great spear point," Gina said. "In fact, you have the best private collection I've ever seen." The only private collection she'd ever seen.

"I make you nervous, don't I," Mack said with a nerve-provoking expression.

"You don't make me comfortable, let's put it that way."

"If you'd grown up in Creed, we'd have been neighbors. Think about it: what if Susan had gone downstate and you'd gone here?"

Then would she have been Mack's lover and Dal's wife. Would she have made the same choices as Susan?

"We're talking ifs here, not maybes. Mack, the things you liked about Susan you're not going to find in me. I know bullet points, not spear points—and you don't know a damn thing about me."

He was standing too close, much too close. Any moment now, the door could open.

"I don't know your favorite color or what movies you like, but I know you have a birthmark right there."

He pointed to her stomach, and took a step forward.

She took a step backward.

"You knew Susan. You don't know me. You have a pretty wife, two kids who think you hung the moon, and if you're ever going to be faithful to them, you need to start right now. Frankly, I'm not interested."

Mack looked mortified. He seemed to know that he'd gone too far.

"I'm sorry." He laid the spear point back in its case, then gazed at her pensively. "I can't believe she's gone. It don't seem real. You know, sometimes, I'd look out my office at the gin, and there she'd be, riding bicycles with him. I could tell she was holding back on his account, 'cause if she wanted to, she could've outraced the moon. We weren't hurting anyone, doing what we did. I loved her. I'm sorry I acted up now. I didn't mean to upset you."

"You're not the first one to forget who I really am," Gina conceded.

"It's okay. Let's get back to the others, shall we?"

On the way to Rosanna' house, Dal read her mood.

"He made a move on you."

She nodded.

"If you like, I can have a talk with him. He shouldn't have come on to you like that. What if one of the boys had walked in?"

What if one of the boys had walked in on Mack and Susan, for that matter. Mack didn't strike her as being a careful person, for Gina believed that Oralia had somehow found out, while Dal remained willfully ignorant.

"Fortunately, they didn't. I'm not going back there. Mack won't have a second opportunity to try and jump my bones."

***

Beautiful bones. How many times had he drawn that face, yet there was something different about Gina, who possessed a subtler side to her personality than Susan.

An instinctual preference for action over reflection had been basic to Susan's makeup. What Susan felt, you saw in her eyes that instant.

Gina, on the other hand, seemed to keep a little of herself in reserve, doling out only what personal data she believed necessary. Once Susan trusted you, she emptied her shelves. Gina's sexuality was at the root of her reserve, obviously.

"Do you plan to tell Rosanna you're bisexual?"

"Not this go-around. Perhaps next time."

"Then you're coming back. Good. Rosanna's more open-minded than you think. You can tell her."

"All these people today, because I'm Susan's sister, they were sweet and caring. If they knew one minor fact about me, how friendly would they have been?"

"Mack would take it as a personal insult to his masculine desirability, but as for the others—attitudes have changed the last few years. Not everyone around here is knee-jerk hostile to your lifestyle."

He stopped the car a few yards from the Wintersole place. He saw another difference between the twins. From a raw attraction in the beginning to a wary rapprochement at the end, Susan's feelings toward him were always apparent.

"The other night, when we were close, what were you feeling? Believe me, this isn't a come-on. Something happened. I don't know what to call it. There's something between us."

"Susan. She's what's between us."

"Gina, I'm not out to find a replacement."

"You think that, but in your heart, you—"

"You don't know what's in my heart. I don't assume you're the same as Susan. You're single, you date around—that's a big difference right there from Susan. I don't fault you for it. You were raised differently."

"We're done now." She gathered her purse and jacket.

"I'm not through."

She bolted from the car.

Following her on foot, he said, "What's upsetting you now?"

She pointed to the surrounding grassland. "What was there?"

"Huh? A church. Don't change the subject."

"Mack and Susan had an affair," Gina said distractedly. "A friend of hers from work told me. Mack didn't deny it, so, right. I was the one raised differently, me and my big city ways."

She started at a fast clip for Rosanna' house.

Dal tried to speak, but he'd lost all control of his voice.

## CHAPTER TWENTY-NINE

Told the reason for the argument, Rosanna never broke her rhythm as she breaded catfish strips. She remarked that she knew all along that Mack and Susan were lovers. Had known it for years, ever since she noticed the two of them arguing in the gym entrance while on her daily walk.

"I didn't hear a word of it, but something told me what was up. Later, Susan came by and told me. I got the impression they were breaking up."

"One of her co-workers told me they kept seeing each other. I shouldn't have told Dal, though."

"Sometimes, the truth is better off not being told."

"Is that how you feel about us?"

Catfish sizzing in the pan, Rosanna washed her hands and dried them on a hand-stitched towel. "Your parents may feel that way. I don't, not anymore. Well, I better go give Dal the invite. He's been listening to that car radio long enough."

An uneasy meal. Rosanna and Gina took turns trying to resuscitate the conversation through stabs at humor and ostrich lore. Nothing worked. As he got into his car, Gina tried apologizing again, only to be faced with yet another placid, unreadable nod.

"I'll give you a call in the morning before you leave," he said.

"I blew it, didn't I."

"No, I did." His face crumpled.

"She loved you."

"Right. She loved me, but not enough to be faithful. You love—you love yourselves. Shit, I don't know. Maybe I should have screwed her, and be done with it. Been like you, and dumped that girlfriend you mentioned."

What an ass. "Don't take it out on me, Dal."

"I know what your girlfriend did wrong. She loved you."

"Terry was a liar. Took my favorite necklace, then claimed she lost it. Then, lo and behold, she has money to burn. To hell with her. You don't think I'm real. I'm a copy, and a lousy one at that. You're a cartoonist. Draw your own clown."

Midway to the ostrich shed, he caught up with her.

"Gina."

"It's getting late, Dal. Go on home."

"Let's start over again, please."

With a rough spasm, she threw his hand off her shoulder. Seeing her expression, he moved back, but continued sidestepping beside her.

"Gina, I'm sorry. Your personal life is none of my business. I don't want you to leave town hating me."

Slowing to a stop by the pen, she stared at him with disbelief.

"What town? There's nothing here. Dal, I don't hate you. I think the way you trusted her was—"

"Stupid."

"Touching. I've never had someone who believed in me that way."

Such a blind, yet pure devotion. She'd never given it, so why would she receive it from anyone? It had nothing to do with being bisexual; she simply wasn't wired for relationships.

Susan risked her marriage for a farmboy stud when she had Dal at home. A man who probably struck Susan as being boring, yet he could carry on an intelligent conversation, hold his liquor, and not push his luck in a clinch.

"Did Susan like to dance?"

***

A leftfield question.

"Yes, mostly two-stepping and disco. She hated line dancing. She would have liked Freddie's with all those tempo changes. She preferred a challenge."

A southern gust, nudging at them like a pouty child, fluttered ostrich feathers lodged in the fence.

"If you like, we can go back in."

"No, I don't mind the wind. Dal, you don't have to stand way over there. I won't bite."

Elbow to elbow, they talked about sunsets as they watched the ostriches snooze. She claimed to have never seen any as beautiful as those in Creed. He nattered on about his still amorphous graphic novel plans while he listened to her body language. Receptive and friendly.

Susan would have gone on a run, trimmed trees, or driven into Lubbock. She wouldn't have stayed around to make amends. Tired, he was so tired of trying to ignore the effect Gina had on him. He wanted her—no matter how twisted it looked, or how crazy it made him feel.

"Come back to my place," he said. "Let's talk a little longer."

Back home, he downed shots of tequila as they lounged on the sofa and listened to a Dixie Chicks CD.

Wobbly on his feet, he said, "Come sleep with me. Sleep, that's all I want."

She rose too quickly. "Dal, I'm sorry, but I can't."

He stumbled over to a chair and fell into the seat. She came over and sat on the rug next to him.

His brain unhinged from his skull and floated toward the ceiling. He'd finally gotten drunk. Susan did it better. A freakish energy let her outlast anyone in the room. He, on the other hand, was a boring, soppy failure. Gina seemed to be saying something, but he couldn't concentrate to save his life.

When he opened his eyes again, the room was dark. He could see Susan outlined on the sofa, sleeping. Dal pulled up his blanket and drifted away.

# CHAPTER THIRTY

"How did the night go?" Raymond paused while grating cheese.

Gina was in the shower. Not until his friend showed up, did Dal remember inviting him to breakfast.

Omelets were in order, he thought. Omelets, then he'd run her over to Rosanna, go back home, and lose his mind—hopefully, in that order.

"Strange, very strange."

"Yeah, I can imagine. No, I can't imagine, but yeah, it must have been weird, touching her, and knowing she wasn't Susan."

"We didn't go to bed together."

"She spent the night."

"On the sofa. I sat there passed out in the chair, making a great impression on her."

"You're acting like a human being. What's wrong with that?" Raymond said. "You're always too tough on yourself. I'm actually glad you didn't do the twin. Knowing you, you'd be in sackcloth and ashes forever."

"Am I that much of a prig?"

"No, but you don't give yourself any leeway, and you give other people way too much."

"Meaning?"

Raymond looked at him meaningfully. "Gina's a grown woman. She knows what shape you're in, yet she came over here last night. She thought about doing the deed. Thought about it, and changed her mind, lucky for you."

"You know Gina so well without ever having met her."

"I knew your wife. I even know their mom. Isn't that a trip? They're ballbreakers, but in a good way. They're not much on hearts and flowers—oh my God."

Gina entered the kitchen. Raymond wore a bug-eyed, seen-an-alien cartoon face. Raymond, for the first time in their long friendship, had been rendered speechless.

***

Dal's friend seemed overwhelmed by the Face. People here have yet to see me, she thought. They're still looking at Susan. Rosanna seemed to have processed the difference, though Gina wasn't altogether certain about Dal.

Dal, who showed no ill signs of the drinking, blandly dispensed omelets and weather bulletins, acting as though last night occurred in an alternate universe. Maybe it had.

"Gina, oh, Gina." Raymond, a burly man with intense eyes, broke her concentration. "Do you have a headache? You're frowning."

"I'm thinking."

Raymond left immediately after breakfast, so attuned to the tension in the house he didn't bother to mouth social niceties about looking forward to any future visits.

That struck her as a good idea, to avoid dragging out the farewells. Dal stood at the door, preparing to say something, but she brushed by him and headed down the road. As she drew closer to the Wintersole place, she could see Rosanna chugging along in her morning constitutional.

A few minutes later, enjoying a light breeze that whisked through the front porch, Gina and Rosanna drank glasses of iced tea.

Finally, Gina broke. "Dumb, huh."

"Pardon?"

"I must look like a sleaze, going over there when I know how torn up he still is. I watched him get drunk and I didn't say a word. But, I didn't go to bed with him."

"I'm not passing judgment." Rosanna seemed transfixed by the highway.

"I am. Ever since I got here, he's been looking at me as though I have the answer."

"Don't take all the blame. There's been too much of that."

"Dal said you were the one who found her."

Fanning herself with her hat, Rosanna met Gina's eyes. For once, she didn't look away.

"I had a bad feeling that morning. Felt that I needed to check on her. I went over, and there she was. Dead. Not a blessed thing I could do to change it. Could have told her the truth ages ago. She'd have left this earth knowing who gave birth to her. Gina, I almost lost my mind."

"She knew you loved her. I wish you could have told her the truth, but I don't think it's a tragedy she died not knowing."

"I wish I could be that certain. My pastor says God doesn't care about labels, and what really matters is that I stood by Susan in her times of need. What I think is that I didn't stand by her when it mattered most, when she was born."

The distance in Rosanna's face seemed unbridgeable. Gina left shortly after that. Neither of them talked about future visits.

Touching down in Houston, Gina found a fidgety Dianne, instead of Carla, waiting at the gate.

As they zipped down the freeway, Gina interrupted Dianne's opening ceremonies.

"Lupe wants you back. I'm not against it."

"Who told you, Carla?" Dianne said, surprised.

"No one told me. Look, you know and I know it wasn't leading anywhere. You go on back to your ex. You have my blessing."

As if one were needed. Gina had easily rendered the face-saving gesture, the empty phrase, so why did she burst into tears? It ruined the rest of the drive for both of them.

A cumulative effect from too much drama, Carla diagnosed in her visit that evening. Where Carla traveled, psychoanalysis was sure to follow.

"I was tired from the trip," Gina protested. "That's why I became so weepy."

"Same old Gin. No one's ever broken your heart. No one's ever disappointed you. I do think you're right about this one. You thought it'd be a good chance to cry over Terry and your sister, and everything else that's been going on."

Seeing Gina's expression, Carla softened an iota. "Remember the night before my wedding?"

Drunk on retro trashcan punch, Gina admitted to Carla that she still carried a sizeable flame for her, and would run away with her friend that very night if asked.

"I can't imagine my life any different than it is today, yet three little words from you at the right time and we'd have set up housekeeping for life," Carla said.

"Good for you I didn't say them. I'm a better friend than lover, I'll tell you that."

Carla eyed her quizzically. "That's your best excuse? Ms. D'Abruzzo, love starts with like—it might end with hate—but like gets the ball rolling. You have everything it takes to make a relationship work, except confidence. You said your twin was an extreme jock. You need a little of that in your head, then maybe you won't keep talking yourself out of sticking with someone. A certain Murray female comes to mind."

Late that night, an old Meat Puppets CD masking the dryer's fix-me rattle, Gina checked her online banking. According to her estimate, she would have extra spending money to take with her next weekend to Las Vegas. Blackjack and constant neon action, with a wide-eyed Binh in tow.

She needed a diversion, she thought as she closed her laptop. For a second, she thought about messaging Charmaine. No. She had no idea what to text, other than, "Hello, I'm scared."

***

Dal finished writing the email. One more read and off into the ether.

> Gina,
>
> I didn't want go to bed with you because I missed Susan and you were the next best person available. Maybe there was a little of that, but not as much as you might think. I should have waited to contact you. I should have never made a move on you. We're better off as friends, but I do care about you. I want you to know that I'll always be here for you. You're family. I hope you someday will feel the same about me. Pogo sends his love, as do I.
>
> Dal

Immersed in the shadows of his living room, Dal listened to the wind spirit through his front door.

Another Panhandle autumn night, featuring whiskey, Willie Nelson, and ghosts rustling through the nowhere streets of Creed.

Another night to get through.

## CHAPTER THIRTY-ONE

"It's your father again. Do you want me to tell him you're out of the office?" Binh asked with an air of reproach, his finger on the hold button.

"Yes. Don't look at me like I shot your puppy. I'll get with him after our trip to Vegas."

Monday and Tuesday she'd muddled through—Wednesday represented her best hope of nailing down loose ends before their flight Thursday afternoon.

She told Binh to lose any more calls from her father. After studying the vendor list for the convention, she turned to working on a new sales forecast.

Charmaine came in as she sliced a pie chart once too often. Taking a break, Gina kissed her on the cheek. Charmaine barely acknowledged the gesture, but then, Gina had been professionally frosty at the sales circle that morning.

Take it head on. "About the meeting: I think it's important to dial you and me down around the others. Otherwise, it might get complicated."

"If you want to call texting a relationship, fine. Me, I think it takes more than a pair of thumbs. You're like this beautiful ship on the ocean. You take on passengers, you show them a good time on deck, and you always drop them off on shore. Nobody stays. Terry said she knew she'd messed up with you."

"What'd you do, track her down?"

"Terry said—"

"I'm not interested in hearing about her."

"I talked to Carla—yeah, I went backdoor on you. Whatever. Carla told me how to get in touch with your ex. Terry said what happened with the necklace you gave her."

"The necklace she sold."

"She broke it by accident, and the jeweler wanted three hundred bucks to fix it, which she didn't have, but he offered to buy it for five hundred."

A necklace that cost Gina over a grand. The jeweler made out well on that transaction.

"She made the wrong decision, granted, but she spent the money on you. The concert, the dinner—that was all for you. Then, when you noticed the necklace was gone, you froze her out, wouldn't answer her emails. She comes up here and you throw her off the parking lot. Binh thought you were going to hit her."

"No, I wasn't," Gina said. "And another thing, I'm not a cruise ship. I'm under no obligation to be whatever it is people think I should be."

"You're free, baby, free as the wind. Is that it?" Charmaine shrugged. "One day you'll be like Terry, trying to make the person you love care about you, and you'll finally know what it feels like. You'll hate it. It's the worst feeling on earth."

Less than two hours later, Gina sat sipping a Pepsi in an ice cream shop that offered a clear view of the bookstore. I should be home packing, Gina chided herself. What a waste of an evening.

Terry, attired in a sari-wrap green print dress, popped around a book display. She looked unchanged from the last time Gina had seen her. Had it only been a few weeks ago?

A strawberry blonde in her forties, Terry moved back to Texas from North Carolina shortly before meeting Gina at Freddie's. She possessed an undiluted East Texas accent courtesy of her Quitman upbringing, a ready smile, and a taste for nightlife.

What am I doing here, Gina thought. Charmaine lays on a guilt trip so I go see someone who wishes I were dead. A few minutes later, Gina wandered in, picked up a *Texas Monthly* from the magazine rack, and waited for Terry's reaction, which wasn't long in coming.

Steaming over, she whispered fiercely, "I get off in an hour. If you're still around, I'll talk to you then."

Malling around, Gina bought a tube of overpriced lipstick, tried on a sweater, ate a toothpick cube of German sausage, then returned to the ice cream shop, where the waiter asked again if she wanted the banana boat special.

"Maybe later," she said as Terry approached.

Her voice at low volume, Terry demanded, "What's this about? What do you want?"

"I'd like to talk with you."

"What about? I have a partner now. A real one. In fact, we're thinking about getting married."

"Isn't that happening kind of fast?"

"I'm not doing it because I'm on the rebound from you, if that's what you think," Terry said. "When you weren't treating me like trailer trash, you were sort of fun. If we see you at Freddie's now, we'll sit down and have a drink with you—that is, we'll have a drink. I know you can't handle it, just like you can't handle love, or commitment. I'm okay with it. If you hadn't dumped me, I'd never have met my partner."

"I'm sorry I said those things to you." Gina knew she was stammering, but she couldn't stop it. "I'm sorry I couldn't be what you wanted."

"Couldn't? You never tried. You didn't want to be serious."

Terry turned on her sensible heels and left.

It was well past midnight when Gina rang Charmaine's doorbell. Granted admission, she scavenged a bottle of Chardonnay from the refrigerator. She sat down at the kitchen table and went to work.

Perched on the counter, Charmaine watched for a while before she spoke. "I take it you spoke to Terry."

The bottle half gone, Gina's sense of panic had diminished to a dull pounding in the back of her head.

"Have you had any dinner?" Charmaine asked.

"Not hungry."

Pulling up a chair, Charmaine tried another tack. "Take a break. Talk to me."

"I can't give people what they need. I should tell everyone I get involved with the truth right from the start."

"Tell you what: let's play a game. Let's take turns naming the things we think are scary. I'll start. Rednecks when I'm driving through hick towns."

"Rednecks when I'm driving through hick towns with a dyke."

"Copycat. The middle of the night when I'm alone, and the dog next door starts barking his head off."

Feeling fuzzier by the minute, Gina deliberated. "Two in the morning, walking out of Freddie's."

"My father."

"Cyril scares you? Ah, he's a pussycat."

"You're not his daughter, although you might as well be, as much as he dotes on you. What about your father? Does he scare you?"

"I'm not having a daddy conversation. Not tonight."

"I'm not a shrink, I'm your friend. Nothing else, I guess, but that.

You want to open another bottle?"

"Got anything else?"

"Some single-malt Scotch."

"That'll do."

"What are you scared of? That if you open up, we'll back off?"

As Charmaine started toward the cabinet, Gina snared her around the waist and leaned against her.

"Don't send me home tonight, Charm. Please."

## CHAPTER THIRTY-TWO

"You may as well let me in, Dal. I shan't go away peaceably."

White-haired and erect, Roy J. Davis stood on Dal's front porch, as an excited Pogo whuffled at his feet.

"Your dog doesn't receive enough visitors. You should buy him a companion."

"Maybe I should. Pogo, give the man some room."

"Ah, he's a fine sport." Davis leaned over and patted Pogo on the muzzle. "Pogo, eh? I once had a tabby named Little Nemo. They say cats have nine lives. I can assure you he had but one. A happy life, with an abrupt ending."

Davis, the cartoon genius behind *She's a Doozy*, looked a century older than the last time Dal had seen him, which had been at Junior's funeral. As they went inside, Davis said he'd heard about the decision to shut down Dal's strip.

"I knew I'd be coming through this general direction on my way to the cabin."

"You still have that place in Taos?"

"Indeed, so I decided to come pay respects to the deceased."

Did he know about Susan?

"It's a strange feeling, isn't it, to bury a cartoon. Milt did it to *Terry and the Pirates*, but I wonder if he didn't want to take the Dragon Lady out of a drawer sometimes, dust her off, and put her back to work corrupting Occidentals. When I gave Doozy her last rites, I wondered if I'd miss the old girl enough to desire a reunion. Haven't yet, never shall."

In fine form, Davis waxed nostalgic over glasses of whiskey, never spilling a drop as he hailed news of Dal's graphic project.

"And what is the name you've chosen for your epistle?"

Dal shrugged.

"My dear fellow conspirator, you must begin with a gat for the gambit, a moniker for the missive, otherwise you're bloody well wasting your time."

"I haven't finished plotting what the story's about."

"I see. You're one of those deep thinkers who must draw a banana peel for every pratfall, when the awful truth, my dear fellow, is that quite often people fall flat on their face with no physical cause to blame. Who's responsible for this alternate world?"

"No one's responsible."

"You've exiled God from the firmament. Ah, then kismet's not a factor. What a pity. Without God, there's no good or evil—merely gradations of gray. Not very interesting to me, although your younger readers may prefer such a universe."

He pondered Dal's work-in-progress sketches on the wall.

"I see Bogart as a bartender serving a flashy dame, and over there, Duke Ellington at a campaign rally."

"He's the President."

"Finally, an intelligent man in the position. What makes them laugh, what makes them cry?"

"The usual things, I guess. Good point. I need to put that stuff in."

"Many of the old-time costume capers relied on muscle and cheesecake, rather than warmth and insight. Pure escapism, yet in all of them a definable good, however so bumbling, triumphed over evil."

"Things change, Roy."

"Good and evil: they're not obsolete terms. Since the murder of your wife, surely you're convinced of the latter if not the former."

"I know evil when I see it. I haven't lost all my senses," Dal said heatedly.

Davis switched to talking about Junior and his first visit to Creed, a disappointing visit since he had expected to see rough-hewn, whimsical Windswept County. Then, at Junior's funeral, he realized even that Creed had disappeared.

"'A cartoonist is a mongrel with pretensions of breeding.' Your father used to say that, yet I do believe that people like Hal Foster, Carl Barks, even young Mr. Bode, produced a formidable body of illustrated literature."

"Legitimate literature," Dal said helpfully.

"Who decides what's legitimate? Dickens and Shakespeare wrote for the masses. Cultural legitimacy came along later, a validation by the critical elite. In his heart, your father recognized the value of his work, but I also believe that he would have approved of your decision to move on to a new project."

***

Gina awoke to find Charmaine kissing her goodbye, and delivering messages. Cyril said it was okay for her to take the morning off, but to come by before she and Binh left for the airport.

"And lock the door when you leave," Charmaine said in a rush.

She left before Gina could talk to her about the night, or talk to her about anything.

Back at her apartment, having changed clothes and finished packing, Gina checked her e-mail. Mom had sent a "we're thinking about you" e-card. Gina didn't want to consider how misleading that phrase was, on so many levels.

Picking up a Buckburger special on the way to the office, she made it almost halfway down the hall when she heard Aaron's voice from his opened door.

Closing the door behind him, he spoke with his characteristic briskness. "I heard you got drunk last night. First time in how long?"

"I slipped once at a friend's wedding."

"It's none of my business why. Speaking from experience, I know that one drink can lead to another. That's why I wrote down the address and number of my AA group. I go Tuesdays, eight at night. I won't take it as an insult if you pick a time slot other than that."

"I didn't know you were an alcoholic."

"I know you've done well without AA, but you can't always handle it alone. AA's there for you, and for that matter, so am I. Anything you say on the subject'll stay in this office."

She believed him. Aaron had the tightest mouth in the Murray family, especially in comparison to Cyril, a born leaker.

"Thanks, Aaron. I appreciate your thoughtfulness."

"It's simply a matter of good business, you understand. We need for you to be alert and on the job."

His eyes darted to her face, then back to his note pad.

"Don't worry, I won't let it get around that you're a nice guy," Gina said with a wink.

She headed over to Cyril's office, where she apologized for missing work.

"Do I look worried? Certainly not. Kid, I want you to have a good time in Vegas. Have you picked up your per diem yet?"

"That's where I'm headed next. Thanks, Cyril." She felt compelled to add, "I won't let you down. I promise."

"I know you won't, Bruise. Go kick some butt."

He chucked her playfully on the arm as she left.

She picked up the money envelopes from bookkeeping, then returned to her office. Thrilled with his two hundred dollars, Binh had visions of slot machines dancing in his head, but Gina pointed out that he could blow that amount in thirty minutes if he wasn't careful.

A quick check of her own envelope. A crisp sheaf of eight one-hundred dollar bills. What was this: a bonus, a payoff, what?

"Did you get shortchanged?" Binh asked, trying to read her expression.

She showed him the contents.

"Wow, we're going to party," he said.

Charmaine, who'd agreed to shuttle them over to the airport, followed Gina's car over to the apartment, then went inside to help with the bags. Gina tried to land a kiss, only to be rebuffed.

"What's the matter," she asked, more surprised than offended. "Did I do something wrong last night?"

Charmaine exhaled slowly. "You were more than adequate, but I'd rather you not come over anymore."

"Then I did do something wrong. Tell me what it was, and I promise I won't do it again."

"Don't, don't talk that way." Charmaine leaned against the door, her eyes tired. "I want something you can't give me. I don't only want a lover. I want someone I can imagine spending the rest of my life with. I watched you sleeping this morning, and I thought, yeah, this could work. Everyone in the family thinks you're great. I was thinking like Dad, of how sensible a match you and I would be. How practical, how advantageous. That's the wrong way to look at it."

"Give me time."

"I don't want to wait that long," she said with a bittersweet smile. "There's a knack for knowing when to quit before you start. I hope I've learned it by now."

"Are we still friends?"

"Always."

## CHAPTER THIRTY-THREE

Snake eyes, garish statuary, numb-faced gamblers, and booth after booth of the latest tech marvels.

Day, night, then early, early morning at the Convention Center, the Hard Rock Casino, and other neon haunts.

Collapsed on her bed, Binh moaned, "Don't make me get up, please. I don't think I can make it to my room."

Standing by her seventh-floor window, Gina stared down at the skittering bugs and toy cars.

"Nah, you can sack out here if you want. I'm going downstairs."

"Not again. We're supposed to be at that power brunch at ten-thirty. When am I supposed to get some sleep?"

"Sleep? We don't need no stinking sleep 'round here."

He looked at her oddly.

"You've never seen Treasure of the Sierra Madre?"

"No. You've been kicking it big time ever since we got here. When do you plan to take it easy for a while?"

"When we get home. Binh, I'm doing fine. I've done nothing but caffeine since we got here. We've gotten virtually all of our sales and contacts completed. I've kiss-faced every power butt on the promenade."

"Don't you want to lay back and enjoy the scenery, and not like be the super buyer of all time? If this is what your job is like, put me in the warehouse."

A packet of money fell out of her purse as she was placing it on the bedside table. She'd quadrupled her travel allowance with some ridiculous wagers at the craps and blackjack tables, while Binh had quickly lost all but twenty bucks.

"I'm sorry you're not having a good time. I've got more living to do, sweetheart."

Tossing a couple of hundreds on the bed, she headed to the door.

"If I'm not at the brunch, don't worry. Just eat the free meal, smile a lot, and don't commit to anything."

As she walked out, she could hear Binh protesting about something, but the door shut off further comments. On the way down in the elevator, a butch number kept sneaking looks at her. For the fun of it, Gina gave her a full-throttle bimbo on the prowl stare, which caused the woman to focus on the floor buttons.

As they got off, the woman started to say something to Gina, but thought the better of it as a likely girlfriend approached. Kind of cute, Gina thought on her way to the slot machines. Puppy-dog eyes, and a dancer's physique.

Gina sat down at a slot machine and fed in a hundred, almost immediately drawing the attentions of a casino hostess. Maybe it was Gina's imagination, but the woman seemed almost upset that she was coming away with only an order for a Pepsi.

This place couldn't operate stone cold sober, Gina observed. It's in the air.

Pulling the lever produced an immediate outcry from the machine. Lights and hooplah, then an underplaying slip of paper that read two thousand dollars.

The cashier smiled cheerily when she deposited the money into Gina's hand.

"You're not going to quit now, are you?" she asked.

Probably another professional requirement of the staff. Keep the customers drinking and gambling at all cost. It wasn't until Gina was halfway to the elevator that she realized she hadn't bothered to answer the cashier.

Binh wasn't lying on her bed, nor was he in his side of the suite.

Hearing a noise behind her, she returned to her bedroom, calling out, "Okay, Mister Binh, come out, come out, wherever you are."

No Binh—not in the bathroom, the closet, under the bed—yet she had an almost palpable sense that she wasn't alone.

In a casual tone of voice she said, "If you're here for the money, it's all in my purse. Just take it and leave."

No response. Get a grip on yourself, she lectured silently. You haven't slept since you left home. No wonder you're on edge. Just lie back and close your eyes. Breathe deeply. Think pleasant thoughts.

An image of Terry from their last argument came into her mind unbidden. "I don't care if you're gay or bi. I just want to know that you're human. I want to know if you actually give a damn," Terry yelled before Gina started in again about the necklace.

Why was she still thinking about Terry? Why was she still thinking about the woman she loved.

It would be so easy to call up room service and start a good old-fashioned raving drunk. A bottle of champagne for starters. Make that two. Instead, she pulled out a freebie pad and began scribbling a note to Binh.

Midway through the noon flight to Lubbock, she thought to count her money. Eight thousand bucks. If she'd stayed, she might have broken the bank and lost her mind, not necessarily in that order. Perhaps the cash she left with the note would make it up to Binh for ditching him.

A tidy fellow with an Indian accent nudged her in the side and asked, "What is bringing you to Lubbock?"

"Beats me."

She and Rosanna didn't have much to say to one another on the way to the Wintersole place. Collapsed in the porch swing, she didn't notice that Rosanna had sat down beside her until she felt a tap on her shoulder. Opening her eyes, she saw an enormous glass of iced tea, and Rosanna's green eyes crinkled with concern.

"Rough trip?"

"Awful. I made loads of contacts, set up some great deals, and, to top it off, I made a boatload of money at the casinos."

Politely skeptical, Rosanna commented, "Most folks count themselves lucky if they break even. I'd like to have that bad a time."

A prolonged swallow. A person could get hooked on the stuff.

"It didn't mean anything. I'll get back to my apartment and do what, call my friends? Pat myself on the back? There's nobody waiting for me."

"You'll find someone."

"I already did, and I blew it by being Little Miss Nonchalant with her. Like Daddy was with you. Spread that sugar on the phone, but let's not get serious. Let's not do something rash like fall in love."

"It wasn't love, Gina. That's not what I felt for your father. It was an idea of love. An idea can keep you going for a long time, but if you grow up, you find out love's a whole lot more complicated than that. It grabs you."

Rosanna took Gina's free hand.

"It grabs you, and you don't ever want to let go. What I felt for your father was an infatuation. There's no comparison between that, and what Tom and I had."

"Do you regret having us?"

"No," she said firmly. "Dovie deserved to have Susan. And, anyway, you did get to be with your natural family."

"But not with Susan."

Rosanna gave a little smile. "I know I wasn't thinking too clearly at the time, but I do remember thinking it wouldn't be right for Danny to walk away with, well, with all the marbles after the way he'd lied about not being married. It didn't seem fair."

"To whom?"

"To me. I thought I'd lost my husband. Thought I could never go back to Creed. Here he was asking about Susan, as though I could tear her away from Dovie without blinking an eye. I was hurt. I was flat-out angry. As it is, I fretted over having given you to your father. Frannie thought I was a fool."

A gray and gold pickup passed by, turned around, then pulled into the driveway. Mack Wender sat at the wheel.

"You can go inside if you like," Rosanna said.

"No, I'll be fine."

Rolling down his window, Mack drawled, "Y'all enjoying this good weather?"

"Yes, we are, Mack," Rosanna said. "How're Oralia and the boys?"

"They're doing fine. If you're looking for Dal, I saw him walking to the Shinnery. That's his new route these days. I can take you down there."

"Just to the house. I can wait for him there."

Giving Rosanna her glass, Gina gave her a pat on the shoulder then joined Mack.

"I've been wanting to show you something," Mack said shyly.

"What is it?"

"Don't get ahead of yourself. Be patient."

Parking at the gym entrance, Mack took a flashlight out of the glove compartment and beckoned her to follow him past the piles of old machinery through a set of double doors, then down a dark, musty hallway. His voice palpably nervous, Mack shone a light on a stand of lockers, opening one on the far left.

"That one belonged to Susan, the next one was mine, and the next Levon."

"That's interesting." To a historian, perhaps.

"It gets better."

Down another hallway, then through what must have been the cafeteria. With the kitchen gutted and windows boarded up, it was more like a hamburger surprise mausoleum.

Leading her through another door, Mack announced, "This is it."

A sheeted mattress, pillows, an ice chest, a blanket.

"Your home away from home?"

"In a matter of speaking. This is where Susan and I.... We had candles and stuff. It was kind of nice. Hard to tell now, I guess."

"Hard to tell."

Sad and tacky at the same time. Susan showed horrendous judgment screwing this flake so close to home, though in a weird way it made sense. No one would ever see this building as a lover's nest.

"Right over here." He flicked the beam over to the near wall. "I'd slide the window off its hinge so we'd have some air from underneath the boards. Gets hot in here during the summer. And see, I made a kind of door out of it. Kept it tied down so you couldn't see how it worked unless you got real close."

"Why'd you do this?" As he moved the flashlight around, the beam reflected off an object in the far corner. Her eyes were beginning to adjust somewhat, as beams of light trickled through the boarded windows.

"It was real convenient."

"No, I mean why did you keep it going so long?"

The object was square and flat, about the size of a—yes, a DVD player. That's what happened to Dal and Susan's DVD player. That's what happened. Oh God.

"Because I loved her," Mack said agitatedly. "I told you that already. Gina, come over here. I want to say something to you."

"So say it."

He knows I saw it, she thought with a rising sense of panic. Maybe the robber left it here, and this is all a terrible fluke.

"No, I want you to come over here."

Elaborately calm, Gina moved toward him, the flashlight's beam hitting her squarely in the face.

"Mack, I really do need to go over to Dal's."

"You don't understand how much I loved Susan. I only wanted the best for her." His breath sounded ragged and all too close.

"I told her I'd get a divorce, but she didn't give a damn. Wanted to stay with that asshole. Wanted to break it off."

Mack had ramped up to full rant.

"Hadn't she said that before?"

"Yeah, but I'd talked her out of it. All she cared about was how Dal felt. She wouldn't back down."

"Women can be that way."

"She wasn't going to leave her gravy train. I bet that's why you came back, to get in good with the Cartoon King. Bet you already screwed him.

Right. Right?"

On impulse, Gina crashed into the boarded window, her weight carrying her halfway through, before Mack jerked her into reverse. She caught a glimpse of sunlight, amidst the blobs and stars left from the spotlight solo.

Stabs of pain along her arms and shoulder, Gina kicked hard, gaining a measure of freedom, then another kick and she was all the way out.

Clambering to her feet, she managed a few steps before being slammed down onto a hard, warm surface.

"Don't say a word, don't even think of it." Mack's weight crushed down upon her.

***

He might want to sell the trees to the Marroquins, Dal thought as he wound his way through the orchard. He felt a touch winded from an excursion to the Shinnery mounds that proved to be more walking than jogging. A slapping sound started up abruptly from a familiar place.

"Damn," Dal said aloud.

Not even a stiff wind as an excuse. He had half a mind to rip off boards from the offending window completely, to allow the elements to take their toll. In a high dudgeon, striding briskly down the dirt path leading to the U-court, Dal heard other sounds. A falling object. Urgent voices. The Marroquin kids playing hooky, perhaps, except the voices sounded like adults. Vandals, that's what.

Whipping around the corner, Dal prepared to say "A-hah," only to stand in shock. A bleeding Gina sprawled face down on the court under Mack, who looked up at Dal, his face manic and distorted.

"Come here, you son of a bitch." Mack started to rise, only to be pushed to one side by Gina.

Dal threw himself at Mack. They fell in a tangle. He delivered one solid punch in before Mack rocked his head back into the concrete.

Instantly giddy, Dal saw the goal net flickering in the breeze, a stretch of weathered brick behind it, then the concrete rapidly approaching his face. A thudding sound kept repeating. For a while, Dal thought it was his head, but he didn't appear to be moving.

Weakly lifting his head, Dal saw Gina crouched next to a supine Mack. She looked awash in blood, yet was able to slam a flashlight into Mack's face. And again.

"Gina?" She stopped in mid-motion.

She looked at him with anguish. "He killed Susan. He killed her."

Dal pulled himself up to a sitting position and felt a wave of nausea come over him. Fighting to keep it in check, he got to his feet unsteadily.

His face a caved-in mess, Mack lay unconscious on the cracked concrete.

"Dal?" Gina's body was trembling.

Dal staggered over to her side. She looked…bad. Blood streamed from a host of places on her shoulder and arms.

He pulled the flashlight from her hand and threw it down.

"Come on," he said. "Let's go to the house."

"I don't want him to get away," she said weakly.

"I don't think Mack's going to bother us for a while." If he wasn't already dead. "We need to call the Sheriff's office."

Gina's eyes rolled up into her skull and she slumped to the ground. Not good. In her jeans pocket, he found a cell phone and pressed the emergency numbers.

He heard himself call for help. He listened to his voice—measured and informing—describe the situation as he stared at her in a blind panic. He picked the flashlight off the ground with his free hand and decided that, if he thought he might pass out, he'd try to give Mack a few more shots.

The largest of the splinters removed from her arm measured over two inches, said the E.R. doctor, who had spent the better part of an hour debriding wounds on her arms and shoulders. Cuts, scratches, and deep bone bruises. No fractures.

Mack was still in surgery and would be for at least an hour longer. He had sustained severe facial lacerations and fractures of the facial bones. The vision in one eye might be affected.

All in all, Gina had done well in upholding the family honor. Better than Dal had. A reporter from the Lubbock Avalanche-Journal came over after the doctor left, and asked again for an interview.

"I understand that this is a difficult time for all concerned, but Wender's aunt has already given me a quote and the sheriff's department spokesman has given me its statement, such as it is. I need something giving your side of the story."

Something broke inside of Dal as he looked at the young man clutching a small digital recorder.

"My side? Wender took my wife's sister inside the school and tried to kill her. It was pure luck that I happened on it this time."

"This time." The reporter seized on that eagerly. "You believe Wender's a suspect in the killing of your wife."

"Damn right he's a suspect."

There was an unreal quality to the scene. Jimmy Olson questioning a

Dark Knight character. With Dick Tracy, no doubt, holding forth in the hospital lobby for any TV crews that happened to come by. I'm getting sucked in, he thought.

Walking away from the reporter toward the E.R., he heard Rosanna call out to him.

"Are you a friend of Ms. D'Abruzzo?" the reporter asked.

"I'm her mother," Rosanna said sharply.

Dal paused for a moment, appalled by how that revelation would play out in the media.

"Come on, Dal," she said. "Gina needs us."

"Was Wender good friends with Ms. D'Abruzzo and your wife?" The reporter's next words were drowned out by the E.R. hum of personnel and machinery.

Rosanna swept aside the curtain around Gina's cubicle.

Dal saw a beautiful, long-legged woman, her arms and shoulder heavily bandaged. Susan, if he'd been there the first time.

Glassy-eyed and thick-tongued, Gina slurred, "Rosanna, I should've stayed with you. I should've known better."

"No," Rosanna said. "There's no blame here. You couldn't have known what was in Mack's head. He got caught this time. He won't ever get away again."

Her look wrought and accusatory, Gina said to Dal, "You took it away."

"I had to."

"You shouldn't have." Her voiced trailed out, and she closed her eyes.

The nurse came in at that point and bustled them out. Worried about reporters, he led Rosanna through a side door and they headed to the parking garage. Rosanna kept him silent company until she opened the driver's side door.

Dal felt the ache in his temple intensify. "It's not about the damn flashlight. It's about me making Susan so unhappy that a lunatic could get next to her."

Rosanna's volume abruptly went up about six notches.

"You may have messed up, but so did Susan. I made my mistakes, still making them, but I'm not going to beat myself up over it any longer."

Her voice turned softer. "You're holding on to the guilt 'cause that's your way of dealing with what happened. It can't be blind fate, or a twisted fool of a man who couldn't let go. It has to be you and you alone, but that's not how it is. Mack created a terrible emptiness when he killed Susan. You filled it with shame, with guilt, because you weren't the man you could have been. Don't let him win. Don't let him have the last word."

## CHAPTER THIRTY-FOUR

Gina tried to turn on her side, but managed only a bug-like wiggle until, with a strenuous effort, she rose to a seated position, surveyed the blue paisley wallpaper, then collapsed onto her back.

When she awoke again, Rosanna was straightening her covers.

"I want to lie on my side," Gina said.

"You're better off lying flat. Either way you go, it's going to hurt."

Rosanna reached for a glass of water on the bedside table. "Here, take this."

She had an assortment of pills in her hand.

"Don't want to sleep," Gina said.

"These aren't for sleep. There's one for pain, and a muscle relaxant, and an antibiotic."

"Antibiotic?"

"Dr. Rao said he was worried about you getting an infection, since the wood was so rotten in places."

Gina swallowed the pills and tried to find a clock in the room.

"What time is it?"

"Along about ten in the morning. You've been asleep quite a while. Just to bring you up to date: I called your parents to let them know what happened. Your sister, Linda, should be getting in anytime now. Your boss and a man named Aaron called, also your friends Charmaine and Carla. Ben Kong called. I think he's your assistant. Dal would like to come over, but there's a cameraman hanging by his house. He can't get away right now."

"How is he?"

"He has an awful cut on his scalp. It took fifteen stitches to close it. He thinks you're mad at him, that he should've known about Mack somehow."

"He's wrong," Gina said.

"Mack made it through surgery okay. Alive, anyway."

"How's Oralia?"

"Stunned. Absolutely stunned. Mack had been acting strange lately, but she thought it was because of the problems with the gin."

"She knew Mack and Susan were lovers."

"She had no reason to think Mack was responsible for Susan's death."

"Murder."

Rosanna carried on. "The kids are staying with Levon's family for the time being. Oralia's mother's blood pressure went through the roof over this, so her father has a full plate dealing with her being in the hospital."

"What about Mack's family?"

"His aunt called me this morning. They're all in shock over this."

Rosanna pulled back the curtain on the west window. Gina could see cotton fields stretching out to the horizon.

"We've made the news, I imagine," she said with a leaden sense of fatality.

"Dal's a fairly well-known cartoonist, and, well, the circumstances are a bit unusual," Rosanna said.

"Bizarre is more like it. It'll only get worse. They'll start off with Mack and Susan, then work their way over to you and Daddy. It'll be a freak show before you know it."

"I won't talk to the press," Rosanna said, her face blurred by a shaft of sunshine.

"You won't have to. There'll be someone around to make money off of this. God, I wish I'd never come here. I wish I'd sent Dal on his way. None of this would've happened."

"Mack's not one to keep a secret. That's why he took you to the school. He wanted you to see the DVD player, to put two and two together. Oralia, Dal, Levon, me—someone would've ended up in that room, ended up dead most likely."

"Oralia must be crushed over this."

"You know what she said? She hopes you'll forgive her for not knowing Mack was the killer."

A husband likely headed to death row. Two small children, and probably a mountain of bills.

Foundering on a mix of complicated emotions, Gina managed to stammer out, "I can't imagine being in her situation."

Rosanna patted Gina's head softly, then leaned closer as Gina tugged on her sleeve.

Without quite knowing how it happened, Gina found herself in

Rosanna's arms, chest aching from pent-up tears, yet she felt as though she was crying. Neither seemed to feel like talking for a while, then Rosanna withdrew tactfully.

As she left, Rosanna said, "I'll bring you something to eat in a bit."

"I'm not hungry."

"You will be."

She was right. Rosanna returned with a plate of biscuits, sausage, and gravy, along with a glass of milk. Gina could manage part of the process, the piling of food on a fork, but not the delivery. Rosanna took over, covering Gina's embarrassment with chatter about non-Mack news events, and the Texas Tech women's basketball team.

"They're going to have a good year, I just know it. Susan." She stopped for a moment, then continued. "Susan and I took in as many games as we could. Those were about the only times she ever talked much about when she played basketball."

"Why didn't she play in college?"

Feeding Gina another bite, Rosanna said, "She'd always told me it was because Dovie needed her at home to help with the farm and take care of Floyd. When we were at a game last year, she said the real reason was because she thought she was nothing but a big fish in a small pond. She wasn't, you know."

Rosanna had an almost fierce look about her. "She was as good as any of the players we've seen."

"Don't do that," Gina said softly. "Everyone does that with Susan. They make up their own alternate history for her. Don't do that anymore. Susan lived full-tilt. That doesn't sound like a woman who missed out on her own life. Right now, I feel that way about myself. I've been living second-hand, not making my own way."

She had lost her train of thought. Rosanna looked at her strangely.

"The thing is, what you don't know about me is that, I'm not like Susan in my dating material."

Rosanna waited.

"I broke up with someone recently who meant a lot to me, but I sabotaged it. I made sure it wouldn't work. And now, I'm interested in someone who I think could be the one, but I'm afraid I'll do the same thing as before."

Bathroom. Gina couldn't wait any longer.

"I'm sorry, but could you give me a hand up?"

Minutes later, Gina was back in bed, trying haplessly to arrange her covers.

"Let me do that." Rosanna took over with a minimum of fuss.

"Gina, I realize you think I'm someone who's never seen the world, and Lord knows you're probably right, but I get what you're trying to tell me. You're gay. I'd already figured that out."

"I'm actually bisexual, but yes, mainly women."

Appearing neither shocked nor dismayed, Rosanna located a pick in the dresser and gently began untangling Gina's hair.

"Look, I almost got killed yesterday, and what could people have said about me? 'She was a good employee, she had a lot of friends.' That's it."

"That's more than a lot of folks could say," Rosanna said with a quiet smile.

"Anyway, I hope you're not disappointed that I'm so unlike Susan."

Her face turning sober, Rosanna said, "Even if the two of you had grown up together, I think there would have been major differences, but some things would've been the same, regardless. There's something I want to tell you: I don't want it to go out of this room. Susan had a streak of what you're talking about. I don't know how much she acted on it, but she did tell me that she kissed a fellow nurse from the nursing home after they'd been out at a bar. There might've been more to it than that. Susan blamed it on drinking, but at the time I thought of how close she and Oralia had been in high school—how they'd hug and carry on."

"Straight girls do that, Rosanna. I wouldn't read too much into it."

"I grew up with Frannie. I know how she acted when she was young. I've always thought that for some women it must be an awfully thin line between needing men, and needing other women."

"Maybe you misread the signals." Gina felt distressed for some reason.

"Gina," Rosanna said, seeing her expression. "What does it matter now?"

"I've been resisting people making comparisons between us, and it bugs me how much alike we are—were, whatever—and no, I don't know why it would bother me."

Gina felt fretful, and itchy under the bandages. And, despite all that, sleepy.

"I've seen you in all kinds of light, yet it amazes me how much you look like Susan," Rosanna said pensively. "Some angles I think, yes, they're different, but then I realize I'm imagining the differences. But, if you and Susan had come into the same room with the same hair and same clothes, I still could've told you apart. It's the attitude, the expressions. So close some ways, so different other ways."

Rosanna began crying. "I was so angry at Danny for lying. Now, all I can do is tell you stories about Susan. I don't blame you for hating me. I don't blame you at all."

"I don't hate you," Gina said haltingly. "I don't know that I would have done it differently if I'd been in your situation."

Too much to think about, and she felt too tired to do it properly. "I can tell you this. My father has changed since you knew him. He doesn't mess around the way he he used to."

Gina felt fuzzier by the minute.

Rosanne looked dubious. "After he filed for bankruptcy, he couldn't keep up the big spender image, then all those cigarettes finally got to him. It's not so much that he changed; it's more like everything changed around him. He adjusted. I give him credit for that."

"You weren't there. You weren't there to see him change. All you got to see was the man who dumped you. You never really knew my father."

"I thank God for that. I thank God that Tom took me back. I thank God that Danny wouldn't let me stay with him."

With that, she suddenly went quiet.

"The money was to pay for something else, wasn't it," Gina said. "He wanted you to get an abortion."

Her face stricken, Rosanna raised her head. "I thought about it, then I realized I couldn't do it. I had to pay the price. I couldn't get off scot-free."

"We were your punishment."

"At the time, I thought of it that way, I suppose."

Noticing a hollow look around the woman's eyes, Gina regretted dragging the conversation out. I'm not the only one who feels wiped out, she thought.

"Then I had the two of you, and my thinking changed. God blessed me with this experience. I thought of y'all as a necessary burden, when in fact it was the best thing that ever happened to me. I had to care about others. I had to think of someone other than myself. Lord, I needed that."

Winking out for a moment, Gina came back long enough to hear Rosanna whisper, "Get some rest."

A bare impression of a kiss on her cheek.

***

Levon, who arrived with a bottle of vodka, a carton of orange juice, a bag of ice, and some old Prince CDs, didn't waste any time in easing Dal into a somewhat more relaxed state.

Raymond was already on the scene, having brought his time-tested remedies of spaghetti and tiramisu.

The last cameraman left his stake-out by the mailbox earlier in the day. Raymond said that a drug scandal had erupted involving a well-known

Lubbock surgeon—bad news for the surgeon, but good news for Dal, if it meant fewer headlines that mentioned his name.

Levon claimed he hadn't followed the coverage, then immediately disproved it. "The defense lawyer thinks Mack can avoid the death penalty. I don't see how. Mack obviously set Gina up."

"What he didn't count on was Gina being a lot tougher that she looks. Big city girl like her, she wasn't going to be caught off-guard," Raymond said.

"I'm glad Gina got her licks in. Wish she'd kicked his ass all the way to hell," Levon said.

"You've known him most of your life," Dal said.

The son of a farm foreman, Levon spoke with feeling. "That's just it. Mack was the golden boy, the one with a rich daddy, and a job for life. He ruined that gin, and he blamed your family for kicking out all those people."

"He's right about my grandfather. The old man made this town. He thought he had the perfect right to unmake it."

"Did you ever think, Dal, that maybe he was right in doing it?" Raymond said. "The only reason people moved here in the first place was because they thought the train was going to come. It never happened. This town wasn't meant to be."

"It should've died a natural death," Dal said. "There was no need to hasten it along, to poison their hopes."

"I can see having a little town stuck off in the mountains, or by the sea. Someplace beautiful, or at least with a sense of history. Getting evicted from Creed meant they could move somewhere better," Raymond said.

Dal motioned to Levon for a refill on his drink.

"You see the most unbelievable sunsets and sunrises everyday, but it's not enough for you. Me, I...love this great absence. You have to reach out for the beauty here. It won't come to you, like in the mountains," Dal said. "You have to search out the odd bump in the far horizon, the tangle of golds and greens in the grassland, crows peppered on the high wire, the reddish hints of clay in the sandy loam. You have to come out and meet this land. It's not served to you like a redwood tree in California."

His friends looked at him solemnly.

"Dal, I get your point," Levon said. "But, I like to go fishing sometimes, and there're not many good spots around here."

"That's what the highway's for."

"You're going to stay here?" Raymond said, incredulous.

"Nothing's changed, Ray."

"The hell it hasn't. Oralia'll be selling the gin piece by piece. That leaves you, Rosanna, and the Marroquins out here by yourselves."

"We're not alone." Dal rattled the cubes in his glass.

Levon obliged with a dribble of vodka and a lake of orange juice. "Don't start talking about ghosts. I lived out here. I heard the same stories you did. There's nothing out here but coyotes, and whatever your mind conjures up late at night. You might could make it out here, but I don't know about Gina."

"Gina's not moving out here. I doubt that she'll ever want to see me again. She probably thinks Susan would be alive today if I'd caught on earlier about the affair."

"Really?" said Raymond as he cleared away the trash on the table. "Do you think Rosanna knew?"

"I sort of got that impression. It doesn't matter who knew what, and when. I didn't know, though I should have."

"When I saw you and Gina together, it seemed as though something could develop," Levon said thoughtfully. "In some ways, y'all have more in common that you and Susan did. Gina mentioned some book she'd read, which is something I never heard out of Susan."

"I loved Susan. I don't love Gina." Gone for a few minutes, the headache had returned with a vengeance.

"You've been really torn up about Susan. Who wouldn't be? The fact is, Mother Teresa could come here in the body of Beyonce, and she still wouldn't measure up," Raymond said. "Brother, it's too damn soon to say what you feel about Gina. You don't know."

"Maybe so, but I know what she feels about me. She's no sister of charity."

## CHAPTER THIRTY-FIVE

It took several rings of the phone to rouse Dal, and several hellos before he realized some woman wanted to talk to him about Gina.

"I'm not giving interviews. There's nothing more to say."

He glanced at the clock. Seven in the morning. He must have finally found the right combination of Vicodins and screwdrivers.

"I'm not a reporter. I'm Marilyn D'Abruzzo, Gina's mother. Mrs. Wintersole has been helpful, but I'd feel a lot more comfortable talking to someone else."

"Why don't you talk to Linda? She's been over there since yesterday."

"She can't talk freely, not with the others there. I need to know: how's Gina really doing? She's not answering her cell phone."

"You're asking me?"

For the first time since before the attack, Dal felt a smile, however faint, on his face.

"Mrs. D'Abruzzo, I haven't seen Gina since the hospital. I'm not exactly on her A- list."

"Why is that? From what Mrs. Wintersole told me, you saved Gina's life."

"I provided a moment's diversion, is more the way it happened. Your daughter's quite capable of self-defense. At any rate, Rosanna said the doctor will probably be releasing her to travel in two or three days, plus I imagine the law still has questions for her. She's not in any trouble, you understand. They're making sure they have the strongest case they can make against Wender."

"I wish we could come up and see her, but I'm afraid that would be difficult," Marilyn said.

"I can understand that. Your husband's not in the best of health."

"Oh, it's not that particularly. His breathing machine's portable, and as long as we take it easy, Danny does okay. I wouldn't want to take him on long car trips, but he's in better shape now than he has been in several months."

"Maybe he's turning the corner."

"He has advanced COPD. The doctors say he won't get any better. Mr. Creed—"

"Call me Dal."

"Danny and I can't afford to go up there right now, and maybe it's better that we don't, given how angry Gina has been at us."

There they go again, backing away, refusing to communicate.

"Frankly, Mrs. D'Abruzzo, if you have any hope of working things out with your daughter, now is the best time. For one thing, she can't run out of the room—not too quickly, anyway."

That was meant to be a mild joke. Too mild, apparently.

"I'm afraid it'll have to wait until she's away from that woman. I've tried to be patient, to not push too hard, but I'm scared that she'll never talk to us again."

"You didn't talk to her about Susan—I'm sorry. That's none of my business."

"You were married to Gina's sister. You have a right to be angry at us."

"I'm beyond that these days. I can't get too angry at you people, not while Mack Wender's in the world."

An idea occurred to him. "What I can do is get you a couple of plane tickets."

"Pardon? I wouldn't want to put you through any trouble."

Translation: yes.

"Start getting packed. I'll call you back with the departure time."

Not waiting for an answer, he hung up. Looking around, he saw a bedroom in disarray. The living room was probably a wreck.

"Get a grip, Dal," he said aloud. "Your in-laws are coming over. Time to do some straightening up."

***

"You need to seriously consider suing the Wenders," Linda said as she pulled a tank top over Gina's head.

They'd already managed the jeans surprisingly well.

Since she arrived last night, Linda had been on a tear about her sister's financial losses. Gina tried telling her that TopSound offered excellent insurance, and that everyone at work, from Cyril to Charmaine, advised her to take as many sick days as needed. Plus, she had her gambling winnings. The trip to Las Vegas felt as though it happened a lifetime ago.

On the phone, Charmaine also promised personalized nursing once

Gina made it back home, this after Gina blurted out that she wanted them to get serious—or, as she actually put it, "Let's get together, for real."

Gina, still the poet of romance.

"Oralia doesn't have the money, and we're not hitting up Mack's relatives. Forget it."

Linda shook her head at Gina. "You need to be prepared for Mack's lawyer claiming that you set Mack up."

"You're kidding."

"What else can he claim? Temporary insanity, two times running? No, he has to make it look like you're a whack job."

"What about the DVD player, and the fact that several people know he and Susan were having an affair?"

"Preach on, baby girl."

Linda smiled as they sat down at the kitchen table.

Rosanna, who was out checking on the ostriches, had left flour tortillas and huevos rancheros on the warmer.

"I'll fix us plates to eat," Linda volunteered.

"Thanks, but we can't let Mack's lawyer get away with telling lies to the jury. Rosanna said that there's no way Mack can avoid the death penalty, based on the evidence."

Oh-h-h. Sitting in a hard chair made her realize how many bruises she'd collected, including on her butt.

Looking bemused as she made the tacos, Linda said, "I can't get over how well the two of you are getting along. The last time I talked to Carla, she said she didn't think you'd ever go back up here again, and now you and Rosanna are practically best friends."

"I wouldn't call it best friends. It's more as though we've come to an understanding."

"And what's that?" Linda returned to the table.

"That I'm not going to blame her, and she's not going to blame Daddy."

"All well and good, Gin, but when are you going to talk to Mom and Daddy?"

"About what, the weather? They're not exactly forthcoming."

"I'm not going to defend them. I feel bad enough not saying anything all these years."

"Don't, don't feel bad. It was their secret to tell, not yours."

A piece of egg went flying out of Linda's taco, unnoticed. She was on a roll.

"If you cut them off, you'd have to deal with the guilt feelings when Daddy dies. Don't give me that look. You know what the doctor says.

One bad case of pneumonia could send him out the door. Do you want that on your conscience?"

"When I go home, I'll drop by the house. I'm telling you right now: I'm not putting up with the silent treatment. They'll have to let it all out, every last detail."

"Why?" Linda asked. "You told me what happened at Daddy's bar with Rosanna, and you already know the how and when and why you and Susan got separated. Case closed."

"I don't know why Daddy cheated on Mom, and why he gave Rosanna money for an abortion. He was raised Catholic."

"It's human nature, Gin. Human nature. Daddy screwed around on Mom, Rosanna got caught in the crossfire, and Susan and you were the upshot. Him being Catholic—c'mon, we're not talking about Daddy being the Pope."

Leave it to Linda to find a relativistic way out. No one's to blame, everyone's to blame. Don't be too upset about it.

"I want him to talk to me, okay? I know it's not in our parents' DNA to talk about anything important—you know, like, feelings?—but I wish they'd try."

Linda laid down the remnants of her taco. "Good luck on that."

***

Another run through with the vacuum cleaner and Dal would pronounce it a done deal, for he needed to be on the road to pick up Gina's parents. Turning off the vacuum, he couldn't help but stop and admire his work. The best it'd looked since...well, since before Susan's murder. There, he could think about it and not get choked up or angry. Doing better, doing better.

"Dal?" A voice spoke softly. He saw Oralia standing at the door, the screen door still open.

"I knocked, but you had the vacuum going." She remained frozen by the door.

"Come on in and have a seat." He sat in the recliner as an inducement.

"I can only stay a minute. The boys are over at my sister's. I've been at the hospital all morning."

"How's he doing?"

Her face crumpled. "I can't believe you can even ask that, knowing what he did to Susan, what he tried to do to you and Gina. He was so woozy yesterday I couldn't get him to listen, but this morning, he was a little more alert. Thank God, 'cause I didn't want to say what I had to say unless I knew for sure he'd remember it."

She sank to the sofa.

"What did you want to tell him?"

"That I've filed for divorce. Papa's helping me on that."

"How's your mother?"

"They let her come home from the hospital last night. She has to take it easy for a few days. The doctor said no TV, no newspaper. There was a reporter at my door yesterday morning. I've told them all to go to hell."

"I should have tried that approach."

"You have every right to say what you want about what happened. They asked me what Mack told me about the murder, as if I was involved in some way. Susan was my best friend in the whole world."

"I know."

"Dal, I want you to know that I called Mack's banker. He's helping me set up an auction for next week, to sell everything at the Culdesac, from the ground up. I don't want anything left of that place, nothing left to remind you of Mack. I'm going to sell the house, and move into Lubbock. I'm going back to school, going to change my name back to Iglesias, and I'll make the school call my kids by that name."

"Sounds like you've been real busy."

Such a banal comment, but he was at a loss as to what to say.

"My sister's already offered to let us stay with her until the house is sold. It's partly my fault, you know. Not what Mack did, but for not doing something or saying something earlier."

"You knew he and Susan were lovers."

She looked at him—correct that, past him—with a level expression. "Almost from the beginning."

"Why didn't you tell me?"

"I thought you knew," she said, surprised. "To me, it was so obvious when they were around each other. They'd exchange little looks and stuff. I didn't see any point in talking to Mack about it. He'd have denied it, just like he tried to do today."

"Why didn't you divorce him earlier? Did you simply not care who he was screwing?"

"Yes, I did," Oralia flared in return. "I cared a hell of a lot."

"You loved him so much that you put up with his lies."

"I loved—I love the kids, and most of the time Mack and I got along."

"What I don't understand is how you could've been friends with Susan, knowing what was going on."

"Susan and I were like that growing up," Oralia said, entwining two of her fingers.

Her voice slowed to a crawl. "The thing is, what you don't understand, is how much Susan meant to me, and what I think I meant to her."

What was she saying? They were so close Oralia could forgive her friend committing adultery with her husband?

"I don't understand."

"Mack always loved Susan, and while I don't think she loved him, she did have feelings toward him. She came real close to spilling the truth to me, but I steered her around it. She knew I knew, and that I wasn't going to make a big deal over it."

"It was okay for them to screw around because you liked Susan."

"I loved her. I don't care how that sounds. I loved her, and you know what, I think that's one reason I married Mack. We had something in common."

"Oh, so you were screwing her, too."

"It's none of your business, but I can tell you this: I never committed adultery. That's all you need to know."

Dal hardly noticed when she left.

Since he found out about Mack and Susan's relationship, he'd placed it in a particular file labeled irrelevant. Susan was dead; the past didn't matter. Almost getting killed by Mack jumbled the order again, but once more Dal had managed—with Levon's vodka intervention—to put that knowledge aside.

Now Oralia had slapped him in the face with yet another damning detail. Susan was a liar from the beginning, said the vows as though she meant them, but couldn't live up to the standard. A liar.

He wasn't much of a husband, but still, he'd managed to stay true to his wife. Stayed with a drunk, barely educated slut who made her sister look like a college professor by comparison.

It wasn't my fault, Dal thought, then realized he had said it aloud.

"It wasn't my fault," he said louder. "Not my fault. Not my fault."

The words barely out of his mouth, he felt as though a gigantic knot had been loosened in his belly. His glance at the clock provided a necessary jolt.

Time to go pick up Gina's parents.

***

A cool breeze slinking through the railing, Gina and Linda swayed back and forth in the front porch swing. While Linda yammered about work, Gina felt content to listen and veg on a serious dosage of pain med. It was a good thing she never ventured into narcotics during her party doll phase, otherwise she'd be a junkie poster child by now.

I must look like a highway pancake, she thought, but damn, I feel good.

"Look." Linda pointed to the slowing car about to turn into the driveway. "It's Mom and Dad."

Dal sat at the wheel. The culprit.

Coming out onto the porch, Rosanna almost immediately started to turn around.

"Don't leave," Gina said.

"I don't think it's such a good idea," Rosanna said with a note of caution.

Dal emerged from the car and helped Mom get Daddy, looking wan and shaky, out of the back seat. They were quickly joined by Linda. An eerie, pointless silence hung over the scene, as Dal and Mom helped Daddy onto the porch.

What were they waiting for? Gina could walk for miles to the main road, then hitch a ride into Lubbock. Book a flight to Houston and be sitting in the airport bar, reverting to alcoholism, before these jokers ever said a word.

So much time wasted. Abused, actually. Deposited in the porch swing, Daddy could only smile at her weakly.

"You need your machine," she said.

"Marilyn's bringing it," Dal volunteered. He turned, as if to leave.

"Stay. I need you here," Rosanna said tensely.

"You're part of the family," Gina said.

"And so are you," her father wheezed.

"Daddy, don't talk right now. Wait 'til Mom can set up the machine. Rosanna, do you have an...I see it," Linda pointed out an extension cord connected to the portable refrigerator by the swing.

Gina felt full to overflowing with conflicting emotions. To tell Daddy off, to help him to the sofa inside, to never say a word again to anyone, to burst into tears.

"Daddy, why didn't you tell me I had another sister?"

The wheezing somewhat improved, he said, "What would have been the point? She had a family. I may be the world's biggest son of a bitch, but I'm not going to tear a kid away from the only parents she's ever known, all because I want to feel better about myself."

Mom worked furiously to set up the breathing machine. While Daddy sucked on the tube, Dal and Linda settled onto the porch steps and Mom sat on the stool. Rosanna remained at the door, giving her best impression of a statue.

"What's bugging you, sweets?" he finally said.

"Just the fact that even after I found out, you couldn't be bothered to say anything about it. Rosanna finally gathered up the nerve to meet me. Granted, I'm not thrilled about her part in all this."

"You don't know what she did," Mom said in a high, panicked voice. "She chased Danny all the way back to Lambert and demanded that he leave me. Then when he refused, she threatened to tell me."

Bemused, Rosanna shook her head. "The last part's not true. I never threatened to tell you. Danny knows the truth."

His breathing starting to clog up again, Daddy put his hand on Gina's knee. How frail, how bony he looked. Blue-veined hands, discolored fingernails, an ashen face, and glassed-over, sleepy eyes. He shouldn't have made the trip.

"Marilyn," he began, then stopped for breath. Propelling herself from the seat, Mom hurtled to the far corner of the porch.

"Sweets, I don't know what to say to you. Used to, I could talk a blue streak, bullshit with the best of them. Sold a lot of cars that way."

"You were the best," Linda said loyally.

"Yeah, I was. I could lie like a Persian rug, make the Pope think he's Jewish. Even when I was stuck selling junk cars to people who couldn't afford them, I could still shoot a line. I think, hell. Solid gold caddy time. That gal over there—"

He pointed to Rosanna. "She's a rattletrap. Who'd believe a word she said? Then it hit me: I couldn't walk away from my own flesh and blood. Maybe I'm not your hero anymore, if I ever was. Maybe there ain't one thing I can tell you that makes you understand why I'd send that girl packing. Why I'd mess with her in the first place."

"Why did you?" Rosanna asked softly.

Daddy regarded her for a long moment. "Because I was Dynamo Danny, the car king of Lambert, and if some pretty young brunette came along, then I had to be the star of the show. Besides, you were stuck with that hayseed. I felt sorry for you."

Rosanna said, almost smiling. "If that's all there was to it, you wouldn't have kept asking me to come down and see you. You promised to set me up in an apartment—you made it sound as though I was special to you."

Gina didn't have to look at Mom to know her reaction.

"I told you a lot of things, some of it I meant at the time, but when you showed up in a family way, that straightened me out in a hurry. I couldn't ditch my wife and kid; I loved them too much. Hell, that wasn't even an option."

"You gave Rosanna money for an abortion," Dal interjected. No answer. "Then when Frannie called, you decided to try to take the kids away from Rosanna. Only you arrived too late."

"He didn't want to steal the twins." Mom advanced a few steps toward the others. "He didn't even want to come, at first. I talked him into it.

He thought I wouldn't accept you, baby, but I told him he was wrong. When I saw you, when I held you in my arms, he believed me. Gina, no matter how horrible you think we are, everything we did from the moment we took you home was strictly out of love."

"And fear," Gina said.

"That, too. I knew if the day came that you found out, you wouldn't want to see us again."

Mom. Mom had been the roadblock all along.

"Mom, you didn't want Daddy to come up and see Susan, did you."

"No, I didn't. I thought it'd lead to trouble."

"What trouble? Did you think he and Rosanna would get back together?"

"Of course not," she snapped.

"And you probably threatened Rosanna with the electric chair if she came back down again and checked on me. It was you. That's why Daddy didn't want to say anything, because he didn't want your part in all this to come out. Oh God, Daddy..."

At a loss for words, she clutched his hand.

He started to say something but Mom intruded, "What was I supposed to do? Let that woman hang around Lambert, stirring up gossip? I didn't care what people said about me, but I'd die before I let you suffer for other people's sins."

Mom's chin was trembling.

***

I'm not a drinker, Dal thought, as the buzzing in his ears threatened to drown out Marilyn D'Abruzzo's tirade. Not sick as a dog, but not overly brimming with good health, either.

Considering the behavior of Marilyn, Danny, and Rosanna, Susan appeared merely feckless by comparison. She never set out to hurt me, he thought. Probably didn't think it counted as adultery, since it was with a man she never, by all accounts, took seriously.

Here Dal was, sitting on Rosanna's front porch in the exact same position as when he was a seventeen-year-old wanting to talk to Tom Wintersole about a summer job, and hoping that Rosanna would pass by the door wearing that sleeveless sundress again.

His rushing off to the altar with Susan constituted the only wild card, the sole rebellion, in a life otherwise marked by risk-free ventures. Mother and Junior were never going to let their only son starve during his independent artist stage.

***

"God, I miss her." Dal's voice broke into Mom's second and

unchanged defense of her actions.

"Pardon?" Linda said, puzzled.

"I miss her, too," Rosanna said huskily.

Surprised by the sudden course change, Mom fell silent.

Dal seemed strangely calm. "Susan was the entire point of my life. The only part that wasn't in the original script. I've been so angry since I found out she messed around on me. Not that I would've admitted it, but that's how I felt. So ironic, that all along I'd tried to keep her wildness in check. Oh no, she's going to get drunk at this party, or she's laughing too loud at the show—but I miss that intensity.

"Somehow, when she turned up my emotions a few notches, I'd feel more, I don't know, alive, even if sometimes it meant feeling absolutely miserable. Do you know what I mean?" He turned to Gina.

"I do. All the time Terry made me nuts I couldn't wait to see her until something came up that was a perfect excuse to dump her," Gina said.

His tone still even, Dal said, "And that's why I went searching for you. You were my rescue, Gina, because Mack took Susan away. I've been divesting myself of Junior—the strip, the contracts—but I have to do more.

"You people want to fight over the past, you're welcome to do so, but as for me, all I've had these years is the past. It's not enough to sustain you; I about starved on it, and so did Susan. Susan..."

Visibly fighting back the surge of emotion, he kept on course. "Susan...made a mistake keeping the affair going with Mack, but I think the night she was killed, she was attempting to let go of all that. Funny how these last few weeks, tracking down Gina and changing my career plans around, I've made a one-eighty degree shift in my life, in my attitudes. Susan would've been thrilled to see all this happen.

"It would've been a dream come true for her, to see me this daring. The old Dal would've never gone off looking for Gina, would never have ditched the strip, would've never sat here on this porch talking like an idiot. I'm doing all the things that would've made her believe in me again. You know what? It took her death to accomplish all this. How ironic that is, how stupid it makes me feel. How stupid."

His face flushed, Dal trailed off into silence, leaving a trashed conversation in his wake. Leaving her post, Rosanna came down the steps and quietly displaced Linda, who went over to comfort Mom. The others seemed unsettled by Dal's outburst, Mom most of all, who turned toward the far pasture, her back shaking.

"Dal's right," Daddy said. "We've been hashing over things that happened years ago, like we can change it. Babe," he said, turning toward

Gina. "I'm sorry for not talking to you like I should've. A screw-up from the start. No excuse, no excuse at all."

Except that Mom was pulling the guilt strings on him. A profound exhaustion overtook Gina, causing her to sigh involuntarily.

Rosanna suggested, "You need to go lie down."

Good advice. Impossible to follow. "Daddy, you can't take all the blame. I'm not asking you to do that."

"So it's my fault," Mom erupted. "I plead guilty. Drag me to jail. I plead guilty to placing my marriage and my children above that woman, to wanting to protect you."

"I don't feel protected. I feel cheated, and not only by you, Mom. I want you and Dad to know about someone. A lady who was great with children. I've met four kids she babysat for, and they miss her terribly. She worked at a nursing home where everybody, and I mean everybody I met, acted as though they'd lost their best friend in the whole world. An old classmate who played basketball with her, he grew up with her. He loved her like a sister. Loved her like a sister. Sometimes when I'm walking through this house, I can almost see her, feel her. She was here hundreds of times. Susan came to know Rosanna, came to rely on her for emotional support. They loved each other. Susan didn't miss out on anything important in life. Maybe she didn't receive the ideal upbringing. So what? She was loved. By Dovie, by Rosanna, by Dal, by everyone."

Her eyes fearful, Mom turned around.

Gina kept talking. "She didn't miss out on anything; we did. Mom, Daddy, Linda, and me. We're the ones who lost something in the transaction. We missed out on knowing a good woman. A daughter, a sister. I'll never know her the way I know you," she said to Linda, who blinked fiercely, holding back tears.

"I wish, God, I wish I could say that I loved Susan, the way Dal and the others did. I wish I could say that I miss her the way they do. But, I can't. She's a picture, and that's all she'll ever be. I do miss her, even if all I'm missing is the picture everyone's painted for me. Daddy—"

She took his hand. "Daddy, Rosanna, I want to thank you for my life. It wasn't planned, but it happened, and I'm grateful for it."

Drawing closer, Rosanna smiled tentatively.

"Mom—"

***

Ducking under the side railing, Marilyn hopped down onto the grass and walked with a sense of urgency toward his car, prompting Dal to attempt an intercept.

"Take me back to the airport," she demanded, her shoulders shaking from either tension or anger.

"Why?"

"I'm the fifth wheel, Dal. I lost." Anger, definitely anger.

"You don't know that."

"Yes, I do. That woman's brainwashed her into thinking I'm the enemy. I knew this would happen, I knew it, but Danny said, no, let's go up there and try to make amends. Right." She spat the words out bitterly. "Now, I've lost my daughter."

"You never trusted Gina enough to tell her the truth. You assumed the worst, and guess what: it happened. What you forget is that Rosanna isn't Gina's real mother. You are. Gina hasn't forgotten that, neither should you. Rosanna's a part of Gina's life now, so get used to it. Don't allow your jealousy to take over."

"I'm not jealous."

"Then prove it," Dal returned. "Don't back off."

Gina's voice behind them sounded timid. "Mom, don't leave, please don't leave."

Turning, Dal saw Gina, the side of her neck purpled with bruises, extend the less-bandaged arm forward, beckoning, then embracing, a weeping Marilyn.

Glancing over to the porch, he saw the screen door close after a retreating Rosanna.

## CHAPTER THIRTY-SIX

Ninteen-15, with Levon in the lead. A thrust fake freeing him from Levon's glue hands, Dal tossed up a shot that rimmed and bounced back over his head, too high to retrieve.

"You need a softer touch," Gina said, causing both of the men to come to a dead stop and turn around. The over-wrap off her arm, he could see the mass of ugly bruises, the pair of long stitches wrapped around her forearm, the clutch of smaller stitches high on her upper arm, and bandages where the gashes were still too raw to breathe.

The smaller stitches would fade, but a plastic surgeon needed to be consulted about that mess on her forearm. Dal decided he'd make a few calls and leave the information with Rosanna, slip some money her way if Gina's insurance couldn't cover. The least he could do, considering how she kept Mack from killing him.

"Up and around, I see."

How beautiful Gina looked, despite the damage. A bit worn, perhaps, yet remarkably relaxed. Not so remarkable. Rosanna said they were leaving today. She's probably thrilled to be getting out of here, he thought.

"Not as well as you." Said with a smile.

"Where's Rosanna?"

"Pogo ambushed her by the car. She'll be along in a moment."

As she spoke, Pogo bounded around the corner and took a proprietary position by her feet. A weakness for brunettes, evidently; a weakness Dal shared.

"Levon, how are the kids?"

"Doing great. Anita was wondering if you'd come over for supper the next time you visit," Levon said too rapidly. "That is, if you're coming up again."

"I am. Rosanna has invited me up for Thanksgiving. I'll be spending that weekend with the folks, but the next weekend after that I'll probably be coming up. Rosanna'll let you know. And yes, I'd love to have supper with y'all."

Her arrival signaled by a merry whistle, Rosanna came around the corner.

"Levon, could you come take a look at my tire? I think it may have a leak."

Rosanna didn't even bother to make it sound convincing. Levon went whole-heartedly for the ploy.

"Let me check it out for you. Nice to see you again, Gina," he said, leaving too hastily with Rosanna.

Waiting a decent interval, Gina said ruefully, "That was believable, wasn't it."

"I guess they thought we needed some time to ourselves."

"They're right. Dal, I've said some awful things to you lately."

"Most of it true."

"Some of it," she allowed. "I'm sorry I unloaded on you. Can you forgive me?"

"Yes. I hope you can forgive me for dragging you up here in the first place."

"I wanted to come, and I'm glad I did."

Her body a mass of stitches and bruises, a family still traumatized despite the hugs that accompanied the D'Abruzzos' departure—no, he couldn't see how her life was improved to any degree by the revelation.

Somehow sensing his doubts, Gina said, "I'm a grown-up, Dal. It wasn't easy finding out how my parents had lied to me; it's still not easy. All I know is that I love them, and it's worth it to me to keep on loving them, to not back away."

"Where does Rosanna fit in on this?"

Where do I fit in, he added silently.

"For now, she's someone I care about a great deal. She's not a stranger anymore. I don't want to put any more definition to our relationship than that she's important to me."

"How do your parents feel about that?"

"They're not one hundred percent okay on it, but they'll adjust." Either adjust or perish in the eyes of their daughter. Not an enviable position, but survivable.

"So, you're going to put out a graphic novel, right? That's what Rosanna said."

"There's not much money in that, but I figure I can pick up a few advertising accounts here and there, and still do okay."

"Cyril likes your stuff."

"Hopefully he'll hire me."

"You have my vote."

It thrilled him to have her good will, however cautiously expressed.

"And anyway, the next time I come up, maybe we can go out to dinner. You still owe me a steak."

"I'd like for us to be friends. I don't want you to be worried about things getting complicated."

"Dal, I've been lazy about relationships. I've been content to take the easy route every time. I don't want to do that anymore."

"Going back to Terry, then?"

A gray depression settled into his bones, dug deep into the marrow. Why did he feel as though he was losing Gina when he'd never had her to begin with? Susan. He could rationalize it away, but he'd always see a ghost of Susan in Gina's eyes—a tantalizing glimpse, that's all.

"There's someone else I'm interested in--"

"Charmaine."

"Yes, but it's too soon to tell how that'll work out."

"You're going to try."

"I have to." Another fleeting smile. "I need to go take my lumps like anyone else."

"Looks like you've already started."

"I'm going to try to stay away from crazy people from now on."

"Then you ought to stay away from me."

"You're not crazy. You've been hiding out here for too long. I know, three cheers for the country life, but you don't strike me as that kind of man."

"You may be right. I'm thinking of getting an apartment down in Austin."

"Why Austin?"

"I don't know. I've always liked the town."

True enough. Actually, he had been thinking of getting away for a while.

"Then go, Dal. Go now; otherwise you'll never leave. It's a shame that your grandfather kicked everybody out when he did, but that doesn't mean you have to stay here forever. At least get out every now and then. It'd do you a world of good."

"Thanks, I think I will."

"And come by and see me. Don't be a stranger."

Leaning toward him, she tucked her good arm around his waist and gave him a hug, which worked into a kiss without too much trouble.

Breaking away, he said, "Maybe I'll drop by sometime. I'll call ahead, not the way I did before."

"I'd appreciate that. Well, time for me to head on out."

"Let me walk you back to the car."

Halfway to Rosanna and Levon, Pogo joined the progression, his tail wagging at a furious rate, as if to bat down the wind, which was starting to pick up. There were hugs all around, cheerful farewells, then Gina eased into the car's passenger side, hindered somewhat by a passionately friendly Pogo.

"Pogo, you can't come with me," she said with an affectionate ruffle of his fur. "But I'll be back. We'll chase some rabbits."

Grabbing his collar, Dal pulled him back so Levon could close her door. Waves, smiles, then they were gone.

"That's one strong lady," Levon remarked.

"What do you mean?"

"She nearly got killed back there, yet she came for a visit anyway. I don't know if I could've done that."

"Runs in the family. For a woman who cried over commercials, Susan was tough as nails."

"That's right."

Levon sailed into an anecdote involving a hard foul from Levon, Susan's twisted ankle, and his subsequent 21-12 loss.

"She kicked my butt so hard I thought she was on a mission from God," Levon finished.

"That was Susan."

Dal remembered a dark-haired woman racing Pogo down the dirt road to the Shinnery, winning, then waiting for Pogo to catch up. Then off again, until they were both dots on the horizon.

Don't ever stop, Susan, don't ever stop.

"I seem to recall we have a sporting engagement."

"Speaking of a butt-kicking."

"We'll see about that."

***

Waiting to board the airplane, Gina listened to Rosanna talk.

"Mack's not going to contest custody on the boys. Oralia thinks he's gone insane."

"He may have gone overboard for a while, but he's not crazy."

The last thing she wanted to do was hear about Mack, when all she had to do was look at the Frankenstein patterns on her arm and be reminded of the man.

"Listen, do you think Dal's going to be okay?"

"Yes. I don't think he's going to stay out at Creed anymore, except perhaps for occasional visits," Rosanna said.

"I got the impression that he hadn't really thought about it, when he was talking about buying a place in Austin."

"Maybe not the specifics, but he's thought about it. It'll be hard to sell the house at a profit, so I'm thinking he'll rent it out to the Marroquins. Elsa and Lupe have done wonders with that little place of theirs. I know they'd love to have a bigger house for the kids, and it'd be on the highway."

"Sounds like you've thought it out in detail."

Rosanna shrugged. "It'd be a perfect solution. He's barely been outside except to go shoot baskets over at the school, which he won't even be able to do that soon."

"Why's that?"

"Oralia got Mack's signature on the auction papers, so everything'll be up for grabs next week."

"Mack owned the school?"

"You didn't know that? The Creeds donated the land to the Creed school district. When the school closed, the board deeded it over to Mack Wender's father for a dollar, then of course when he died, Mack inherited the land."

"Who'd want a school building?"

"No one. It's the material they'd want. I expect in a few months nothing'll be left but the concrete foundation, and the same over at the Culdesac."

"Are you staying?"

"Of course I am. And no, I'm not living in the past. I have my college classes—I'm starting Art Appreciation in the spring—and my ostriches. That, and the church'll keep me plenty busy. Creed's my home."

"There's no Creed anymore."

"Yes, there is. Here." She pointed to her heart. "It's not schools and gins, it's people, and as long as I think I'm living in Creed, it's Creed."

The woman had taken entirely too mystical an approach to country living. A stirring of passengers cuing them both, she opened her arms and Rosanna entered, careful of the stitches.

"Be careful," Rosanna said.

"I will."

"You're going to see your doctor tomorrow, right?"

"Day after. Some of the stitches'll be taken out then. Don't worry, Rosanna. I'm going to be fine."

"Your mother's familiar with the airport, right?"

"I'm sure she'll be on time. Don't worry."

"You need anything, anything at all, let me know."

"I will." So much tension in her face. "Rosanna, I'll be back. This is goodbye for a little while."

The strain eased visibly. "I know you will. I love you," Rosanna said with an air of 'should I have said that?'

"I love you, too."

Another hug, then Gina boarded the plane, attracting more than a few stares for her post-mugging appearance. Something memorable for each to report.

"Excuse me," a plump woman at the beginning of her row said as she stood to allow Gina passage. "Excuse me, but I know you from somewhere."

Rosanna said a reporter had obtained an old TopSound corporate video of Gina, and used it during a piece about the murder/attack/well-known cartoonist/twins 'shocker.'

"Ma'am, I don't think we're acquainted."

"I know where I saw you. At the nursing home, where my father-in-law's staying. I remember you 'cause you're so tall, we thought you might have played for the Lady Raiders. Did you?"

Thank God, a woman with no grasp of current events. "No, ma'am. And I think you're talking about my sister."

She looked dubious. "If you say so. Anyway, she was a real sweet gal. Carl sure has been missing her. You tell her to get well and come back to work."

"Yes, ma'am. I will."

The double whammy of pain med and muscle relaxant having kicked in, she arrived at the Houston airport in a pleasant daze. Mom pushed her through the airport in a courtesy wheelchair.

"It's really not necessary," she thought she said.

"What?" Mom hollered through the P.A. announcer's spiel. "I'd rather do it, honey. You sit back and enjoy the ride."

A ride she barely noticed all the way to her apartment, as Mom kept up a steady chatter about work and neighbors. Daddy was waiting at the door. He insisted on escorting her to the sofa, although Gina pointed out in vain that she was quite capable of walking. Wobbly, perhaps, but functional.

How strange it felt, to be with these people again in her place. A mother, a father, a daughter. Same scenario as before Dal's first visit, but so much had changed since then. Still a mother, still a father, desperate to reestablish the old order. Let them. So long as the truth isn't erased once more, let them.

"Mom, Daddy, it's great to be home again," she said with a surge of emotion that surprised her.

"Yeah, doll, it's great to have you here," he said. "All I ask is that you don't run into any more crazy bastards."

"I promise."

***

Susan had him jammed in close to the basket, feinting left, faking right, trying to get off a shot, which, when delivered, had no arch and no chance of swishing.

Corralling the rebound, she announced, "Get ready, Dalhart, your butt is mine."

"I know that already."

Smiling widely, she reached out without warning and tapped him on the nose.

"Stay here," she said, and whoosh, she was halfway to the basket before he could react.

Easy bucket. He turned and saw Mack creeping out of the half-shuttered window behind the goal post.

"No," Susan said sternly. "You get back in there."

Chastened, Mack threaded back through the window.

"Thanks," Dal said.

"That's all you've got to do. Tell him no."

"I will."

Tossing the basketball to him, she took up a defensive position and waited while he pivoted anxiously, his back to the goal, then, making up his mind, he whirled suddenly to his right and awoke sitting up in bed, for a moment disoriented. He had been dreaming. A good dream, though. No walkabouts, no Pogo barking instructions.

He flipped his pillow so that he could lie on the cool side, then went back to sleep.

***

"Certainly, certainly, but I'd much prefer you to come back on Monday and maybe work half-days until you're moving around better," Cyril said fretfully, turning a gold letter opener over and over in his hand.

"Cyril, all I want to do is get with Binh, work down some of the messages on my desk, and give him some instructions."

She worked on her clothes, hair, and makeup assiduously before she came into work, yet she knew she still looked like walking wounded.

"That's all, then I'll go back home. I am planning on taking the laptop so I can get some work done."

"No, Gina, no work at home, no work up here. If you want to make arrangements with Binh, that's fine, but nothing too complicated. When I talked to your mother—the one here—she told me the kind of injuries you've suffered. You've had an awful time, so don't push yourself too hard."

"I won't. And thanks for caring about me."

That embarrassed him. "You and me, we've been through the wars together. Go home, kid. Get healed up, so we can kick some more butt."

Creeping down the hall, she was waylaid by Aaron, who offered condolences and a Diet Big Red, then disappeared into his office. The next Murray was considerably more energetic, as Charmaine did her best to hug Gina without touching any possibly injured parts.

"You don't look near as shitty as I thought you would."

"Thanks," Gina said gratefully. "Everybody else has been acting as though I came from a beauty pageant when I know how awful I look."

"You look like one of those billboards about the abused women's shelter, but as though you're one of those upscale broads who's had a few days away from the jackass. Not too trashed out. But enough about you. I'm moving to a new house."

"When?"

"First of next month. I'm signing the papers Thursday."

"You're making changes."

"So are you," Charmaine said with significant eyebrows.

"More like changes have been made on me."

"No, it's not all that. I noticed it when we talked on the phone. You seem, I don't know, more down to earth or something."

"Less bullshit, you mean."

"Maybe that. Anyhow, I'm glad you're back."

"So am I. For a while, I didn't know if I would be coming back in one piece."

"I saw it on CNN, but they didn't really push it that hard. Not more than a day or two, tops. Really. Dal Creed's not a big celebrity."

"Stick a couple of twins in there and add a mad killer, and you have yourself a story."

"They're on to the next scandal. Turns out the man who directed that Angelina Jolie flick I liked, he's secretly married to a soap opera hunk."

"No, really?"

"Really," Charmaine said breezily. "You're old news, except with me."

Gina surveyed her friend for a long moment. "I don't want to disappoint you. I've done that too much in my life."

"Gina, we don't know yet if we like the same coffee, much less if we're meant for each other. Let's take it easy, let things happen."

Let things happen. What a novel concept.

"We can order in pepperoni pizza tonight and watch a movie. Mom left a copy of The Color Purple, for some reason."

"I don't know if I have the tear ducts to last through that one, but sure, I'll come over."

Standing on her tiptoes, Charmaine gave her a peck on the cheek.

"Glad you're back, Bruise. Got some calls to make. See you tonight."

Left alone in the hallway, Gina found herself barely able to move. Back in familiar territory, on unfamiliar ground. The closer she crept to her office, the better she could hear Binh's jambox pulsing out a mordant slice of Arcade Fire.

Unaccountably, the music cheered her up so much she was beaming when she came into the office, encountering Binh, resplendent in a flaming purple jacket and melon shirt.

"Damn, Binh, turn down that suit. I'm going blind."

"Gina, you're back," he said, pleased albeit startled.

"That's right."

She'd get some work done, go home and chill out until Charmaine came, then after Charmaine left, she'd go to bed, get up in the morning, and live the rest of her life.

All in all, she was on a tight schedule.

"Let's get busy."

The End

## ABOUT THE AUTHOR

A native of the Texas Panhandle, Kelly Sinclair currently resides in Central Texas. Her previous three novels are "Accidental Rebels," "Lesser Prophets," and "If the Wind Were a Woman," all published by Blue Feather Books. She is a singer-songwriter.

www.ingramcontent.com/pod-product-compliance
Lightning Source LLC
Chambersburg PA
CBHW050929120626
46552CB00001B/122

* 9 7 8 0 6 1 5 5 3 2 4 6 2 *